SIGNET

REGENCY ROMANCE

Patricia Oliver

Double Deception

MORE BREATHTAKING REGENCY ROMANCES BY PATRICIA OLIVER

from SIGNET

A KISS SO RIGHT—
AND SO WRONG

It had been the darkness and excitement of the storm, Athena told herself. Otherwise she would have known that the man kissing her was not Perry—but one as different from her intended as night from day. She would not have yielded so—not only to his passion but her own.

Now she looked into the darkly handsome face of the Earl of St. Aubyn and said, "Put me down instantly."

"You fainted, my dear Athena," St. Aubyn said, ignoring her request.

"I did not give you leave to use my name," she declared.

St. Aubyn looked into her eyes and smiled. "After what just passed between us, I wonder at such modesty."

"I thought you were Peregrine," she protested.

"Does he always kiss you so?" St. Aubyn asked.

"Perry has never kissed me like that at all," she said. "I merely thought that he . . . I th-thought he—"

"You thought a boy had suddenly turned into a man, is that it, my dear?" St. Aubyn said softly.

Double Deception

by

Patricia Oliver

A SIGNET BOOK

SIGNET
Published by the Penguin Group
Penguin Books USA Inc., 375 Hudson Street,
New York, New York 10014, U.S.A.
Penguin Books Ltd, 27 Wrights Lane,
London W8 5TZ, England
Penguin Books Australia Ltd, Ringwood,
Victoria, Australia
Penguin Books Canada Ltd, 10 Alcorn Avenue,
Toronto, Ontario, Canada M4V 3B2
Penguin Books (N.Z.) Ltd, 182-190 Wairau Road,
Auckland 10, New Zealand

Penguin Books Ltd, Registered Offices:
Harmondsworth, Middlesex, England

First published by Signet, an imprint of Dutton Signet,
a division of Penguin Books USA Inc.

First Printing, August, 1997
10 9 8 7 6 5 4 3 2 1

PROLOGUE

The Garden Party

London, Spring 1811

Athena Standish glanced around at the chattering groups of muslin-clad young ladies gathered on the wide, gently sloping lawns of Hereford House and wished most fervently that she had stayed at home.

If she was forced to agree one more time that yes, indeed, the afternoon had turned out to be very fine for Lady Hereford's alfresco breakfast, Athena thought, she would disgrace herself by answering with the first scathing remark that rose to her lips.

By rights she should not have been invited at all, and after an hour of strolling about the luxuriant gardens on what appeared to be the hottest day of the Season, Athena wished she had never received her ladyship's condescending invitation.

"Lady Hereford obviously mistook me for a simpering miss in her first Season," she remarked to her aunt when the gilt-edged card had been delivered earlier that week.

"Nonsense, my dear," Mrs. Mary Easton replied with unusual vigor. "You know that Lord Hereford is a retired colonel from poor, dear John's regiment and takes a personal interest in the affairs of his officers. Lady Hereford is well known for taking on her husband's causes."

Athena winced at the mention of her late husband. "I do not wish to be one of their *causes*," she said firmly. "And I can think of a dozen things I would prefer to do on a hot afternoon than listen to that totty-headed niece of theirs rattle on about her latest purchases from Madame Lucille on Harley Street." Athena glanced speculatively at her aunt, who sat fanning herself half-heartedly on the faded green settee. "Perhaps I should decline her invitation."

Mrs. Easton had uttered a little shriek of horror.

"How you do love to tease, my dear Athena," she tittered breathlessly, her plump little hands fluttering about aimlessly.

"I know you cannot mean to offend her ladyship, so let us hear no more of this nonsense. Doubtless it will be quite pleasant down by the river. And only think, dear, we shall be able to sample Lady Hereford's famous crab patties and iced creams. I declare, I am quite looking forward to it."

Athena threw her aunt a brief, compassionate smile and resumed her needlework. Aunt Mary enjoyed her food, and Athena told herself that to deny her aunt this opportunity to indulge her taste for delicacies her small pension did not allow would be heartless indeed. Athena's own tastes were Spartan by comparison and had been so even before the untimely death of her husband two years ago in Spain. Besides, the thought of eating crab patties in the heat of the day nauseated her.

"It will be dreadfully hot, Aunt," she warned, half hoping that her aunt would balk at another afternoon spent enduring the unseasonably warm weather they were having that Season in London.

Mrs. Easton gave a gurgle of laughter. "Nonsense, child! The Herefords live outside the Metropolis beside the Thames. It is bound to be cooler under the trees by the water, dear. And besides, this is a heaven-sent opportunity to show off our new parasols."

Athena had sighed at the childish delight her aunt took in such small pleasures and made no further attempt to dissuade her. Now, as she glanced about the crowded terrace and the brilliantly green lawn dotted with young ladies barely out of the schoolroom, clad in pale muslins of every conceivable hue, she wondered if the sacrifice had been worth it. She felt positively ancient in the presence of so many giggling innocents, and her dove-gray gown was definitely not in the first stare of fashion. Had she ever been that young and naive? she wondered.

Throwing off these morbid thoughts, Athena drifted down the terraced steps towards the river. Perhaps it would be cooler beside the water, she thought, forcing herself to nod and smile at an enormous dowager in purple who appeared to have collapsed in a garden chair, perspiration standing out visibly on her round face. Pretending not to see the spark of curiosity in the dowager's eyes, which heralded a flow of chatter, Athena moved on without a pause until she stood on the riverbank beneath a huge chestnut tree.

Even the water appeared sluggish to Athena's jaundiced eye, and she was disappointed to find no relief from the oppressive heat that had caused her shift to stick uncomfortably to her extremities as she walked. Removing a damp wisp of handkerchief from her reticule, she dabbed discreetly at the perspiration on her upper lip, wishing herself safely at home in the cool music room, listening to Penelope struggle with her scales.

Penelope. Athena's spirits rose at the thought of her precious daughter. The only person in the world who really mattered to her, now that John was gone, and her poor Papa irrevocably riveted to that brassy widow from Brighton, she mused, her gaze idly following the lazy approach of a swan trailed by a fleet of half-grown cygnets. The swan made straight for the spot where Athena stood, stretching her elegant neck and hissing imperiously—rather in the manner adopted by her new stepmother once she became Lady Rothingham, Athena reflected bitterly. The former Gracie Hopkins, relict of a prosperous Brighton merchant and possessed of an overweening ambition to step up in the world, had made it abundantly clear—once Sir Henry's ring was safely on her finger—that she was not prepared to share her newly acquired prominence with the baronet's widowed daughter.

The cygnets imitated their mother's aggressiveness, one cheeky fellow scrambling up onto the bank and eyeing Athena expectantly. Athena drew back in alarm, clutching her furled parasol tightly. She had heard that these royal birds could be temperamental and dangerous.

"There is no need for alarm, miss," a masculine voice said from close behind her, causing Athena to jump. "They expect to be fed, and will not give you any peace until you oblige them."

Athena glanced nervously over her shoulder and found herself staring into a pair of guileless blue eyes the color of wild cornflowers.

The young man smiled, and, without knowing quite why she did so, Athena relaxed. He was definitely young, although he stood a good seven or eight inches above her. Young and with the aura of a boy still clinging to him, she thought, instantly beguiled by the innocence in his smile.

"I am afraid I have nothing to give them," she murmured. "It seemed too hot to eat anything."

"Not for these greedy birds," the young man remarked, laughter making his blue eyes dance. "And it really is too hot to eat, but I saw you being accosted by this brood and came prepared to fend off your attackers with a piece of seed cake."

He carried a small blue Limoges plate piled high not only with an enormous slice of seed cake fit for a giant, but various other delicacies, including two of their hostess's famous crab patties.

The brood of swans immediately set up a noisy clamor, evidently anticipating the forthcoming feast.

The young man held out the plate. "Will you do the honors, miss?" he said. "Food is the only thing that will keep these beasts at bay."

Athena gingerly broke off a piece of cake and tossed it into the water. Instant pandemonium broke out. The cygnets squawked and beat their wings furiously to fend off competitors for the treat, while their mother looked on complacently, daintily salvaging a stray crumb here and there.

"Do you really think we should feed Lady Hereford's crab patties to the birds?" Athena asked hesitantly, glancing around to make sure they were unobserved in the commission of such a crime.

The young man let out a crack of laughter. "Better the birds suffer acute indigestion than us, would you not agree?"

His grin was so contagious that Athena could not resist the temptation to speak her mind. "My thoughts exactly, sir," she said gaily, seizing the plate and emptying it recklessly into the river. "There," she exclaimed, watching in delight as the swan family fought long and bitterly over the delicacies. "I trust you have strong stomachs to digest such rich food." A sudden thought occurred to her and she glanced anxiously at the young man at her side. "They will come to no harm on our account, I trust," she murmured.

His smile was utterly charming and devoid of any hint of flirtation. "I fear they are a good deal hardier than one might suspect," he said with apparent regret. "I harbor distinctly painful memories of being tweaked unmercifully by the swans on my father's estate in Cornwall when I was a boy. I cannot claim to waste any sympathy on the brutes."

He looked at her, his boyish smile open and honest. Then a shadow flashed across his face and he flushed like a schoolboy. "I do beg your pardon, miss," he stammered, so like the seven-year-old Penelope caught in some childish misdeed that Athena's heart gave a lurch. "My wits seem to have gone begging. I have not introduced myself to you. Peregrine Steele at your service, miss." He reached awkwardly for her hand and raised it self-consciously to his lips.

Athena gazed at him in frank delight. There was something so refreshingly innocent and untainted about this young man, who was not yet quite a man, who lacked all the vices and deceptions she found all too often in the men of her acquaintance. Athena suspected she would find nothing duplicitous about Peregrine Steele. She sensed it instinctively, and for a fleeting moment was filled with a deep regret that she herself was not equally innocent and naive enough to accept without question the open admiration she saw in the young man's transparent blue eyes.

No, she thought, quelling this regret instantly, her days of innocence were long past. At eight-and-twenty she knew herself to be forever excluded from the brief innocence that still hung about Peregrine Steele's tousled blond head like an invisible halo. All too soon he would lose that sheen of childhood that reminded her of Penelope. But for now, for this brief moment, Athena thought he was the most beautiful creature she had ever seen.

She gave him her most brilliant smile.

"And I am Athena Standish," she murmured, already regretting the passing of this afternoon that would make him that much older and less innocent.

"Athena?" he repeated, unable to hide his surprise as his eyes took in her small stature and delicate features. "A b-beautiful name, of course," he added quickly, "b-but . . ." His voice trailed off and a bright flush spread over his beardless cheeks.

"But hardly appropriate, you mean, sir?" Athena laughed softly at his evident embarrassment.

"I would not presume to be so rude as to think it, miss," he insisted, his face giving the lie to his attempt to deny what had been so plainly writ upon his face.

Athena smiled with genuine amusement. "It would not surprise me if you had, sir. I have often thought so myself. My father rather fancied the classics as a youth, and even though I was reportedly a tiny bit of a thing when I first saw the light, he insisted upon naming me after the most belligerent of the Greek goddesses."

"Pallas Athena was also the goddess of wisdom and purity, if I remember correctly," he responded immediately, a grin replacing his former embarrassment. "And was she not the patroness of weaving and other gentler arts?"

"I believe she was," Athena conceded, returning the grin. "But you cannot deny, sir, that she is usually represented in full armor with the Gorgon's head on her shield."

"A female of many talents, to be sure."

The words were spoken almost reverently, and Athena realized with sudden insight that Peregrine Steele had intended them as a compliment.

For the first time that afternoon, Athena found herself enjoying the alfresco setting. Even the heat felt less stifling, and when a light breeze drifted in off the water, she made no objection when Peregrine Steele offered his arm and proposed a stroll along the grassy verge in the shade of the giant chestnut trees.

For a magical hour that sunny afternoon, Athena allowed herself to feel young and carefree again. In the youthful Peregrine—and almost before she became aware of it, they were on familiar terms—she discovered an amusing and attentive companion. In his lighthearted banter and unfeigned interest in everything about her, he brought back the memory of John's protective presence, touching a chord of longing in her she had thought long buried. Peregrine reminded her of her late husband in other, less innocent ways, as well, evoking with his awkward compliments and shy glances a yearning for the sensuous male companionship she had shared with the late Major Standish.

What harm would it do, Athena asked herself several times during that blissful hour in Peregrine Steele's company, if she let down her guard briefly to savor the reassurance of a man's arm beneath her fingers again? She sighed at these unfamiliar, maudlin thoughts, and then had to laugh at Peregrine's instant anxiety that perhaps he had tired her with so much walking.

"Oh, no," she assured him, marveling at the tenderness in blue eyes he was too young to veil. "I am not such a poor creature as you seem to think, sir. I am country born and bred, and have even campaigned in Spain with my husband."

She stopped abruptly, wondering why she had not revealed her married state sooner.

"Your husband?" the young man repeated blankly, his face suddenly serious. "I thought . . ."

"My late husband," Athena amended quickly. "John was killed at Talavera and left me a widow with a small daughter," she added in a rush, wishing to leave no doubt in this innocent young man's mind how unfitting she was of his notice.

His reaction startled her.

"The widow of one of England's heroes," he murmured reverently, his eyes revealing none of the withdrawal she had anticipated. "How I envy your husband, Athena," he added simply, without the slightest hint of flattery. "It must have been a terrible experience for you, of course, but how glorious to give one's life for England like that."

Peregrine had spoken fervently, his blue eyes shining with passion, confirming to Athena, as nothing else could, his extreme youth and innocence. Only the very young and naive would glorify what had always seemed to her a shameful waste of England's best young men. The soldiers she had encountered in Spain had not glorified the war; they had endured it, and all too often died for it, as John had.

No, she thought, gazing sadly into Peregrine's shining eyes, only an innocent could possibly believe in the glory of a soldier's death in battle. Her own eyes misted over, and she turned away.

"I have upset you," Peregrine blurted, instantly contrite. "Forgive me, Athena. I am a perfect brute. It is just that my father refused to buy me a pair of colors, and it is my dearest wish to fight with Wellesley in the Peninsular campaign."

"He is a wise man, your father," Athena said, feeling the weight of her years descend upon her again as they wandered back towards the thinning flock of guests on Lady Hereford's pristine lawns. "And I am sure that your mother would agree with me."

"I am sure she would, too," Peregrine responded in a sober voice. "But my mother was taken from us several years ago. Influenza. It carried off half the village."

Athena gently squeezed his arm. "I am sorry to hear it," she said. "My own mother died ten years ago of the same thing."

They walked along in silence for several minutes before Peregrine seemed to pull himself out of the gloom that had fallen over them.

"What is your daughter's name?" he wanted to know.

"Penelope."

He laughed, and Athena was unaccountably relieved to hear the sound. "I see that a love of the classics runs in the family. My father is a bit of a scholar himself. I think you would like him, Athena. In fact, I am sure you would."

Athena smiled but made no reply. Since her chances of meeting the elder Mr. Steele were too remote to merit consideration, she dismissed the thought. Instead, she concentrated on committing to memory the enchanted hour she had spent with his son.

CHAPTER ONE

Uneasy Betrothal

Cornwall, Summer 1811

"Are we nearly there, Perry?"

The elegant traveling chaise had made yet another stop, this time at the Swan Inn at Okehampton, for refreshments and a change of horse, and young Penelope had posed her oft-repeated question to Viscount Fairmont.

It had come as a shock to Athena to discover, the very afternoon following that riverside encounter at Hereford House, that her new acquaintance had not been simply a delightfully naive young man who could make her laugh at his nonsensical starts, but the only son and heir to the Earl of St. Aubyn.

Athena glanced at him now, marveling as she had so many times in the past tempestuous weeks at the unfailing good humor the viscount showed to the eager child who clung confidently to his hand and danced along at his side. Perry—she could not think of him as a viscount in the privacy of her mind—had been an instant success with Penelope. From the very first, he had insisted upon including her daughter in their frequent drives about London in his smart curricle, in the impromptu picnics he organized on particularly pleasant days, and on the long, leisurely expeditions into the countryside that had come to make up the texture of her days after Peregrine's boisterous eruption into their lives.

"We shall be at St. Aubyn Castle in plenty of time for dinner," Athena heard him say. "But if you get to feeling a mite peckish before then, Penny," he added with a deep, infectious chuckle, "there is a wee pastry shop in Launceston where they have the best cream buns in all England. I daresay your mother will let us stop to buy a dozen or so to tide us over 'til dinnertime."

He glanced at her then, his blue eyes dancing with mischief, and Athena was struck again with the boyishness of this man she had promised to marry. Had she done the right thing? she asked herself for the umpteenth time since that afternoon when she had finally succumbed to his insistence that only as her husband could he take care of and cherish her and Penelope as they deserved. This argument had swayed her as none of his protestations of undying love had been able to. The notion of protecting her darling daughter from the rough edges of life had demolished Athena's resistance. By accepting Peregrine's offer, she would escape the skimping and scrounging to eke out an inadequate pension, the genteel poverty of her aunt's existence, and the humiliation of having to pretend that she had not been cast off both by her husband's family and by her own father.

The realization that the late Major Standish's pension would never allow her to provide her daughter with even the smallest luxuries she herself had taken for granted as a child had caused Athena to relax her scruples. But in moments such as these, when Peregrine appeared even younger than his nineteen years, doubts assailed her, and she wondered if perhaps she had been selfish in thinking only of the benefits marriage to a wealthy viscount, even one who had yet to reach his majority, could bring them.

These benefits had made themselves felt almost immediately. Athena felt a twinge of conscience at Penelope's new bonnet and pale blue pelisse, both purchased on what she still considered a rash spending spree organized by Peregrine one afternoon soon after he became a regular visitor to her aunt's modest house on Mount Street. Her protests at Perry's extravagances had been drowned out by Penelope's squeals of delight and her aunt's exclamations of approval.

She herself had not escaped the bounty of Perry's generosity. The very afternoon following their betrothal, Perry had escorted her to the best warehouse on Piccadilly Street and—despite her urgent protestations that she was well provided with gowns for her modest needs—purchased a dazzling array of Indian silks, shimmering satins, the softest muslins, and other materials that he insisted his future bride should not be without. These purchases had been made up into a rare assortment of fashionable gowns by none other than Madame Lucille on Harley Street, who was only too happy to add a future viscountess to her distinguished clientele.

"May we, Mama? *Do* say we may."

Distracted from her guilty thoughts by her daughter's voice, Athena raised an eyebrow.

"May you do what, darling?"

"Stop at Launceston for cream buns, of course," Penelope said eagerly.

Athena smiled. The notion of stopping on a whim to purchase a dozen cream buns seemed so incongruous after their previously sparse diet of butterless bread and boiled vegetables that Athena winced.

"Perhaps you will not be hungry again before dinner, dear," she murmured, unwilling to admit that she considered the consumption of cream buns in the middle of the afternoon an unnecessary extravagance. "After all, we have yet to eat our nuncheon."

"Oh, my dear Athena," her aunt cut in quickly. "I do think that is a wonderful treat for us all that Perry is proposing. And remember that our darling Penny is a growing girl. Besides, we shall be stopping for a cup of tea anyway, so why not include these famous cream buns? I do declare my mouth is watering already."

Athena could well believe that Aunt Mary's sweet tooth had been titillated by the mention of cream buns, so she made no further protest and was rewarded by a dazzling smile from Perry.

"You will not be disappointed, love," he murmured, his irrepressible grin melting her resistance.

The proposed stop at Launceston was an undeniable success, as Peregrine had promised. The cream buns were pronounced beyond anything delicious by Aunt Mary, and Penelope had to be severely reminded that well-brought-up young ladies did not make pigs of themselves at the tea-table.

For Athena, however, the delay at the Blue Stag Inn at Launceston—where Perry was greeted with genuine delight by the stout innkeeper and his wife—was a welcome postponement of what she could only anticipate as an uncomfortable encounter with the Earl of St. Aubyn. Despite Perry's insistence that his father was a great gun, top-of-the-trees as a parent and completely up-to-snuff as a friend to his only son, Athena felt her apprehension grow the closer their carriage came to the Cornwall estate of Perry's family.

"Great-Aunt Sarah will love you to death," her betrothed had assured her with his usual exuberance. "I have written expressly to tell her all about you, Athena, and I do not doubt she will receive you with open arms."

Athena was not at all convinced. From Perry's ingenious

flow of reminiscences, Lady Sarah Steele had emerged as more of a dragon than a benign personage. She also considered Perry's choice of words rather unfortunate under the circumstances. The notion of being loved to death by a formidable female, who might naturally be expected to look upon her great-nephew's nuptials to a widow of eight-and-twenty with disfavor, caused Athena to quake in her new kid half-boots.

When the chaise turned into the well-kept grounds of the park in the early summer twilight, Athena found she could not give the magnificent centenary oaks that lined the driveway the admiration they deserved. Her thoughts were too full of the enigmatic figure of the earl, the master of all this splendor. Although Perry had assured her that his father was far too engrossed in his lifelong obsession with Oriental treasures to pay much heed to the pedigree of his future daughter-in-law, Athena dreaded this encounter more than she had imagined. In Lady Sarah she hoped to find, if not an ally and friend, at least a female whose sensibilities might allow her to understand if not condone the pressures that had driven Athena to accept Perry's offer.

She had no such expectations about the Earl of St. Aubyn, and as she allowed Perry to hand her down from the carriage before the imposing entrance to the austere mass of stone and mullioned windows that was St. Aubyn Castle, Athena's heart sank even further. How foolish she had been to believe for a moment that she could ever be accepted as the mistress of this magnificent residence, home of the Steele family for countless generations. Doubtless they would be back in London within the week, seeking new ways to stretch the scanty pension John had left her.

The thought was utterly depressing.

The Earl of St. Aubyn rose to his feet when his son and heir burst unceremoniously into the library, but he made no attempt to move out from behind the heavily inlaid mahogany desk that had belonged to his great-grandfather.

"We are here, Father," Perry said, with a hint of defiance in his voice that Lord St. Aubyn did not fail to notice. "I hope I find you well, sir," he added, when his father made no reply.

Peregrine paused and cleared his throat nervously.

The earl did not smile.

"We?" he inquired softly, his tone deceptively mild. "Whom have you brought down to the Castle this time, boy? I trust it is not another parcel of young bucks who will turn the place upside-down again?"

Perry winced visibly at this reminder of a recent debacle perpetrated over the Christmas holidays by some of his London cronies, but the earl's stern gaze did not waver. He knew whom his son had brought to the Castle, for his butler had informed him of that fact not ten minutes past, after ushering the viscount's party into the Blue Dragon Saloon, where Lady Sarah sat at her needlework.

"No, sir," Perry stammered. "Nothing like that. I have brought Mrs. Standish with me as I wrote in my last letter to you, sir. Surely you received—"

"I received it all right," the earl cut in sharply. "And I distinctly remember writing by return post to inform you that I do not welcome fortune hunters here at St. Aubyn's."

The earl noted that his son looked acutely uncomfortable, but he refused to relent.

"Mrs. Standish is no fortune hunter, Father," Perry protested, his chin rising defiantly. "I know that, when you meet her, you will find her as well-bred and charming as I do myself. And as for Penelope, why she is a treasure of a child—"

"This widow has a child?" the earl demanded in ominous tones.

"Why, yes," Peregrine stammered. "Did I not include that in my letter, sir? I could have sworn that I did."

"Do not prevaricate, Peregrine," Lord St. Aubyn said shortly. "You know perfectly well that you said nothing of any child. How old is this . . . this treasure?"

"Penelope is nearly seven, sir. And you can take it from me—"

"Seven?" Lord St. Aubyn's voice exploded into the tense atmosphere of the library like a rifle shot. His lips thinned into a forbidding line, and he felt his temper rise as the full import of his son's irresponsible action dawned upon him.

Perry's face turned a sickly white, but he held his ground.

When the earl spoke again, his voice was icy. "Am I to understand that you have dared to bring your doxy and her child to St. Aubyn's?"

Peregrine gasped at his father's harsh words. "A-Athena is n-no such thing, Father," he stammered. "She has a-accepted my offer of m-marriage. We are b-betrothed."

"Betrothed?" The earl's voice was a sneer. "What utter nonsense! Did I not warn you—repeatedly, I might add—to avoid the company of destitute females masquerading as members of the *ton*. This Standish female is obviously one of these encroaching creatures who aspire to entrap just such a country flat as you have turned out to be. How could you be so taken in, Peregrine?"

"Athena is not like that at all," his son retorted, spots of color appearing in his white cheeks. "I cannot tell you how many times she refused my offer before I convinced her that my intentions were indeed honorable. She insisted that I was too young for marriage, if you must know the truth."

Lord St. Aubyn gazed upon his son pityingly. "How touching," he drawled sarcastically. "And how much blunt have you dropped on this pious paragon of yours?"

Peregrine bristled. "Nothing to speak of, Father, so you are off the mark if you imagine Athena is out to fleece me."

"How much?"

"Not above fifty pounds, I would say," his son answered hesitantly. "To tell the truth, Father, I did not regard it. I never imagined children could be such fun. Penelope was delighted with any little thing I purchased for her."

The earl's lips curled contemptuously. "And the widow?"

"Athena would accept nothing at all until we became betrothed. Father. And then a paltry length of silk or two."

"No expensive baubles?"

"Oh, no, sir." Peregrine assayed a small smile. "To tell the truth, Father, I had always believed females to be insatiably frivolous, but Athena is quite embarrassingly frugal. I thought that would please you," he added with such naiveté that the earl felt his anger waver.

"How convenient," he replied, with deliberate cynicism. "I shall not have to spend a fortune to buy her off and send her back to London."

"Buy her off?" Peregrine looked puzzled, and his clear blue eyes clouded as he gazed quizzically at his father.

Lord St. Aubyn winced at his son's innocence. He had no wish to cause Peregrine any more pain than he had to, but there was no way he would allow his only son to fall into the clutches of a female who was obviously an adventuress of the craftiest sort.

He shrugged. "Yes," he replied quietly. "Pay the lady for the excellent job she had done in hoodwinking you into making an offer. She must be very good, although there is no denying you are not quite up to snuff where the petticoat company is concerned, Perry. Just let me handle your Mrs. Standish, lad. I can guarantee you will be free of her in no time."

The earl knew he was in for an argument when he saw Peregrine's chin go up and his eyes turn stormy.

"You have misunderstood the matter entirely, Father," his son said quietly. "I have no wish to be free of Athena. On the contrary, I wish to spend the rest of my life with her. I had hoped you would welcome her here to the Castle, but if necessary, we will remove to London."

An uncomfortable silence followed this piece of plain speaking, and for the first time, Lord St. Aubyn felt a glimmer of apprehension.

"And how would you support a wife and child?" he asked softly, quelling his rising impatience at his son's foolhardiness.

"My allowance will hardly be sufficient, of course," Peregrine said innocently. "But I understand it is to be increased upon my marriage."

"Upon my sole discretion," the earl replied bluntly, hating himself for dispelling the expectant light from his son's eyes.

"I have a much better suggestion, Perry," he continued swiftly, wishing that a certain captivating widow had not brought out this unsuspected chivalrous streak in his son. "If I were you, I would install Mrs. Standish in London in a style befitting her station." He carefully kept any hint of irony from his voice and forced his lips into a smile. "A female in her situation, with a seven-year-old daughter to care for, will jump at the chance of having a young and wealthy protector. And to sweeten the transaction, I will pay the rent myself and double your allowance so that you can keep her in gewgaws and gowns and all the fripperies so dear to a female's heart."

The shocked look in his son's eyes made the earl pause. This approach was not going to work, he realized, sensing that he had not played his cards as carefully as he should have.

"Look, Peregrine," he said brusquely, "let us face the truth. Gentlemen like you and I do not marry penniless widows of dubious pedigree, however charming they may be. Set up this Mrs. Standish as your mistress and I will frank you generously. But understand one thing, Peregrine, and understand it clearly. I will not countenance any marriage between you."

Lord St. Aubyn regretted the words instantly, but it was already too late to withdraw them. Peregrine's handsome face—so like his mother's that the earl's heart ached at the sight of him—took on the stubborn expression Adrienne's always had when she was irrevocably set upon something. It was rare for father and son to argue, but the earl recognized the grim set of Peregrine's mouth and the pugnacious glint in his blue eyes. He sighed.

"I am sorry to hear that, Father," Peregrine said stiffly. "I was sure that you, of all people, would understand. Were you not barely twenty yourself when you met my mother? Was she not your elder by several years? Was her family not in dire straits?"

Lord St. Aubyn felt as though he had been suddenly and violently deprived of air. "How *dare* you mention your mother in the same breath as this . . . this *widow* you wish to thrust into the family?" he roared, frustration at his son's callousness exacerbating the ache in his heart, still tender five years after the loss of his beloved Adrienne. "Your mother was a lady, the daughter of a marquess," he continued, making a valiant attempt to control his temper. "And if she was two-and-twenty to my twenty, it was no great matter. Adrienne was always a girl at heart." He stopped abruptly, quite unable to say another word about the wife he had loved so much and lost.

"And how much did grandfather have to pay to salvage Mother's family from ruin?" Peregrine insisted quietly. "He paid it gladly because you loved her, did he not? Mother told me the tale many times. An enormous sum, she always said. She did not tell me the exact amount, of course, but I shall never forget how her eyes would shine when she spoke of you."

The earl turned away to stare out of the window at the gathering dusk. His son's words had touched him deeply, bringing back memories twenty years buried in his heart. Memories of Adrienne as he had first seen her, radiant in pale blue muslin that matched her eyes, her golden ringlets dancing as she laughed at something one of her cousins whispered in her ear. He had seen his future in that instant, stretching out before him with Lady Adrienne at his side, almost as though he had already lived it. There had never been any other female for him after that first dazzling glance. He had never wanted another.

Peregrine's voice, strangely gentle now, brought the earl back from his nostalgic journey into the past.

"I meant no disrespect to Mama, you must know that, Father. I grieve for her, too, just as you do. But the Castle needs a mistress again, and if you have no wish to—"

"Your Great-Aunt Sarah is all the hostess I need," the earl cut in brusquely, his voice harsh with emotion.

"I love Aunt Sarah dearly, Father, but it is time for me to bring a bride of my own to the Castle."

"A bride worthy of our name, perhaps," the earl insisted. "You might look as high as you pleased for a suitable wife, Perry. Why settle for a widow with a seven-year-old daughter? I cannot like it. How can you be sure she is not an adventuress?"

He winced at the sudden besotted grin that spread over his son's face.

"When you meet her, you will see that for yourself, Father."

"I have no desire to meet her," the earl retorted. His words sounded peevish even to his own ears, and he watched the brief joy fade from his son's eyes.

"Then I shall escort Athena back to London in the morning, sir," Peregrine said with a quiet dignity that sat oddly on his boyish face.

As his son turned to go, Lord St. Aubyn stopped him. "Wait," he said flatly, the fear of losing his son as well as his wife curling up inside him. "If you are set on this freakish start, Perry, I shall talk to the woman tomorrow. If she is what I suspect she is, I will not countenance her presence as a guest at the Castle, much less as your wife." He paused for a moment wondering how far he could bend Peregrine to his will. "If I find she is a fortune hunter, you will abide by my decision and send her packing immediately. If not . . ." He shrugged. There was not much chance of the widow being anything else, of course, but he dared not cut off all hope if he wished to convince Peregrine to accept his conditions.

"If she is not a fortune hunter, I shall reconsider the issue. Do you agree, Peregrine?"

The light of hope had reappeared in his son's eyes, and the earl felt quite the villain for inflicting pain, however necessary, on his only offspring.

"Is that a promise, Father?"

"Of course."

"And you will be fair, will you not?"

"Of course."

Peregrine's face broke into a delighted grin. "Thank you, sir. I know that once you see her, you cannot fail to love her as I do. And now, if you will excuse me, sir, I must go to her. I do not scruple to tell you, Father, that Athena has been anxious for your approval."

Fairness had little or nothing to do with the matter, Lord St.

Aubyn mused as the door closed behind his son after that artless speech. And he could well believe that the mysterious Athena—the name suggested precisely the aggressive kind of female the earl deplored—had been anxious about her reception at the Castle.

She had every reason to be, he though grimly.

The following morning, Athena was awakened by the sparrows chirping happily in the plane trees outside her window. Her night had not been entirely restful, partly because her arrival at St. Aubyn Castle had been every bit as awkward as she had feared.

Her reception by Lady Sarah Steele, Perry's great-aunt, had been cool to say the least, although her ladyship had shown genuine warmth at the sight of her great-nephew. When Perry had presented his affianced bride, Lady Sarah's steel-blue eyes had turned several shades cooler, and Athena had endured a rapier-sharp stare that seemed to dissect her to the very bone.

"Standish?" her ladyship had repeated sharply, as soon as the guests were seated in the imposing Blue Dragon Saloon. "Are you perchance related to the Dorset Standishes?"

Athena breathed a small sigh of relief and confirmed that yes, she was indeed related to the Earl of Wentworth by marriage. "My late husband, Major John Standish, was the late earl's youngest son, my lady," she added, hoping that connection would be illustrious enough to satisfy this terrifying dragon dressed in a plum satin gown of a design fashionable fifty years in the past.

"And how many sons did Wentworth have?" Lady Sarah demanded. "Four or five, as far as I remember."

"Four, my lady," Athena replied, resigning herself to what appeared to be an exhaustive examination of her pedigree. "Three after John was lost in the battle of Talavera two years ago."

"I can count very well, thank you, young lady," came the snappish reply. "So you make your home at Standish Park, do you?"

"No," Athena said coolly, hoping she could avoid going into the details of her banishment from her husband's family home. "I have lived with my aunt, Mrs. Easton, in London since John's death."

"Easton?" Lady Sarah pounced upon the name disdainfully, without so much as a glance in Aunt Mary's direction. "Easton?

I do not seem to recall anyone by that name. Your mother's family, I presume?"

"Yes, my lady," Athena responded as civilly as she was able. She cast a speaking glance at Peregrine, who had remained silent since his effusive reception by Lady Sarah.

"Not in *Trade* were they, I sincerely trust?" The tone of her ladyship's voice conveyed more clearly than words the offensive nature of such a connection, the mere suggestion of which made her aristocratic lips curl. Athena glanced nervously at her Aunt Mary, and her heart withered in her breast at the prospect of having to inform Lady Sarah that a tradesman's daughter was at that very moment seated in her drawing room, drinking tea from a porcelain cup bearing the impressive and doubtless ancient crest of St. Aubyn.

"Athena's maternal grandfather was the vicar of Marksbury, near Bath," Peregrine offered, a grin flickering briefly on his handsome face.

"When I wish for your enlightening comments, I shall ask for them, Peregrine," her ladyship remarked with dampening effect on her female guests, although Perry appeared unimpressed.

His grin widened. He winked at Athena and rose to his feet. "In that case, I shall beg to be excused, Aunt Sarah, and leave you in the company of these lovely ladies. I must speak to Father."

Before Athena had gathered her wits, the rascal had bowed and escaped, leaving an oppressive silence behind him.

Lady Sarah uttered a noise astonishingly like a snort and turned her gimlet gaze upon the unfortunate Mrs. Easton, who had been too intimidated to do anything but perch, like some terrified sparrow, on the edge of her chair, her crested tea-cup clutched precariously in her trembling fingers.

Athena had little recollection of what transpired after Peregrine had so cavalierly abandoned them to the dragon, but she must not have said anything too disgraceful, for there had been no summons from Lady Sarah to have them ejected from St. Aubyn.

Dinner had been a trying affair, punctuated by Lady Sarah's endless questions about friends and acquaintances of hers in London whom—as she put it—anyone of any consequence whatsoever must definitely have encountered at the height of the Season. Since the vast majority of these personages were unknown to Athena, it fell to Peregrine to keep his aunt at bay with the latest *on-dits* and crim.-con. stories concerning members of the *haut monde*.

The Earl of St. Aubyn was noticeably absent from the dinner table: the second reason why her first night under his roof had been less than refreshing. After dinner, as Peregrine escorted the ladies into the drawing room, having instructed Jackson to serve his port with the tea-tray, Athena discovered that her premonitions regarding her welcome at St. Aubyn Castle had been painfully accurate. Reluctantly, Peregrine had confessed that his father was less than delighted to discover that his only son was betrothed.

"But I thought you had written to him to ask his permission, Perry," she had chided in a low voice as Lady Sarah launched into a recital of her connections with all the prominent families in Dorset.

"Of course, I wrote to him," Perry protested naively, "but I thought it best to allow Father to get used to the idea gradually."

"And now he knows and does not like it above half?"

"Yes," Perry mumbled sheepishly. "He kicked up rather a dust about the whole notion, so I had to tell him roundly that we are to be wed." His boyish face had turned a deep red during this cryptic explanation, and Athena had little difficulty in divining the source of the earl's hostility.

"He believes me to be a fortune hunter, no doubt," she remarked prosaically.

"I told him you were nothing of the kind," Perry blurted out, innocently confirming Athena's speculations.

"Can you honestly say that I am not, my dear?" she teased him gently. "You know precious little about me when all is said and done."

Peregrine's expression of horror made her laugh. "I know all I need to know, Athena," he said earnestly. "You are an angel, and so I told him."

"You told his lordship that I was an angel?" she repeated in astonishment. "I cannot help thinking that you have exaggerated somewhat, Perry. He will see at once that I am no such thing. If he ever comes out of his lair to take a look, that is."

"You are teasing me again," Perry protested. "By tomorrow all this will be settled. Father wants to talk to you after breakfast, and he has promised to . . . to . . ."

"To what?"

"Well, he has promised to . . . to talk to you, that is all," Peregrine repeated, ignoring the most elementary rules of logic.

"His lordship wishes to quiz me about my intentions, is that it?" Athena remarked without rancor. "I do not blame him, Perry. If you were my son, I would wish to know—"

"I am *not* your son," her betrothed interrupted heatedly. "And I wish you would not talk like that, Athena. You make me feel younger than I am. I hope you will not speak to Father that way; I went to great pains to make him see that I am quite old enough to have a wife of my own. Unfortunately, I do not think he is at all convinced of it."

Neither am I, Athena had thought to herself as she took her place at the elegant rosewood pianoforte at Lady Sarah's instigation. What a mull she would make of the affair if she was forced to agree with his lordship that Perry was not yet ready for the responsibilities of wedded bliss.

Morning had not brought much needed illumination to her muddled thoughts. As Perry escorted her to the library, where the stony-faced Jackson stood poised to throw open the double doors, Athena felt a distinct affinity for the Christian martyrs who must have listened in paralyzed silence for the roar of the lions.

Athena smiled at this fanciful twist of her imagination. Jackson might have the stalwart girth of a Roman centurion, but she was quite sure that Lord St. Aubyn could not be one half as bloodthirsty as Lady Sarah and her merciless inquisition last night.

Keeping this bracing thought foremost in her mind, Athena forced a smile to her lips as she stepped across the threshold into the lion's den.

CHAPTER TWO

The Bribe

The library at St. Aubyn Castle was built on a grand scale, and as she stepped over the threshold, Athena felt herself instantly plunged into an oasis of scholarly calm and refinement. Under normal circumstances the sensation of breathing the air of this hallowed atmosphere might have intoxicated her with its promise of intellectual challenge, but today a more sinister challenge distracted her from the enjoyment of literary treasures.

The Earl of St. Aubyn stood behind the enormous carved desk, an ominously dark figure. Behind him the morning sunlight filtered into the high-ceilinged room, outlining his imposing form but leaving his face in shadow.

With sudden insight, Athena realized that the earl's pose was quite deliberate. Doubtless the massive mahogany desk had been placed before the window with the calculated intention of producing the vaguely mysterious and threatening tableau that now greeted her as she entered this masculine sanctuary. Idly, she wondered how many stewards, solicitors, servants, even neighbors on friendly calls had been cowed—as she was at this moment—by the sight of the tall, shadowy figure behind the desk.

Unwilling to show fear in the face of the enemy—and she no longer doubted that the man who awaited her was hostile—Athena glanced up at Peregrine, an encouraging smile on her lips. To her dismay, she noted that her betrothed's face looked strained and the smile he returned was tentative and fleeting. Good God, she thought, a flicker of panic making her mouth dry, Peregrine was as nervous as she. What had he not told her about this enigmatic father of his?

She turned back to the man behind the desk, willing herself to be calm, and saw instantly that the appearance of shadow and mystery had been an illusion. As Perry led her across the wine-red carpet towards his father, Athena found she could see every detail of the Earl of St. Aubyn's face clearly. She stumbled, knees suddenly unsteady beneath her, and had Peregrine's hand not been firmly on her elbow, she might have fallen.

Flustered and not a little mortified at her *gaucherie*, Athena straightened her shoulders and lifted her chin. It simply would not do to show weakness now; not when so much depended upon the impression she must make before this complete stranger.

And Peregrine's father was more of a stranger than Athena could possible have bargained for. Had it not been for a faint resemblance in the cast of the features, she would not have taken them for father and son. Where Perry was as warm, and innocent, and cuddly as a puppy—how often had she chided herself for regarding her betrothed in such unloverlike terms—his father could only be likened to a wolf.

A darkly handsome, enigmatic, magnificent wolf.

Athena mentally shook herself out of the trance that seemed to have paralyzed her faculties. The first notion that flashed across her mind was that this man could not possibly be Peregrine's father. He was far too young to have a son of nineteen. As she drew closer and listened to Perry's mumbled introductions, Athena gradually changed her mind. Although there was no hint of gray in the black hair that curled youthfully about the earl's ears, and at first glance no sign of aging in the austerely handsome face, Athena detected a delicate web of lines beside his eyes and laugh lines around his sensuous mouth.

There was not even a shadow of a smile on that mouth now.

The earl inclined his head briefly to acknowledge his son's introduction, but his mouth remained closed in a grim line. How could such a coldly arrogant man have sired an unpretentious, happy-go-lucky innocent like Peregrine? she wondered, conscious of a growing sense of despondency at the magnitude of the task ahead of her. How could she expect to break through the earl's icy demeanor long enough to convince him to sanction her marriage to his son?

Particularly—an insistent little voice inside her chided— since she was not quite perfectly sure that she could bring her darling Perry the happiness he seemed to believe she could. And which he most certainly deserved, she added to herself.

Resolutely, Athena brushed these troubling thoughts aside and concentrated on Penelope's future, and the benefits her alliance with Perry would bring her daughter. She was embarked upon this matrimonial venture for better or for worse, and she must see it through without flinching.

Athena gritted her teeth, and for the first time raised her eyes to meet the earl's gaze squarely. She drew in a sharp breath. Athena had never seen a wolf, nor—as far as she could remember—a picture of one, but her mind was fertile and fanciful, and she had little difficulty imagining that the cold, dark eyes that glared back at her from the earl's granite face might well have been those of the four-legged predators of the desolate steppes portrayed in the Russian novels in her father's library.

They sent a chill up her spine.

"Leave us, Peregrine," she heard the earl say softly. "Mrs. Standish and I have things to discuss."

For a wild instant of panic, Athena wanted to cry out to Perry to stay with her; to protect her from the attack she knew in her bones was about to be launched against her, and which she would much rather not have to face alone. She quelled the cowardly impulse and gave her betrothed another encouraging smile. She was being missish and maudlin to imagine that the earl would actually do her bodily harm. He would not dare, would he? And anything else would be bearable; unpleasant and possibly offensive, but bearable.

She sank down in a leather chair facing that implacable desk and listened to the door closing behind Peregrine, who had departed without so much as a whisper.

Unwilling to admit her weakness, Athena clasped her hands firmly in her lap and flung herself into the fray. "I understand, my lord, that you have some misgivings about your son's betrothal to me."

The crack of laughter that greeted this remark held no hint of amusement, and Athena shuddered at the cynicism in it.

"You have a talent for understatement, madam," the earl said shortly, "but you are correct. There is no way I will countenance a marriage between my son—a mere boy of nineteen, as I am sure you are aware—and an unconnected widow of . . ." He paused and glared at her down the length of his aristocratic nose. "Precisely what is your age, madam?"

Athena felt the contempt in the earl's voice like a whiplash across her face. She had to exercise the utmost self-control not to respond with one of her most withering set-downs to this piece of rudeness. She met his flinty gaze calmly for several moments before trusting herself to speak.

"I fail to see what my age has to do with anything, my lord."

"It has a great deal to do with it, as you very well know. And do not try to bamboozle me, madam, for I warn you, I am in no mood for feminine tricks."

Athena forced herself to smile. "In that case you will be happy to know that I am not in the habit of indulging in such subterfuges, my lord. I am eight-and-twenty," she added smoothly, her eyes still fixed defiantly on his harsh face.

"Eight-and-twenty?" he repeated, and Athena caught a note of surprise in his voice.

So, she mused with an odd flash of pleasure that the earl had thought her younger that she was, his lordship was not infallible. He had misjudged her. Briefly, Athena regretted not shaving three or four years off her age, but that was precisely the tack he would expect her to take, she thought, and an outright lie—besides being distasteful to her—would only confirm the unfavorable opinion he already had of her.

An uncomfortable silence pervaded the room, and Athena dropped her eyes to her clasped hands, forcing herself to relax. She could feel the earl's eyes upon her, and knew that he was assessing her, perhaps to discover why his son had fallen within her coils. She was quite sure that St. Aubyn thought of her modest attractions as quagmires into which Peregrine had been lured by a scheming fortune hunter.

"I presume that my son is aware of this fact?"

Athena raised her eyes and smiled faintly. "Oh, yes, indeed, my lord," she replied in her softly modulated voice. She knew that her voice was one of her attractive features—too many gentlemen had remarked upon it for her to believe otherwise—and she wondered whether she could use it to pacify the hostility of the man before her.

"And you thought nothing of enticing an innocent boy of nineteen to make a cake of himself over you, I suppose?"

His tone was harsh, and the words intended to wound. Athena's smile faltered. No, she thought, it would take more than a pleasant tone to deflect the earl's hostility. It would be difficult enough to be minimally civil.

"It was never a case of enticing, my lord. I can assure you that—"

"You will never convince me that a female of your looks and experience had the least trouble bedazzling an impressionable boy into believing himself infatuated."

Athena swallowed the angry retort that rose to her lips. "You overestimate my powers of persuasion, my lord. And my experience, too, I might add. I was married at eighteen and widowed only recently, so I cannot imagine what experience you refer to." She deliberately refrained from acknowledging the earl's casual reference to her looks, although she could not help wondering which of her feminine attributes he considered noteworthy enough to bedazzle a gentleman.

She heard the crack of derisive laughter again and flinched.

"Do not play the innocent with me, madam," the earl drawled, his gaze raking her face with studied insolence. "Do you really expect me to believe that you have received no offers of a more—shall we say—mundane nature during your stay in London? I cannot believe that a penniless widow with a pretty face did not attract the notice of a few of our notorious rakes."

Athena pushed herself out of the chair and stood, her knees trembling, staring at the earl across the wide expanse of the desk. She could not believe what she was hearing. Had this man actually suggested that she was better suited to be some gentleman's light-skirt than Peregrine's wife? It did nothing to mitigate her anger to remember that she had indeed received offers of *carte blanche* from at least two erstwhile protectors.

Lord St. Aubyn smiled wolfishly. "Can you deny it, madam?" he said softly.

Athena kept her voice under control. "No, I do not deny that I have received indecent offers from men who are all too eager to take advantage of an unprotected female. But you are off the mark, my lord, if you believe that I would ever consider such an arrangement. I may be impoverished, but I am not lost to all sense of decency."

"How very touching," he drawled, his dark eyes full of insolence again. "So I take it that you prefer to beguile an innocent boy into taking a step that he will rue for the rest of his life?"

The echo of this ugly accusation hung in the room and reverberated throughout every nerve in Athena's body. She felt herself tremble with the impact of it, for it had struck home. Had she not asked herself the same question more times than she cared to remember? In truth, had she not asked Peregrine himself the very same thing?

Athena closed her eyes briefly, willing this odious man and his impertinent, disturbing interrogation to go away and leave her to enjoy the summer morning exploring the garden she had glimpsed from her bedroom window. She longed for Peregrine's comforting presence. When she was with him, the sunshine of his smile and his perennial good humor kept all these doubts at bay. Lord St. Aubyn's probing questions only magnified her secret reservations about her betrothal to his son.

She opened her eyes and looked at him, wondering whether it would do any good to plead with the earl not to stand in the way of his son's happiness. And of her daughter's future, she reminded herself with her usual honesty.

The look she saw in his cold gaze froze the words on her lips.

"You must think me a veritable harpy, my lord," she murmured instead. "Surely you cannot believe that I would deliberately do anything to hurt Peregrine. He is as dear to me as my own daughter."

The earl snorted derisively. "If that is true—which you will give me leave to doubt—you will pack your trunks and leave St. Aubyn Castle this afternoon. My carriage is at your disposal, madam."

Oh, I am sure it is, Athena thought dispiritedly, watching the angry grimace of disgust mar the handsome lines of the earl's face. She had expected some resistance from Peregrine's family, but what Lord St. Aubyn proposed amounted to open rejection.

The realization that she was not acceptable to her betrothed's father reminded Athena painfully of her betrothal to Major John Standish ten years ago. John's father, the earl, had turned an alarming shade of purple when they had appeared before him to seek his sanction for the match. Athena's father, Sir Henry Rothingham, had been more than pleased with his only daughter's proposed alliance with a prominent family like the Standishes, but John's father had refused to countenance the union. John had argued and pleaded to no avail, and in the end had defied the head of the family and married her anyway. Retribution had been swift and drastic. The earl had cut off John's allowance from the estate and banished them both from Standish lands.

And now the whole ugly situation was repeating itself. Was she doomed to bring strife to all those dear to her? Athena wondered.

"And naturally, you will persuade Peregrine not to accompany you back to London," she heard the earl add.

The thought struck her that Peregrine must have put up a stronger fight for her than she had given him credit for. The earl's words suggested that her easy-going Perry might be prepared to sacrifice his home, his beloved father, and perhaps even his allowance for her sake. The notion of such loyalty, misguided though it was, touched her deeply.

"You are asking me to give up a lot, my lord," she murmured, silently vowing that she would never permit her darling Perry to make the disastrous sacrifice John had made for her so long ago. She had not the heart to subject a boy to the misery of being cut off from his loved ones. Not that John had uttered a single word of complaint, of course, but Athena had discovered over the years just how much it had cost her husband to wed her.

Lord St. Aubyn's smile sent shivers down Athena's spine. "I am prepared to make it well worth your while, madam," he drawled, dark eyes fixed upon her mercilessly.

"Worth my while?" Athena repeated, puzzled at the veiled flash of triumph she glimpsed in the wolfish gaze. "Whatever can you mean, my lord?"

"Do not play the innocent with me, madam," he snapped, lips curled in a cynical sneer. "I am prepared to offer you three thousand pounds to release my son from any imagined obligation he may fancy, in his innocence, he owes you, Mrs. Standish."

Athena gasped and felt a momentary dizziness. She put out a hand to steady herself against the gleaming surface of the desk that stood between them, like some giant bulwark quite impossible to breach. Recovering her breath, she snatched her hand away and clasped it with the other tightly, returning the glittering stare that threatened to undo her.

She drew a deep breath. "Provided I remove to London at my earliest convenience, I take it, my lord?" she said, bitterness at the ease with which this man had dashed all her hopes causing her voice to tremble.

The earl smiled thinly.

"Exactly, madam."

"I believe your wits have gone begging, Sylvester!" Lady Sarah exclaimed two afternoons later when the earl sought her out in her sitting room upstairs and laid his plan before her. He had given a good deal of thought to the idea since his interview with the widow, and was more than a little put out at his aunt's energetic response.

He stood at the window and from that vantage point could see the elaborate gardens laid out by his grandmother and added to by his mother, a lady noted for her interest in foreign specimens. The roses were in their full glory, he noted absent-mindedly. His grandmother, who had designed the extensive rose beds on either side of the brick path that led down from the terrace, through the garden to the artificial pool, would have been pleased with the results of her labors. The exotic Brazilian water lilies—Lady St. Aubyn's pride and joy—spread their erotic pink faces up to the warm sunshine while, even at this distance, Sylvester caught orange glimpses of the fat, lazy gold-fish his grandfather had gone to considerable pains to import from China for her.

The only flaw to this idyllic scene—at least to his jaundiced eye—was the lady seated on one of the stone benches placed conveniently beside the pool. She wore the lightest of muslin gowns in a shade of pink that competed with the water lilies, and her face was half-hidden by a wide-brimmed straw hat, em-bellished with a pink rose. An open book lay neglected on her lap, her attention seemingly focused on the antics of the gold-fish nibbling at the fingers she trailed in the water to tease them.

Had the earl been ignorant of the identity of the lady beside the pool, he might well have been charmed by the picture she presented in the natural setting. The sun glinted off the coppery curls that tumbled informally about her shoulders, and the long, slender limbs were clearly outlined in unconscious grace be-neath the translucent muslin. As it was, all he felt was a vague uneasiness at the undeniable beauty of the female his son had vowed to make his wife.

"I thought the notion of setting another female to snatch the prize away rather clever myself, Aunt," he remarked, his gaze lingering on the romantic scene in the garden.

Lady Sarah snorted as she always did when provoked. "Mrs. Standish refused to take the bribe, did you say? Are you sure of that, Sylvester? Three thousand pounds must be a small fortune to her. I wonder why she did not rise to the bait."

"The witch had the audacity to tell me I was an odious vil-lain," he replied, a hint of reluctant amusement in his voice.

"Well, and so you can be, Sylvester," his aunt replied with-out hesitation. "I do not doubt you appeared so to Mrs. Standish when you dared to offer her that much money to cast poor Perry off."

"I had certainly thought to tempt her with that sum, but I might be willing to raise the stakes to five thousand, if I could be sure she would take it."

"And you are not?"

Reluctantly, the earl tore his eyes away from the window. "No, I am not at all sure, Aunt. I imagine she is set upon becoming a viscountess. After all, Perry is worth far more that three thousand pounds. And although I have warned him that I will not increase his allowance, he is in a mood to be difficult. I fear he might marry the wench and the devil take the consequences."

Lady Sarah laughed shortly. "I remember a similar argument between you and your father when you set eyes on our lovely Adrienne," she said. "As I recall, you were very young yourself at the time, yet you swore to anyone who would listen that it was a true love match."

"And so it was," Sylvester retorted. "And I beg you will not bring my wife into this discussion, Aunt. I did not lose my head over a widow with a seven-year-old daughter." He paused, the memory of Adrienne still painfully vivid. "Tell me, Aunt," he continued, changing the subject abruptly, "do you believe Perry is truly in love with his widow?"

Lady Sarah raised her gaze from her needlework and stared at him before answering. "I think he is well and truly infatuated, if that is what you mean," she said.

The earl shook his head emphatically. "Well, the notion of such a connection is ridiculous. I have no wish to cause my son pain, but I will not allow it. By God, Aunt, she is eight-and-twenty."

"Really?" Lady Sarah glanced up again from her lap. "She is such a little slip of a thing. I had not given her more than four- or five-and-twenty. Are you sure of this?"

"She told me so herself," he answered. "I had rather expected her to lie to me, you know."

"I certainly would have done so," his aunt remarked brusquely. "Actually, she is quite beautiful, you know. All that glorious copper hair and those odd-colored eyes. I quite understand why our dear Perry has lost his heart to the creature."

The earl made a gesture of impatience. "Whose side are you on, Aunt?" he asked harshly.

Lady Sarah smiled at him, and Sylvester realized with a start that, although his aunt was well into her seventies, her mind was as sharp as it had ever been. She could read him like a book, a knack he had found most uncomfortable as a boy. He still found it disconcerting to see the glimmer of understanding in her bright blue gaze.

"Testy this afternoon, are we? Peregrine's betrothal has—"

"He is *not* betrothed," Sylvester interrupted sharply. "I have forbidden it."

His aunt's smiled broadened, and she shook her head. "As I was saying, dear, this *contretemps* has rattled you more than I would have imagined. Let me remind you, Sylvester, that love is an extraordinarily tenacious force. The more it is denied, the fiercer it burns. I am surprised that you have forgotten that elementary truth."

"Are you suggesting that I should sanction this foolishness, madam?" he said coldly.

"Of course not, Sylvester," Lady Sarah replied impatiently. "Your wits really have gone begging if you believe that. After all, the notice has not yet been sent in to the *Gazette*, so no real harm has been done. But if you act the tyrant, as I can see from Perry's glowering face that you have, you will only push the poor boy into doing something rash."

"He has already committed the ultimate foolishness in bringing that female here under false pretenses."

"Your son has given his word, Sylvester, and you may be sure he will keep it. And once the betrothal becomes public, no doubt the Standish clan will rally behind the girl—do not glare at me like that, Sylvester—and it will be impossible to draw back without scandal. Our darling Perry is no small catch, believe me."

The earl stared at his aunt for a long moment, his expression thunderous. "Then you will go along with my plan?" he demanded finally.

"Yes," Lady Sarah said reluctantly. "But you should be warned, Sylvester, that admitting a widowed lady, however impoverished she may be, into this family is a deuced sight better than having a common actress thrust into our midst."

Sylvester stared at his aunt as though she had sprouted wings. "You cannot be suggesting that there is any real danger of that happening. Surely Perry—"

"Perry is young and impressionable," his aunt replied seriously. "Besides, he is far more innocent than you were at that age, Sylvester. He is barely on the verge of manhood, a dangerous and unpredictable time in his life."

"All the more reason for my plan to be successful," the earl pointed out. "A beautiful, younger female—and naturally I insist that she be ravishing—with no inconvenient notions of modesty, should be able to wean Perry away from his widow within a sennight or two. I cannot wait to see it."

He turned once more to the window, but his gaze searched in vain for the lady beside the pool. She had disappeared, as completely as though her presence had been an illusion. Sylvester felt a twist of disappointment, as unexpected as it was disturbing. The sunlit garden below had lost some of its brightness, as though a cloud had passed over the sky.

The earl brushed these mawkish thoughts aside and turned abruptly back to his aunt. "Then you will write to London today?"

Lady Sarah did not look up from her embroidery. "The letter will go out in this afternoon's post, if that will satisfy you, my dear."

"You are a great gun, Aunt," he said feelingly, moving over to place a hand affectionately on Lady Sarah's frail shoulder. "I depend upon you to see me through this tedious business."

His aunt raised her eyes and said with her usual sharpness, "Then let me give you another piece of advice, dear. I suggest you swallow that infernal reserve of yours and put yourself out to be pleasant to Mrs. Standish, Sylvester. If we are to distract Perry from his widow, it is only reasonable that we also strive to distract the widow. Would you not agree?"

Sylvester gazed thoughtfully into his aunt's astute blue eyes, then shrugged. "That sounds like an ingenious strategy, Aunt. But you know I am more at home with my books than in the drawing room amusing ladies."

Lady Sarah smiled enigmatically. "I also know that it is high time you came out of hiding, Sylvester. I shall expect to see you at the dinner table tonight."

"It will be my pleasure, Aunt," the earl replied lightly.

CHAPTER THREE

The Tea Party

The water felt cool to Athena's fingers, a pleasant contrast to the heat of the afternoon sunshine. She wiggled one finger experimentally to entice a sly, fat fellow out from under the water-lily pad. The bright orange fish seemed undecided, then he moved forward lazily to join two others who nibbled gently at her submerged fingers. She sighed. How simple life might be if she were a fish, she thought. Secure in the small watery world of the pond, they knew nothing of the pain of poverty or rejection. Rank and fortune meant nothing to them. Their joys were probably simple, too: snapping up the insects that dared to pause briefly on the surface of the water; drowsing away the summer afternoons in the cool shade of lily pads; blowing lazy bubbles and nibbling at anything that caught their eye.

Athena's attention shifted as happy sounds rose from the energetic game of croquet that was taking place on the green expanse of lawn. She could not see the players from where she sat, but her daughter's shriek of pure joy was unmistakable. As was Perry's merry crack of laughter, so different from his father's cynical laugh. She knew that her aunt would be there, too, sitting beneath the shady oaks, waiting for the earl's footmen to bring out the tea-tray.

With a small sigh, Athena rose to her feet and made her way through the mass of blooming flowerbeds, down the long trellised pathway, awash with climbing roses in yellows and whites and palest pinks, until she came out into the sunshine again. The sight that met her gaze made her pause and brought a lump to her throat. Penelope tugged wildly at one end of the mallet, while Perry, in shirtsleeves and hair falling about his face, seemed determined to wrest it from her. Two excited spaniels rushed around in all directions, adding to the general commotion with their frenzied barks.

"*My* turn, Perry," her daughter yelled boisterously. "You *know* it is."

"No such thing, you saucy minx," Perry cried laughingly. "Fair is fair, Penny. It is my turn. Ask Mrs. Easton, if you do not believe me."

"Penelope!" Athena called out, advancing across the lawn towards the battling pair. "This is no way for a lady to conduct herself, dear. Whatever would Lady Sarah think if she could see you now?"

At the sound of her voice, Peregrine released his hold on the mallet, sending Penny sprawling on the grass amidst a gale of giggles. He turned and grinned at her.

"You are missing all the fun, Athena," he said, his blue eyes dancing with amusement. He reached down and pulled Penny to her feet. "This daughter of yours is a tip-top player, or would be if she could bring herself not to hog the mallet."

"It was *my* turn," Penelope insisted stubbornly.

"That is enough, Penny," Athena admonished. "Perry will not wish to play with you if you do not give him a turn now and then."

"But—"

"Enough, I said," Athena repeated sternly. "If you insist upon acting like a spoiled baby, I shall send you to take tea in the nursery." This awful threat silenced her daughter, who brushed ineffectually at the grass stains on her dress and handed the mallet to the grinning viscount.

"Race you to the table, Perry," she challenged, their squabble forgotten as the portly Jackson issued from the terrace doors, followed by three footmen carrying silver trays of tea things.

"I would offer you my arm, Athena," Perry said ruefully, "but I am lamentably damp from trying to keep up with your daughter. But I trust you intend to join us for tea." He waved negligently at the butler making his way sedately across the lawn towards the centenary oaks that spread their huge branches over the rustic tea-table and array of lawn chairs.

Before Athena could reply, the imposing figure of Lady Sarah appeared on the terrace, where she paused for a moment, as if debating whether or not to join the small group on the lawn.

"Aunt Sarah!" Peregrine called out eagerly. "How delightful! You are just in time for tea. Here, allow me to assist you." He strode across the grass towards the commanding figure of the dragon, but Athena was not surprised when Lady Sarah waved him aside imperiously with her cane.

"I am not an invalid, Perry," she snapped in her strident

voice, which Athena was beginning to suspect was only adopted with her great-nephew and his guests. "I have no need of your assistance, thank you very much."

"But Aunt—"

"Stop coddling me, Peregrine," the old lady said sharply. "And what new fashion is this to appear at the tea-table in your shirtsleeves, boy?" She paused at the foot of the shallow stairs to regard the object of her censure through her lorgnette.

"I have been playing croquet with Penelope, Aunt," Perry replied, unabashed by her ladyship's stare. "An exhausting business, let me assure you. But naturally I shall replace my coat before I sit down to tea with you." He glanced at the terrace. "Is Father to join us?"

Athena caught a note of wistfulness in Peregrine's voice and a familiar stab of guilt shot through her. The earl had been conspicuous for his absence, both at the dinner table and in the drawing room since that dreadful encounter in the library two days ago. The memory of her reluctant host's grim countenance had troubled Athena's sleep ever since, and she had little doubt that Lord St. Aubyn would refuse to acknowledge her presence until she agreed to accept his outrageous suggestion that she betray his son for a paltry sum of money.

Paltry? Three thousand pounds was hardly a paltry sum, Athena reminded herself, disgusted that she had given the earl's offer more than a passing thought. For if truth be told, she had indeed considered it rather more carefully than she would like to admit. Three thousand pounds was a small fortune and, invested wisely, would provide the extra income she had needed to supplement John's meager pension. The earl's offer had tempted her—Athena was too honest not to admit it—but she knew herself to be equal to that challenge. She would never succumb to his nefarious scheme to be rid of her. His odious bribe had only strengthened her determination to wed Peregrine.

If only she could be sure that such a step would not alienate the earl from his son, she mused, watching Lady Sarah shake her head in response to Peregrine's question. Athena's worst fear was that she would be the cause of a second violent disagreement between a father and a son. It was far too late to remedy the damage she had innocently caused between John and his father, the late Earl of Wentworth, who had gone to his grave unrelenting in his anger towards his youngest son. Her darling John had joined his father two years ago now, and

Athena firmly believed that they had made their peace beyond the grave.

But Peregrine was still such a boy, she thought. An adorable, innocent, and naive boy, so obviously devoted to his father. How could she bare to sunder that sweet bond of love that joined them? Too well she remembered the pain and shock of her own estrangement from her father following his unexpected marriage to his Brighton widow. The new Lady Rothingham had cut Athena off not only from her childhood home and her father's love, but from that sense of belonging to a place in time that contained all her most treasured memories.

She could not—*would* not, if it came to a choice—do that to Peregrine. He was so young, almost a child in many ways, Athena thought nostalgically, wishing—as she so often did— that the viscount were ten years older. But then he would not be the Peregrine she knew and loved, she reminded herself, and he would never have offered her the security of marriage.

A shadow seemed to touch her briefly, and Athena shuddered. She had always enjoyed being a wife, and had begun to despair of ever having a home and husband of her own again. And more children. She had grown alarmed and disillusioned at the number of offers she received from London gentlemen only concerned with their own pleasure.

And then she had met Peregrine by the river that sultry afternoon last spring.

His naive adulation had seemed amusing at first, she remembered, and infinitely touching. Until he had made his first offer of marriage.

She had laughed at the absurdity of such a notion. When he had persisted, Athena had felt the first tug of temptation. She thought of the many sleepless nights she had spent weighing the disadvantages of such an unequal union.

And, of course, the benefits.

"Mama!" The shrill voice of her daughter jerked Athena back to the present. "Perry says I cannot have a currant tart until I have eaten my bread and jam."

"Young ladies do not shout, dear." She glanced around the group seated under the trees, pushing her doubts to the back of her mind. "And Peregrine is quite right. Bread and jam comes first, and if you behave, Lady Sarah may allow you to have one tart."

"Only *one?*" Penelope turned her wide blue gaze on their hostess and Athena distinctly saw a roguish smile tug at the corner of her daughter's mouth. "And if I am extra *extra* good?" she added tentatively, in a wheedling voice, "might I have two, my lady?"

Athena held her breath at the audacity of her child, but before she could censure her, Lady Sarah's caustic voice cut into her thoughts.

"Only if you promise never again to scream in my ear, child," her ladyship said sharply. "As I am always telling Peregrine, I am not yet at my last prayers." She cast a glowering look at the culprit, who seemed not the least cowed by this display of displeasure.

"Do you pray a lot, my lady?"

The awkward silence that followed this artless question was broken by a crack of laughter from Peregrine, who made no attempt to hide his amusement when his aunt threw him a blistering look.

"That will do, young man," she snapped, although Athena was convinced she caught a gleam of humor in the old dragon's eyes. "Come, Mrs. Standish," her ladyship continued briskly, "do not sit there gawking, girl. Make yourself useful and pour the tea for us."

Surprised and pleased at this flattering request to take charge of this duty, Athena hastened to settle herself behind the tea-tray. She smiled up at Peregrine, who had jumped forward to assist her, and his tender smile was balm to her troubled thoughts. If her Perry was happy with their betrothal, as he showed every sign of being, then they would have to find a way to win the earl over to the notion of their marriage.

"Perry, look!" Once again her daughter's voice broke into Athena's comfortable thoughts. "Your papa is coming to join us."

And indeed he was, Athena saw with a tremor of apprehension, as her eyes followed the lithe figure striding across the lawn towards them.

Suddenly the summer afternoon seemed less hospitable than it had a moment ago.

The sight of the ladies gathered under the oak trees on the lawn had drawn the earl out of the library into the sunshine. There had been something nostalgic in the cozy intimacy of the scene that awakened memories of happier times. Lazy summer afternoons spent in that very spot with his beloved Adrienne and young Peregrine. Happy memories that had caused him—

on the spur of the moment—to abandon the lengthy treatise on Chinese porcelain of the Ming Dynasty he had been writing, in the middle of a sentence, and throw his quill down on the cluttered desk.

He would not wait until dinner to put his aunt's suggestion into practice, Sylvester thought, striding across the grass towards Lady Sarah and her guests. He would begin his campaign to distract the lovely widow's attention from his son this very afternoon.

Peregrine's two spaniels, Pip and Squeak, were the first to notice his approach, which they announced with excited yaps and frantic leaping around his knees, their plump bodies squirming with ecstasy.

"Father!" Peregrine exclaimed, quickly drawing up a chair for the earl. "I am so glad you could join us. You missed a splendid game of croquet with Penelope. The minx played so well she almost beat me. Can you imagine that?"

The obvious note of pleasure in his son's voice gave the earl pause for thought. Two days ago he had been so sure of the widow's reaction to his offer of a monetary settlement in exchange for her immediate departure from St. Aubyn's Castle. When Athena Standish had turned up her elegant nose at the not inconsiderable sum he had proposed, the earl realized that the widow must be holding out for more. Either that or she actually intended to lure Perry into her net. Little did the witch know the disappointment that awaited her, he mused with no little complaisance, watching from beneath hooded lids the tender glances his son cast upon the lady.

"My lord?"

Sylvester pulled his thoughts back from savoring the outcome of the plan he had so recently set in motion with the collaboration of his aunt, and found the widow's amber eyes looking directly into his. A most extraordinary color, he thought, startled at the warmth lurking in their tawny depths. Two days ago he had seen them flash with anger, but his own fury had prevented him from appreciating their undeniable beauty. Today he looked his fill and was amused when they fell beneath his gaze, a tell-tale shadow of pink staining the lady's cheeks.

"Father takes both milk and plenty of sugar in his tea, Athena," Perry answered for him. "You will learn the terrible truth soon enough," the viscount continued with a wide grin, "so I might as well tell you that Father has a worse sweet tooth than I do myself."

"What is a sweet tooth?" Penelope asked.

Sylvester turned to find the young girl's candid gaze fixed upon him curiously. She was a beautiful child, he had to admit, her pale golden curls and blue eyes oddly reminiscent of Peregrine's. They might well have been brother and sister, he realized, remembering with a jolt how much Adrienne had wished for a daughter. He wondered if the audacious widow had remarked on this curious likeness.

He smiled wryly at the thought, and the child, imagining the gesture was for her, returned a dazzling smile that lit her small face and caused her eyes to dance like two wild cornflowers in the meadow.

Quite of its own accord, the earl's heart constricted, and he had to look away, the memory of his wife and the daughter they had not had together vivid in his mind.

"A sweet tooth is something to be wary of, child," Lady Sarah answered unexpectedly. "Unless, of course, you wish your teeth to rot away and fall out before you are twenty."

Penelope's eyes opened wide. "Oh, Perry!" she exclaimed, turning to the viscount, "never say that your teeth—"

"That is quite enough, Penny," her mother cut in, rather prudently the earl thought, since the child was undoubtedly poised to utter something quite outrageous. He was surprised at the sense of disappointment he felt at being deprived of this childish chatter. It had been far too long since he had been around children, and this young girl reminded him vividly of dreams that had passed him by.

Shaking these maudlin thoughts from his mind, Sylvester smiled at the child. "I daresay Perry has a few years to go before his teeth turn black," he murmured, enjoying the way her eyes grew round with wonder. "But I hear that if little girls eat too many tarts at tea-time, they will be fat and ugly for their come-out."

"And no gentleman will wish to dance with them," Perry put in with a laugh.

"I shall *never* be fat and ugly," Penelope protested with conviction. "I shall look just like Mama when I grow up. And Perry will dance with me, will you not, Perry?"

"Of course, sweetheart," the viscount responded promptly, passing the plate of tarts. "Here, love. Have one."

Penelope glanced apprehensively at Lady Sarah. "I have not

finished my bread and jam, Perry. And neither have you," she added with a saucy smile. "So we shall both have to wait, shall we not?"

Sylvester turned to Lady Sarah and was startled to see the softening of her expression as she gazed fondly at the child.

"How soon can we expect to welcome the Rathbones, Aunt?" he inquired smoothly, amused at the slightly flustered look that flashed briefly in Lady Sarah's eyes.

"The Rathbones?" Peregrine repeated, a puzzled frown on his face. "Who are the Rathbones, Aunt Sarah? I do not recall—"

Lady Sarah interrupted rather brusquely. "You do not know them, Perry, so it does not surprise me that you cannot remember anyone by that name."

"Oh, but I do," Peregrine said quickly, his frown deepening. "The name is definitely familiar, Aunt, but I cannot for the life of me make the connection."

The earl shot a warning glance at his aunt, but Lady Sarah rose admirably to the challenge. "You are probably thinking of Colonel James Rathbone from the Dorset Rathbones, dear. He and his sister visited the Castle briefly one summer when your dear mother was still with us. As far as I know, he is now married and residing in London. He married one of the Harrison girls, I believe." She paused and appeared to consider her words. "Or was it Lord Sheffield's youngest daughter, I wonder?"

"Never heard of any of them," Perry said briefly. "And I do not recall any Colonel Rathbone coming to the Castle either."

Sylvester glanced at his aunt admiringly. It did not surprise him that his son remembered nothing of such a visit, for the earl was convinced that the whole episode was pure invention on Lady Sarah's part.

It was a great pity, he mused, that his great-grandfather had cut short his youngest daughter's highly improper career on the stage so many years ago. The scandal had occurred in Sarah's youth, when she and another of the pupils of Mrs. Hawthorne's Academy for Young Ladies in Bath had escaped through an upstairs window and gone off to London in the company of a groom in the unfortunate Mrs. Hawthorne's household. Everything had been hushed up, naturally, but while Lady Sarah had been rescued from a life of shame by her irate father, her companion in sin had remained in London and gone on to become an actress of some note. Her stage name—and the rumors of her legions of lovers—had been all the crack in his father's time,

Sylvester recalled, but he knew for a fact that the woman had been a Rathbone, although her family had very publicly disowned her.

And now she was coming to St. Aubyn Castle.

"Augusta Rathbone is an old school friend of mine," Lady Sarah said dismissively. "She has promised to spend a few weeks with me this summer, and will be accompanied by her granddaughter, Viviana, by all accounts a charming young person. Do pass your father his tea-cup, Perry," she added sharply, forestalling any further questions on the subject of their mysterious guest.

"I am sure we shall all enjoy the addition of a charming young lady to our party, my lady," piped a bright voice from a low chair on the other side of his aunt.

For the first time since his arrival, Sylvester looked at the frumpish, rosy-faced woman who had uttered these prophetic words. Mrs. Easton radiated banality from the tip of the crimped curls clustering atop her small head to the profusion of ribbons, bows, and furbelows that adorned her excessively bright afternoon gown of dubious vintage.

Nobody paid the slightest attention to this odd, diminutive creature except Mrs. Standish, who threw her aunt a small smile. Mrs. Easton appeared not the least put out by the lack of reaction to her innocuous comment, merely reaching for another currant tart with plump, eager fingers.

The earl looked away. The lady's remark struck him as eerily ironic, and he could not help smiling to himself. How many of this odd party gathered on his ancestral lawn would actually derive any enjoyment from the addition of Viviana Rathbone to their number? he wondered.

He could think of only one. Himself.

Long after tea was over and Lord St. Aubyn had escorted his aunt back to the house, and after Mrs. Easton had excused herself to retire to her room for a rest before dressing for dinner, Athena sat on beneath the old oaks, her mind in a turmoil. She had resisted Perry's entreaties to join him in a game of croquet, and now listened with only half an ear to his shouts of encouragement and Penelope's squeals of delight as she maneuvered the wooden ball through the hoops.

Something about the earl's sudden appearance at the tea party that afternoon did not ring quite right. He had stared at her rather brazenly, she thought, and she had been disconcerted by the glint of amusement she had detected in his eyes. Those eyes had disconcerted her, too. She had thought them black, or at least a dark brown, that morning they had met in the library. But in the summer sunlight they had been blue—a deep, startling, midnight blue that hovered on the edge of black.

And he had been amused, she was sure of it. Or could she have imagined that flicker of laughter in those blue depths? The question that intrigued and, she had to admit, alarmed her was why he had abruptly changed from the fiercely outraged parent of two days ago to the almost benevolent pose he had adopted at the tea-table.

Athena was sure the earl's cordiality had been assumed. She could think of no other explanation, and the notion that he had abandoned his plan to bribe her disturbed her even more. At least when faced with the earl's open attack, she knew where she stood. His false cordiality—for what else could it be? she asked herself for the tenth time—made her increasingly uneasy. What perverse strategy was he planning to drive her back to London? she wondered.

"A penny for your thoughts, love."

Athena glanced wryly at her betrothed, who threw himself into a chair beside her. Peregrine was such an innocent. He had been visibly pleased at his father's appearance, and Athena doubted that he had given a thought to the earl's sudden change of mood. His second remark proved her wrong.

"I do believe that Father is reconciled to our marriage, Athena. Did I not tell you he would come around when he got to know you better?" he said with such enthusiasm that Athena had not the heart to confide her fears. What would the viscount say if he knew that his beloved father had offered his chosen bride three thousand pounds to jilt him? she wondered. Her heart cringed at the notion of inflicting so much hurt on poor Perry. An open breach between father and son was one thing she earnestly wished to avoid.

"You are not still worried about his disapproval, are you, Athena?" Perry inquired with an infectious grin. "I promise that we will be able to post the banns within a week. Sooner if you like, for I am certain Father will not hold out much longer against us."

Athena forced herself to return a cheerful smile she was far from feeling. "I believe you may be right, Perry. But humor me in this, dear. Let us wait until we all feel more comfortable with one another. There is no need to rush into anything, after all, is there?"

Peregrine looked slightly downcast. "No, I suppose not," he replied dubiously. "But I do so wish to provide you and Penny with a secure future, my dear."

Not for the first time Athena fancied her betrothed sounded perilously like a little boy who had been deprived of a special treat. She put the unkind thought aside and suggested that it was time to dress for dinner.

For the rest of that week Athena could find no real complaint to make about her host. The earl appeared regularly at the dinner table, and occasionally took tea with the family in the garden. He was pleasant enough, she admitted to her aunt one evening as Mrs. Easton accompanied her into Penelope's room to say good night, as they were in the habit of doing, before retiring for the night.

"You are making a big pother over nothing, my dear Athena," her aunt scolded in her lighthearted way. "I cannot believe that his lordship could find anything amiss with you if he tried, dear. And I got the distinct impression this evening that he is more than a little taken with you himself."

Athena stared at her aunt, aghast. "You are certainly exaggerating, Aunt," she replied curtly.

But her aunt's words chased all thoughts of a peaceful night from her mind. The more Athena argued to herself that her aunt had grossly mistaken the matter, the more a reckless voice in her heart urged her to take advantage of the earl's mellowing disposition—and there was no denying that he had, for whatever reason, mellowed towards her—to gain his approval of her marriage to his son.

A dangerous game, to be sure, her common sense warned her. But if played with discretion, one that could well yield bountiful rewards.

CHAPTER FOUR

The Rival

Two days later Athena began to suspect that she had seriously underestimated the mellowing of Lord St. Aubyn's feelings towards her.

The first indication she had that anything was amiss occurred during the tea hour, which had become a ritual gathering under the oaks on the lawn, often attended by the earl.

That particular afternoon, the pleasant rural tea-party that Athena had come to enjoy as the highlight of her day had been interrupted. Shortly after nuncheon the sun had disappeared and a misty drizzle drove the ladies indoors. Peregrine and Lord St. Aubyn took advantage of the cooler weather to go on a tramp through Hangman's Wood, so called ever since an early Baron St. Aubyn had hanged a marauding Saxon there in the uneasy days of the Norman Conqueror.

There had been no question of serving tea in the garden, and Lady Sarah had insisted upon gathering in the formal Blue Dragon Saloon. Since Aunt Mary excused herself to accompany Penelope upstairs to the nursery to have her tea, Athena and her hostess sat together in Oriental splendor surrounded by what Athena supposed must be a small fortune in exotic furnishings.

It was not an ambiance conducive to comfortable conversation, and Lady Sarah seemed more than usually withdrawn into her aristocratic cocoon of aloofness and condescending small talk. After fifteen minutes of such stilted exchange, Athena wished she had gone upstairs with her daughter. She could well imagine the lively conversation that would be going on at that very moment between her Aunt Mary and the irrepressible Penny.

Could she get away by pleading a megrim? she wondered rather desperately. Or dare she introduce a topic more inspiring than the unseasonable break in the weather, upon which her ladyship had droned on for quite five minutes? Or should she try something quite unpardonably gauche, like dropping the fragile Limoges tea-cup Lady Sarah had just passed her onto the writhing mass of blue dragons, whose furious golden eyes glared up at her from the floor?

Athena was rescued from having to resort to mayhem by the sound of the Saloon doors opening. She turned eagerly, expecting to see Perry come bounding in, a contagious smile on his handsome face.

She was disappointed.

The butler stood on the threshold, his impassive features set in their normal rigidity, his colorless eyes fixed on a point in the far distance, his mouth pursed into what Penelope had dubbed his stewed-prune look.

"Mrs. Augusta Rathbone and Miss Viviana Rathbone, milady," he intoned in his driest, most toneless voice.

Lady Sarah moved not a muscle, but Athena, who was looking directly at the butler, received the full force of the Rathbone ladies' entrance.

Mrs. Rathbone entered first, and her aplomb and style were such that, for a moment, Athena fancied the newcomer to be Lady Macbeth herself, borne along by the force of her overweening passions. She was a splendid figure of a woman, tall and stately, her white hair swept up into a fashionable knot beneath an elaborate straw bonnet that even Athena's untutored senses recognized as the *dernier cri*. Her traveling gown, in a warm wine-red lustring trimmed with blond lace, was deceptively simple in its elegance, and Athena did not doubt that it had cost more than she herself spent on clothes in a year.

Although Athena knew that Mrs. Rathbone could not be much less than seventy years old, she had to admire the youthful manner in which the visitor swept into the Saloon and advanced upon her childhood friend with arms outstretched in a charming gesture of affection.

"Sarah!" she exclaimed in a throaty contralto that filled the room with resounding echoes. "My dearest, dearest Sarah! We meet again after so long. Do not get up, dear," she added in that wonderfully musical voice, although she must have seen as well as anyone, Athena noted with amusement, that Lady Sarah had made no move to do so. That did not prevent her from embracing her hostess effusively.

"I shall just sit here beside you and be comfortable," she continued, suiting action to words by seating herself gracefully on the blue-striped brocade settee and removing her red kid gloves. "You have no idea how I long to recall those marvelous times we had at Mrs. . . . Mrs. . . . what was that dreadful woman's name, dear? Hawkins?"

"Hawthorne," her hostess supplied, with a faint smile breaking through the sedate mask she had worn all afternoon. "Mrs. Iphigenia Hawthorne, I believe. And surely you exaggerate, my dear Gussie, when you call those days marvelous. The woman was a veritable dragon, as far as I recall. If your brother had not kept us supplied with pastries during his visits, we might well have starved to death."

"Ah, yes, dearest, dearest Adrian." Mrs. Rathbone sighed theatrically, one elegant white hand brushing her brow briefly. "What a handsome devil he was, too, Sarah. And more than a little taken with you, my dear, as I recall."

Had Athena considered it at all possible, she might have said that Lady Sarah blushed, but her attention was drawn to a second visitor who appeared suddenly—and with quite deliberate theatricality, Athena thought—in the doorway.

"Ah, there you are, love," Mrs. Rathbone purred in her wonderful voice. "Allow me to introduce my darling granddaughter to you, Sarah," she said, flinging out an arm dramatically in the direction of the young lady who stood poised on the threshold, as though awaiting just such a cue to make her entrance.

Miss Viviana Rathbone quite literally took Athena's breath away.

The young girl was a vision in palest pink muslin, gathered beneath the bosom in tiny pleats and festooned with dozens of silk rosebuds in a deeper shade of pink around the neckline, on the cuffs of the tiny puffed sleeves, and on the deep flounce around the hem. Her gloves, in the same shade of pink as the rosebuds, revealed an expanse of unblemished, softly rounded arms that might well be likened to a statue of Aphrodite, while the pink straw bonnet, adorned with a single pink rose amidst a nest of lace, framed a face so perfect that Athena simply could not drag her eyes away.

"Come and make your curtsy to Lady Sarah Steele, my love," Mrs. Rathbone urged, and the vision floated—or so it appeared to Athena's stunned senses—across the Saloon and sank into as graceful a curtsy as Athena had ever witnessed.

"Dearest Sarah," Mrs. Rathbone gushed in richly toned accents, "this is my darling granddaughter, Viviana, who has been dying to make your acquaintance, dear. She has heard me speak of you many times, of course, and is quite in alt at your invitation to accompany me to St. Aubyn Castle, are you not, love?"

"Yes, Grandmama," the vision responded in a tinkling, chime-like voice that made Athena think of Christmas sleigh bells on clear winter evenings.

"Well," Mrs. Rathbone said with evident pleasure. "A beautiful creature, my granddaughter, would you not agree, Sarah? Quite lovely enough to turn any man's head, I warrant you."

This seemed an odd thing to say, but Athena had little time to ponder on it, for at that moment Lady Sarah appeared to remember her presence and changed the subject abruptly.

"Gussie, meet Mrs. Athena Standish, who is staying at the Castle for a few weeks."

Mrs. Rathbone turned her gaze upon Athena, who experienced the uncomfortable sensation of being dissected piece by piece by that lady's shrewd gray eyes.

"Athena? Your parents must surely have been addicted to the classics, my dear," Mrs. Rathbone remarked in her splendid voice. "I never could abide them myself, of course. Perhaps that would explain my aversion for such pretentious monikers as Achilles, Hector, Ajax, Cassandra; even Helen smacks of false grandeur. Although one could hardly accuse you of that, Mrs. Standish," she added with a brilliant smile that did nothing to diminish the implied snub.

Quite unprepared for such rudeness, Athena held her tongue and turned to the young lady in pink.

"Viviana, my love," Mrs. Rathbone continued, gesturing towards the younger woman with a glittering smile. "My dearest, dearest granddaughter," she repeated, as though savoring the sound of the words on her silver tongue. "I trust you will be patient with her, Mrs. Standish. Young girls can be so astonishingly shy in company. Perhaps with you as her friend, my darling will acquire more confidence in herself."

Startled at the notion of playing mentor to such a divine-looking creature, Athena smiled faintly. "I am delighted to make your acquaintance, Miss Rathbone," she said, watching enviously the perfect curtsy the lady in pink executed for her benefit. "Would you care to sit here beside me and let me serve you a cup of tea?"

"Yes, darling!" Mrs. Rathbone exclaimed before the Beauty had a chance to respond. "What a delightful suggestion! Do accept Mrs. Standish's kind invitation, my dear. You cannot go wrong if you take her lead in such things."

At her grandmother's words, a slight frown seemed to mar the perfection of Miss Rathbone's porcelain countenance, and Athena imagined she detected a faint pout on the rosebud lips. But it was the Beauty's large pansy-blue eyes that confirmed her fleeting impression that the lady in pink was not entirely at ease in the sumptuous drawing room. As she rose from the curtsy, Miss Rathbone's gaze flicked over Athena, surprising her with the animosity reflected there.

Was it dislike? Athena asked herself, calming her sudden agitation with the familiar motions of pouring tea and passing the cup to the Beauty, now seated demurely at her side on the Chinese settee. No, that was patently impossible; they had only just met. Or was it annoyance at being thrust into the company of a strange female so soon after her arrival? Or perhaps contempt, Athena reasoned, suddenly conscious that her simple green afternoon gown paled in comparison to the Beauty's profusion of pink rosebuds.

Or perhaps she had imagined that sullen glare in those intense blue eyes? Yes, she told herself firmly. She was being uncommonly sensitive over a casual glance that probably meant nothing at all. She turned to Miss Rathbone, with a friendly smile.

"I trust you will enjoy your stay in the country," she remarked, determined to draw the girl out.

"I hate the rain," came the faintly petulant response.

"Oh, this drizzle is only temporary, they say," Athena countered. "We have had simply glorious weather for the past week, and Lady Sarah has organized an outing to the ruins of a Norman abbey for tomorrow afternoon. I am quite looking forward to it myself."

"Will the earl be one of the party?"

Athena looked at the Beauty sharply, but the luminous eyes were downcast and the face expressionless. "Oh, yes. Lord St. Aubyn was the one who suggested exploring the ruins, which are reported in the Guide Books as picturesque as well as of historical value."

"And his son?"

Athena paused, her cup suspended midway between the saucer and her lips. It was not the question so much as the inflection of the Beauty's voice that triggered a warning note in her head. Of course Peregrine would be there, she thought. He had promised to guide her through the dark and—according to his highly dramatic version of the Abbey's history—dangerous passageways to the dungeons beneath the stone floors of the chapel. She had been looking forward to spending a delightful afternoon in his company.

"Yes, naturally Viscount Fairmont will accompany us," she answered shortly. "And I advise you to wear sensible shoes, Miss Rathbone," she added on impulse. "The ground may be rough."

"I hate sensible shoes," came the pettish reply. "And I do not intend to do any walking. I shall sit in the shade and drink lemonade." She paused for a moment, as though considering the prospect.

"You may be bored," Athena suggested.

"If the viscount is with us, I shall not be bored," the Beauty remarked confidently. A faint smile—oddly sensuous for one so young—curved her shapely lips, and Athena felt a rising sense of unease.

"I hear he is dashingly handsome," Miss Rathbone remarked in her bell-like voice. "Would you not agree, Mrs. Standish? You must know him well."

The deep blue eyes regarded her coyly from beneath indecently long lashes.

Yes, Athena thought crossly, how could she not agree that Peregrine—her own darling Perry—was blindingly handsome in the first flush of his youthful innocence? But before she could find a suitable set-down for this impertinent miss, the Saloon doors swung open and the object of her thoughts appeared in the doorway, a wide grin on his flushed face.

Perry's gaze sought her out, but a movement from beside her drew his gaze to the Beauty. With no little amazement, Athena saw that an elegant pink fan had appeared mysteriously in Miss Rathbone's white hand and was being used with consummate grace to draw the gentleman's eyes to her lovely face.

The wanton minx was actually flirting with her betrothed! Athena could only watch in horror as Perry's grin slipped into a fatuous grimace, and his eyes glazed over as he continued to stare at Miss Rathbone, an idiotic expression on his handsome face.

A movement behind Peregrine distracted her, and Athena found herself gazing into the blue-black eyes of Lord St. Aubyn. When he raised one rakish eyebrow and treated her to a lazy smile, Athena knew the earl had seen her distress, perhaps even read her horrified thoughts, which she had been too startled to hide. He appeared to be vastly amused.

Athena felt suddenly ill as the implications of that smile dawned on her.

Peregrine's entrance into the Blue Dragon Saloon had been boisterous enough to incur Lady Sarah's censure, but the earl did not hear her familiar reproof as he strolled in behind his son. He paused to glance over Perry's shoulder and the reason for the sudden silence became abundantly clear. His son's gaze was riveted upon the two ladies seated on the Chinese settee facing the door. A cursory glance at the ladies, however, convinced Sylvester that he had mistaken the matter. Peregrine was gaping like a veritable rudesby at only one of the ladies.

Ignoring the vision in pink and cream that had reduced his son and heir to unnatural silence, Sylvester's gaze sought the other occupant of the settee. He had been prepared to gloat over Athena Standish's defeat. The notion of seeing her ousted from Peregrine's affections by a younger, more beautiful female had appealed to his sense of justice. But as Sylvester stared into the anguished amber eyes of the widow, he experienced a moment of doubt.

He raised a quizzical eyebrow and favored Athena Standish with a faintly ironic smile.

Was it possible that Athena Standish truly harbored tender feelings for his son? he wondered. The notion had never occurred to him before, and for some odd reason, Sylvester found it disagreeable. He had assumed the widow as after Perry's fortune, an entirely natural conclusion given the circumstances. But she had refused to be bribed. He had been convinced that she would jump at three thousand pounds; another false conclusion, as it happened. Should he have offered five thousand? Perhaps an additional two thousand might have tempted her, he thought, and she might have been gone by now. He might have been spared this disturbing glimpse into a woman's soul.

Impatiently, the earl dragged his eyes away from that agonizing amber gaze. He was being fanciful, he told himself. The widow had made her choice, and he had made his. The die was cast, so to speak. There was no turning back; and had there been a way to halt the farce that was unfolding before his eyes, Sylvester would not have changed his mind. Peregrine had made a foolish mistake, and it was up to him to protect his son from his own folly.

Running an experienced eye over the vision in pink seated beside the widow, the earl grimaced to himself. His aunt's school friend had outdone herself. The young female sitting so primly beside the widow had already earned part of the money he was paying her. She had drawn Perry's attention away from Athena Standish, not only with her pale, stunning beauty, but with the inviting movements of her pink fan, the coy fluttering of her lashes, and the unmistakable admiration in her limpid blue eyes. She was the incarnation of delightful femininity that would have caught his own eye had he been twenty years younger, Sylvester admitted. As it was, his tastes ran to females with less blatant charms.

His gaze shifted to the widow, whose auburn head was bent over her tea-cup. Her face was expressionless, and were it not for her unnatural pallor, Sylvester might have thought he had imagined the pain he had so recently witnessed in her eyes.

"Come in, come in," Lady Sarah called impatiently, breaking into the silent tableau. "My dear friend Mrs. Rathbone and her granddaughter are with us at last, Sylvester. Come over and make their acquaintance," she commanded. "Mrs. Standish, be so good as to serve the gentlemen their tea," she added, after the introductions had been made. "And Peregrine, make yourself useful and ring for Jackson. We shall need another plate of tarts now that you have arrived, dear."

Peregrine complied with alacrity and then managed to find a seat close to the Beauty, Sylvester noticed, grimacing at his son's lack of finesse. As Mrs. Rathbone claimed his attention with the latest *on-dits* from London, the earl observed, with grudging admiration, her granddaughter's skill at capturing and holding the unsuspecting Peregrine's interest.

"I am told that you have a delightful surprise in store for us tomorrow, my lord," she trilled, directing a blinding smile at Peregrine.

"S-surprise?" Perry stammered, obviously reeling under the force of Miss Rathbone's charm.

"The visit to the Abbey," Mrs. Standish reminded him gently.

"Ah, of c-course," Perry stammered. "We are g-getting up a party to explore the ruins of the Abbey. I hope you will join us, Miss Rathbone," he added, with such obvious eagerness in his voice that the earl glanced uneasily at Mrs. Standish.

The widow was munching disinterestedly on a watercress sandwich, her eyes fixed on the plate in her lap. Her color had returned, and there was a polite smile on her lips. Sylvester could not but admire her courage. She made no attempt to compete with the Beauty, which would probably have been a fruitless endeavor, the earl admitted, watching the besotted expression on his son's face as Miss Rathbone leaned forward to rap him gently with her fan and tinkle at him in her bell-like voice.

Peregrine had the grace to blush, the earl noted, amused to see the guilty glance his son threw in the direction of his widow, whose attention seemed to be wholly engrossed in her sandwich.

"I would not miss it for the world," Miss Rathbone breathed with a pretty display of fluttering eyelashes. "What a delightful notion, my lord. How clever of you to think of it."

Peregrine blushed a deeper shade of pink, and to the earl's chagrin, he saw a fatuous smirk spread over his son's face at the compliment. An undeserved compliment, the earl thought wryly, since only the new guests were unaware that it had been his own suggestion to organize the drive to the ruins. Sylvester dared not look at the widow, but for the second time since the arrival of the Rathbones, he felt a twinge of pity for her.

Shortly before the party broke up, Mrs. Standish excused herself to go up to the nursery. Sylvester did not miss the satisfied smile on the Beauty's perfect face as the door closed behind her rival, nor the way she took advantage of the widow's absence to whisper something into Perry's ear that made him blush again. No doubt she considered herself the winner of the first round, he thought. And perhaps she was right, if the widow's retreat might be considered a defeat. But Sylvester doubted that the stalwart Mrs. Standish would cave in so easily.

In truth, he found himself hoping she would put the petulant Beauty's nose out of joint.

Alarmed at these mixed feelings regarding the very female he had hoped to dispatch back to London as soon as possible, the earl rose abruptly to his feet, excused himself to the ladies, and reminded Perry that they had an appointment in the stables to look at a new hunter.

His normally loquacious son was oddly silent as they walked down to the stables. Sylvester wondered if Perry's thoughts had remained behind in the Blue Dragon Saloon with the captivating Miss Rathbone.

Was his son's conscience troubling him? he wondered.

Or was it merely his own that had become unexpectedly fastidious?

*   *   *

Athena's rest was disturbed by fleeting dreams in which she attempted fruitlessly to escape from vaguely familiar assailants, who assumed various disguises to confuse her. First it was the incomparable Miss Rathbone, all smiles and pretty dimples, who suddenly became a witch with sagging jowls and hollow eyes. Then Lord St. Aubyn's handsome face, smiling at her seductively, turned into a leering monster before her horrified gaze. Even her fair-haired, innocent Perry changed from an adoring boy into a thin-faced, lecherous roué who grasped at her with evil intent. When Lady Sarah and the elegant Mrs. Rathbone appeared riding on broomsticks and attired in witches' habits, Athena gave up and scrambled out of bed to sit by the window, waiting impatiently for the dawn.

Quite unable to face either her hosts or their latest house guests, she spent the morning in the nursery with Aunt Mary and Penny. For a short while she was able to forget that they were in Cornwall, unwelcome guests of the Earl of St. Aubyn, but as the hour appointed for the excursion to the Abbey approached, Penny insisted upon hearing once again the history of the ruined Norman Abbey and the events surrounding its decay. Perry had already told the story several times, adding grim details—most assuredly invented on the spur of the moment, Athena guessed—of ghostly monks haunting the walled gardens and shrieks reportedly heard from the dungeons by local farmers. Penny had made the grinning Peregrine promise her a guided tour of the dungeons, where—or so he claimed—fragments of bones belonging to the unfortunate monks could still be found if one knew where to look.

Athena had looked forward to the outing as a chance to talk privately with Peregrine as they had done so frequently in London. She had agreed to ride with him rather than go in the carriage with the other ladies. Lord St. Aubyn had declined to accompany them, pleading a prior engagement, and Athena was relieved to know that she would have Perry to herself without his father's dampening presence.

Now she was not so sure. The arrival of the Rathbone ladies threatened to disrupt the delicate balance of relationships at the Castle. But what form would this disruption take? Athena wondered as she descended to the hall with Penelope and Mrs. Easton. In view of Perry's quite inexcusable behavior yesterday at tea, and again in the drawing room after dinner, when he had appeared to hang on every inconsequential word uttered by the beautiful Miss Rathbone, Athena did not dare to examine the alternatives too closely.

"Will we see the monks in the garden, Mama?" Penelope demanded for the fifth time since breakfast, her voice hushed in anticipation.

"Perry said the ghosts only appear at night, dear," she replied calmly, wishing, not for the first time, that her betrothed had more sense than to intrigue a seven-year-old with tales of phantoms and long-buried bones.

"Mama, I want to ride with you and Perry," her daughter declared, airing one of her chief protests about the planned excursion.

"You do not know how to ride, love," Athena explained patiently, nodding to Jackson as she stepped out into the morning sunshine.

"Perry said he would teach me, Mama. If you agree. Do say you will agree, Mama," she pleaded. "Perry," she called excitedly to the viscount, who stood talking to one of the grooms, "you did promise to teach me to ride, did you not?"

Penelope ran down the shallow steps to pull impetuously on Perry's arm, but Athena's attention was drawn to the third horse held by the earl's groom. Her heart sank. It was the earl's big chestnut, Ajax.

Athena came down to stand beside Tarantella, the dappled gray mare she had ridden during the past week. The mare nipped playfully at the sleeve of her bottle-green riding habit, and Athena rummaged in her pocket for the lump of sugar she had remembered to bring with her. Tarantella accepted the offering greedily, rolling it around with her tongue and nodding her head up and down, eyes closed contentedly.

"Mama!" Her daughter's voice distracted Athena from the somber thoughts that had intruded upon her at the sight of the earl's mount. "Did you hear what Perry said, Mama? He is going to teach me to ride tomorrow. On his old pony Buttercup. He says that you may come, too, if you like," Penny added, her voice high with excitement.

Before Athena could reply, there was a commotion at the top of the stair, and a chatter of female voices. Or rather the chatter of one particular female voice, she thought, listening to the tinkling laughter and light teasing banter of Miss Rathbone. The deeper contralto of her grandmother remarking on the splendid weather, quite as though she had arranged it personally, told Athena that the party was getting ready to depart.

"Help me to mount, will you, Perry," she said, glancing over her shoulder at her betrothed. "Perry!" she repeated when it became obvious that the viscount was paying her not the slightest heed. Following his gaze, Athena saw what had captured his rapt attention.

The Beauty was advancing slowly down the steps towards the carriage, and even the grooms were staring at her, their mouths agape. If Miss Rathbone had appeared beautiful yesterday in pink, this morning she was absolutely ravishing in the palest of blues. Her hair, arranged in elaborate ringlets around her heart-shaped face, gleamed golden in the sunlight, and her pansy-blue eyes danced with anticipation.

Those hypnotic eyes, Athena noticed with a sinking feeling, were riveted firmly on Peregrine's face. The viscount appeared oblivious of everything else.

Athena turned back to the mare, murderous thoughts concerning the delectable person of Miss Rathbone chasing one another through her head.

"Allow me, my dear Mrs. Standish." The faintly amused voice came from immediately behind her, and Athena did not need to turn her head to know that the earl had witnessed her mortification.

What could she do, she fumed, but allow herself to be tossed up into the saddle by the very gentleman she had hoped to avoid? She was so incensed at Perry's rudeness—for what else could it be? she told herself—that Athena could barely bring herself to thank the earl civilly before urging the mare away from the crowd gathering around the carriages.

Repressing the sudden desire to give the mare her head and gallop away from the source of her frustration, Athena drew rein under one of the massive oaks that dotted the Park. The mare danced about nervously, tossing her small head and rattling the bit. She would have to pull herself together, Athena thought, or Tarantella might take it into her head to bolt. The last thing she needed was to take a fall in front of all these people.

The sound of hooves on gravel caused her to turn sharply, but her smile died when she saw Lord St. Aubyn approaching on his big chestnut. In the distance, the number of people milling around the carriages seemed to have increased, as servants hurried out with baskets of food and wine, blankets, cushions, folding tables and even chairs that they loaded into a sturdy gig drawn up behind the open carriages that had been ordered to convey the ladies to the Abbey ruins.

In the center of this pandemonium, Athena could clearly see the Beauty standing up in the first carriage, gesturing to Perry to place a cushion here, a rug there. Her tinkling voice could also be heard instructing her dear viscount to hand up her parasol, and to make sure that the book of poetry she intended to read aloud after their picnic lunch was stowed safely under the seat.

Not once did Peregrine glance in her direction, Athena noted, her lips settling into thin lines. Only after Miss Rathbone finally nestled herself on the velvet seat did Perry turn to hand up Lady Sarah and Mrs. Rathbone. Penelope and Aunt Mary had been relegated to the second carriage with the baskets of crockery, presumably because dear Viviana's nerves could not support the chatter of children, Mrs. Rathbone's dramatic voice was heard explaining to Lady Sarah and everyone else within two miles of the front door.

Athena sighed with relief when she saw Perry mount his horse, but when he trotted up it was not to join her as they had planned.

"Aunt Sarah has asked me to ride beside her carriage to point out the landmarks on the estate to Mrs. Rathbone, who has expressed an interest in them," he explained hurriedly, an embarrassed grin on his face. "Perhaps we can ride back together, Athena," he added lamely. "I shall ask Father to accompany you in my stead."

Without trusting herself to speak, Athena swung her mare and cantered off, her back ramrod-straight, her temper barely under control.

CHAPTER FIVE

The Dungeon

Several minutes passed before Athena heard the sound of the chestnut's hooves behind her, but she was relieved when the earl did not immediately appear at her side. At least he had the sense to know that his company would not be welcome, she thought grimly, holding the mare down to a canter with some difficulty. Her emotions had suffered such a severe shock that Athena felt her hands trembling, and the mare, sensing her anger as horses always do, was looking for a chance to bolt.

Athena was tempted to drop her hands and allow the mare to work out her fidgets in a wild gallop. Her own agitated spirit might find some solace in the rush of the wind against her face; but prudence prevailed. A mile down the road Athena remembered they would have to ford a stream, so she reluctantly brought Tarantella down to a trot.

As if on signal, the earl brought his chestnut up beside her, and Athena waited tensely for him to make some mocking remark. When he remained silent, she relaxed slightly.

"You are an excellent horsewoman, Mrs. Standish," he remarked, his deep voice oddly soothing.

Athena glanced at him. "I am country-born, my lord," she said shortly, hoping he would not expect her to carry on a polite conversation. After the mortification she had suffered at his son's hands, she was not at all sure she wished to be civil to Lord St. Aubyn.

He said no more until they had crossed the ford, then unexpectedly, he asked her about her childhood.

"I understand you were a Rothingham before you married Standish," he began. "Would you by any chance be related to Sir Henry Rothingham up in Somerset?"

"Why, yes," she exclaimed, surprised and not a little pleased that her family was known to the earl. "Sir Henry is my father. Rothingham Manor, where I grew up, is not far from Bath. It was there, at one of the summer assemblies, that I met John."

She stopped abruptly, conscious of the old ache in her heart at the memory of her lost husband.

Why was she speaking of John to this man? she wondered. What could he possibly know of her painful memories? Or care, for that matter? His was a privileged life here at his ancestral castle. He knew nothing of rejection; how could he? While she still carried those invisible scars, inflicted first by her husband's family in denying her status as John's wife, then by her father in refusing to give her a home with him when John's regiment was sent to Spain. And then of course, there was the loss of John himself, a shattering experience Athena knew she would never entirely get over. Now it appeared that she was to lose Peregrine, too.

She felt her throat tighten and fixed her eyes rigidly on the road ahead. It had been a terrible mistake to come here, she thought. She should have allowed Perry to send the announcement of their betrothal to the *Gazette*, and married him in London, as he had begged her to. By now she would have been safe as his viscountess. She and Penelope would have had a home again. They would have been a family with Perry, whose affection for her daughter she had never doubted.

Had they stayed in London, she would never have met this odious man who rode beside her, exuding confidence that he could and would prevent her from achieving that romantic dream she had yearned for. Neither would they have encountered the ravishing Miss Rathbone, who obviously imagined Viscount Fairmont to be a prize ripe for the taking. She was unaware of Perry's betrothal, naturally, but would that have made the slightest difference to the fair-haired Beauty?

Perhaps she should have agreed to make their attachment public, Athena mused. Perry had certainly urged her to do so. But then again perhaps not, an unexpected voice whispered perversely. Might it not be that Peregrine was also a mistake?

This thought came so unexpectedly into her mind that Athena gasped. Quickly, she pushed it aside. If she once admitted such a heresy, her fragile dreams would irrevocably crumble, and Lord St. Aubyn would be proved correct. She could not allow that to happen.

"Rothingham was one of my father's Oxford cronies," the earl was saying, just as though she had never mentioned John. "From the tales he used to tell, I gather they both belonged to a hell-raising coterie of young blades who spent more energy on senseless wagers than on their studies. After he came into the title, of course, my father had other responsibilities and lost touch with his old friends."

She could well believe that, Athena thought with sudden bitterness. The grand new Earl of St. Aubyn would hardly wish to continue a connection with an obscure baronet in Somerset. Startled at her sudden and unreasonable cynicism, Athena glanced at the earl.

"Father never mentioned the connection, my lord," she said. "But that does not surprise me; it was all so long ago."

"When you next see Sir Henry, you might tell him that Father always spoke of those days at Oxford with nostalgia. My own memories of the place are rather less pleasant, I must admit."

Athena took a deep breath and spoke without looking at him. "I can hardly tell my father anything, my lord, since I am *persona non grata* at Rothingham Manor."

There was an awkward silence, during which Athena wished she had held her tongue. Her emotions had betrayed her into confiding some of her painful secrets to this man who obviously cared not a fig for her.

"How long have you been estranged from your father, my dear?"

Beguiled by the gentleness of his voice, Athena replied without thinking. "Ever since my marriage. My stepmother made it quite clear that she would not welcome me back when John returned to his regiment."

"And Sir Henry? Did he agree to this?"

"He must have done so," she responded quietly. "I wrote to him several times, begging him to let my child be born at Rothingham Manor, but he never replied. So John took me with him, and Penelope was born in Spain, in General Wellesley's baggage train." A bitter little laugh escaped her.

"How much farther to the ruins, my lord?" she asked, abruptly changing the subject.

The earl appeared not to have heard her question. "That must have been difficult for you," he said in a low voice.

"No more so than for everyone else in that god-forsaken place," she replied softly. "And better than for others—all those who died." She paused for a moment as the memories of that horrifying time came rushing back. "But I do not regret a moment of it. I was there when they brought John back after Talavera. He spoke to me, and I was able to give him some comfort at the end. . . ." Her voice died away and Athena felt the tears sting her eyes. If she lived to be a hundred, she would never forget that dreadful day. There had been so many wounded to care for that she had been unable to mourn John until much later, after the dead and dying had been separated from the wounded.

No, she thought, it had not been easy. Nothing in her life seemed to be easy anymore. And all she wanted was to make Penelope's life a little easier than her own had been. Could he not see that?

Much to Athena's relief, no more was said until the walled garden of the ancient Abbey came into view. Behind the imposing walls of stone, breached here and there by the eroding effects of time and weather, the Abbey itself crouched, dark and menacing even in the early afternoon sunlight. Athena shuddered.

What stories this place might tell if it only had a voice, she thought. How many lovers had sought the sanctuary of the chapel to confirm their unions before God? she wondered. How many holy men had lived out their unblemished lives within its walls? And how many unhappy souls had languished in the dank dungeons, adding their poor bones to the others that Perry had said were buried there? And what of the ghosts who haunted the Abbey gardens?

She shuddered again at the thought.

"The ghostly monks are said to walk only at midnight."

The deep, faintly amused voice came from close beside her, and Athena looked down to find the earl standing by the mare, his deep blue-black eyes fixed on her face.

The horses had stopped beneath a huge, gnarled oak tree, whose limbs stretched out protectively, offering a welcome canopy of shade. Athena tore her eyes away from the earl's amused gaze and looked up into the branches towering above her. Hardly a glimpse of the summer sky was visible through the thickly clustering leaves. How many terrible events had this tree witnessed? she wondered. And how much celebration and joy? She hoped that the joys had outweighed the disasters. She truly hoped that today would not be one of the disasters.

"This is the official picnic site," the earl was saying in his deep, oddly melodic voice. He was obviously waiting to lift her down from the mare, and Athena felt a tremor of apprehension. It was an ordinary enough courtesy that a gentleman provided for a lady. Perry had lifted her out of his curricle many a time in London, and she had thought nothing of it. But somehow the thought of the earl's hands . . .

Athena shook herself mentally. She was being very missish about this, she told herself firmly. She was a grown woman of eight-and-twenty. And she could not sit here forever. Resolutely, she turned to him and put out her arms.

"If you would be so kind, my lord," she murmured, avoiding his gaze.

And then his hands were on her, and he lifted her out of the saddle, setting her down slowly beside the mare. Had she merely imagined he did it in slow motion? His hands held her, encircling her waist with a warmth that burned right through the riding habit to her bare skin, a fraction longer than was strictly necessary. Or seemly. A rather long fraction, she thought. As she had known they would.

It was only after Athena had removed her hands from his arms, where she had rested them for support, and stepped back that she realized that the pressure of Lord St. Aubyn's hands on her had terrified her far more than any of the ghostly fathers said to roam the Abbey gardens at midnight.

The Earl of St. Aubyn had every reason to feel pleased with himself. Was not his plan to divert Peregrine's attention from the widow progressing admirably? he thought. And Lady Sarah's notion to keep Perry riding beside the carriage to entertain the Rathbone ladies had been positively inspired. He tied his chestnut and Mrs. Standish's mare to a hawthorn bush beside the Abbey wall, and turned back to the female whose ambitions he had sworn to thwart.

The truth was, he admitted with a wry grin, Athena Standish did not stand a chance against the ravishing Rathbone chit. It was not that the widow was unattractive. Actually, her face was rather lovely, and when she smiled—as she often did to that graceless son of his—her eyes glowed with unsuspected warmth and tenderness. No, Sylvester admitted, the widow was no antidote; it was only in contrast to the overstated pink and white perfection of the Beauty that she paled.

His gaze rested on her slight figure, and he smiled to himself. There was definitely nothing wrong with her shape. His palms still tingled with the feel of her small waist beneath the light fabric of her riding habit. He had been suddenly reluctant to release her, and had deliberately held her a moment or two beyond what was proper. She had refused to meet his gaze, and

Sylvester could have sworn she had held her breath until he released her. Had he flustered the little widow? he wondered. So much the better. Perhaps she would be distracted from the spectacle of his son making a complete cake of himself over a brainless twit with a perfect face.

He strolled over to stand beside her, wondering what else he might do—within the bounds of propriety, of course—that would wrest her attention from Peregrine. Several rather pleasant alternatives did occur to him, but Sylvester regretfully dismissed them as highly improper methods of captivating a lady's attention.

His musings were interrupted by the noisy arrival of the carriages, and Sylvester leaned against the old oak to enjoy the spectacle of his Aunt Sarah's preparations for a small family picnic. It was a family joke that Lady Sarah's picnics were grander and involved more fanfare and preparation than a state dinner in the Great Hall at the Castle. She had brought seven footmen and three maids, besides an army of grooms and the undercook, whose sole task it was to see to the arrangement of the various dishes on the tables being set up in the shade of the spreading oak.

From the vantage point of her carriage, Lady Sarah directed the goings-on with military precision, although Sylvester knew from experience that the servants could manage very well without her supervision. He remembered with a stab of nostalgia how Adrienne had hugely enjoyed the incongruity of Lady Sarah's simple pastoral outings, as his aunt always called her forays into the countryside.

Mrs. Standish appeared to find the proceedings equally astonishing, for she moved to stand beside him, a tentative smile on her lips.

"Your aunt does not believe in doing things by half measures, my lord," she murmured after a moment, eyeing two burly footmen struggling with a hamper stuffed full of dishes of cold chicken, roast venison, pigeon pie, sausages, and other delicacies.

Sylvester laughed. "Aunt Sarah's idea of a simple country repast rivals Henry the Eighth's most sumptuous banquets," he replied lightly. "And we all know how much that illustrious monarch enjoyed his food." He motioned to a footman carrying the wine basket. "Allow me to pour you a glass of wine, Mrs. Standish," he invited, watching out of the corner of his eye as

Perry settled the two Rathbone ladies in comfortable chairs and poured them glasses of lemonade.

The widow must have observed him, too, for the gaze she turned upon him was troubled. "I should be drinking lemonade, my lord," she murmured.

"But wine sounds so much more appetizing, does it not?" he suggested with a smile. "And it is nicely chilled, too," he added, drawing the cork from the bottle of champagne and pouring two glasses. "I shall join you, madam, if you have no objection. But allow me to commandeer a chair for you first." He motioned to a footman, who immediately set up two chairs a little apart from the group around the table.

Sylvester caught his son casting a worried glance in the widow's direction, and before long the viscount approached with a glass of lemonade in his hand.

"I have b-brought you some l-lemonade, Athena," he stammered, blushing like a schoolboy. "You must be w-warm after your ride."

The widow did not respond immediately, and when she did there was a definite chill in her voice. "I am well taken care of, thank you," she said flatly, without looking at him.

Sylvester saw his son wince at the rebuff and intervened to soften the blow. "I am sure Mrs. Standish would enjoy some cold chicken, Perry. And perhaps some of Cook's fresh bread. I know I would."

He was rewarded with a grateful look before Perry strode away on his errand. Before his son reached the table, Sylvester heard the tinkling voice of Miss Rathbone calling out teasingly.

"I do declare, my dear Lord Fairmont," she trilled with enervating gaiety, "you have abandoned me to starve to death. Oh, do bring me some of that delicious-looking pigeon pie, and perhaps a sliver of cold chicken."

Quite twenty minutes later, when Peregrine had not returned, Sylvester thought it best to bestir himself on the widow's behalf. He had intended her to be slighted, but certainly not left without her nuncheon. When he returned with two plates of food, he noted that Mrs. Standish was fit to be tied, her amber eyes glowing with suppressed fury. He did not envy Peregrine when the widow caught up with him.

"I am not hungry, my lord," she said, abruptly rising to her feet and shaking out her skirts. "I think I will take a stroll down by the stream." Without another word, she swooped off with an angry swishing of skirts, leaving the earl with a curious smile on his face. He resumed his seat, took a healthy bite of chicken, and watched with interest to see how Peregrine would react to his betrothed's departure.

It was Penelope, however, not Peregrine, who flew after the widow and took her hand.

"Let me come with you, Mama," the child cried, skipping along in the grass. "Perry says there are minnows and frogs in the stream. May I keep a frog if I find one? Please, Mama?"

Sylvester did not catch the widow's response, but he saw the affectionate hug she bestowed on her daughter, and an unexpected twinge of envy touched his heart. If things had been different, he thought, he might have had a daughter of his own. Adrienne's daughter.

His eyes followed the lithesome widow and her daughter down the grassy slope to the edge of the small stream. It struck him quite suddenly that mother and child made a delightful picture in the pastoral setting, a sight to warm any man's heart.

For the first time in many months, Sylvester felt the old ache of loneliness swell up in his chest.

"When is Perry going to take us to see the dungeons, Mama? Do you suppose he can have forgotten his promise?"

Penelope had asked the question four times since they left the party to walk beside the stream, but Athena had no answer for her. She dared not glance over her shoulder for fear the earl might be staring at her. She *knew* he was staring at her, that cynical half-smile on his face. He had been staring at her—she was sure of it—since she left him so abruptly holding two plates of food.

It had been unpardonably rude of her, she realized. His lordship had merely been the attentive host, and she had behaved like some gauche miss straight out of the schoolroom. Considering how much he disliked her, he had actually been quite charming. Except for that moment when his hands had held her longer than they should have, of course. Although, now that she looked back upon the scene, Athena could hardly credit it. Perhaps she had imagined it. Her nerves had been distraught over her betrothed's inappropriate attentions to Miss Rathbone.

And now her flash of temper had landed her in this awkward impasse. How the earl must be laughing at her, she fumed, for there was not the least doubt in Athena's mind that the odious man had enjoyed her discomfort and understood only too well the cause of her peevishness.

Her daughter naturally had no such reservations, and Athena saw Penelope's eyes stray wistfully to the group under the old oak. She felt a cold fury at Perry's thoughtlessness building inside her. If the wretch did not keep his promise to her daughter, she would box his lying ears for him, she vowed. No doubt his smug lordship would vastly enjoy seeing his son's betrothed behave like a veritable fishwife. Indeed he would, and the thought of giving the earl that satisfaction dampened her anger.

"Oh, here he comes," Penny cried suddenly, her elfin face brightening perceptibly. "You see, Mama, Perry did not forget his promise." She paused and Athena saw a shadow cross her daughter's face. "But why is he bringing Miss Rathbone with him?" she asked with the naiveté of childhood. "I do not like her very much, Mama. She is so silly—"

"Hush, darling," Athena said, turning to observe the progress of the Beauty towards the stream, clinging to the viscount's arm as though she were in dire peril of falling. One would think Miss Rathbone were navigating a rocky hillside instead of a gentle, grassy slope, Athena thought disgustedly.

But her worst fears were soon confirmed.

"Miss Rathbone is anxious to explore the ruins, too," Peregrine said, an apologetic smile on his face. "So I invited her—"

"He was reluctant at first, of course," the Beauty interrupted in that clear, caressing voice of hers, casting a brilliant smile in Athena's direction. "But I assured our dear viscount that you would not object in the least, Mrs. Standish. And darling Penelope will not mind either, will you, dear?"

The honeyed tones were so patently false that Athena wondered how Perry could not see the web the Beauty was intent upon weaving about him. She would have liked to give the sly minx a piece of her mind, but politeness forbade it, so she merely looked straight into Perry's blue eyes until he was forced to lower them in confusion.

Penelope, unhampered by such niceties, looked up at the Beauty with one of her deceptively angelic smiles. Athena held her breath. "You are very welcome, Miss Rathbone," her daughter said politely. "I am so glad to see someone besides me is fond of spiders."

"*Spiders?*" The Beauty's voice was no longer musical, Athena noted.

"Yes, spiders," Penelope responded nonchalantly. "Spiders like dark places, you know. There are bound to be millions of them in the dungeons."

The Beauty let out a squeak of terror and turned anxious eyes to Peregrine, who was looking rather bemused.

"You never told me there would be *spiders* in the ruins, my lord," Miss Rathbone whispered plaintively. "I cannot go if I am to be attacked by millions of the nasty creatures. Escort me back to my grandmother at once, if you will."

"But you promised me you would show me the dungeons, Perry," Penelope cut in, the threat of imminent tears in her voice. "You *promised*."

Athena regarded the flustered viscount with interest. He was evidently feeling very uncomfortable. Perry knew from past experience that Penny's tears would be loud and copious if she felt herself cheated out of the promised treat. On the other hand, the Beauty might prove to be equally intractable. He glanced appealingly at her, but Athena refused to come to his rescue.

"You are exaggerating, as usual, Penny," he said after a brief pause. "There are no spiders in the dungeons, Miss Rathbone." He turned to look at the Beauty, who was clinging frantically to his arm and quite mangling the sleeve of his new coat. "I have been there hundreds of times, and I have yet to see a single spider."

"What a bouncer!" Penelope exclaimed with a giggle. "If Miss Rathbone is scared of a few spiders, she should stay behind."

"I am not scared of a few spiders," the Beauty protested, her voice edged with anger. "I merely do not wish to have millions of them crawling all over me, that is all." She shuddered visibly and clung more firmly to Perry's arm.

"They do not bite, you know," Penelope remarked casually. "Unless you squish them, of course. They do not like to be squished."

The Beauty let out another faint scream and sagged against the viscount in what Athena considered a really impeccable semblance of a swoon. The girl should have been on the stage, she thought viciously. She might have made her fortune.

It required the combined efforts of the viscount and her daughter—Penelope having realized that without Miss Rathbone's presence there would be no visit to the dungeons—to convince the distraught Beauty that she would be quite safe from the occasional arachnid that might so far forget itself as to venture within ten feet of their party.

In the end she very prettily agreed to put herself into the viscount's capable hands—an expression that jarred Athena's already exacerbated sensibilities—and allowed herself to be led into the dim interior of the Abbey, her hands still firmly attached to Perry's arm.

CHAPTER SIX

The Kiss

The Earl of St. Aubyn had been amused at the little tableau enacted on the bank of the stream between his son and the three females, all of whom appeared to be annoyed with him. Mrs. Standish glared at poor Perry stonily, while her daughter bandied words with him quite shamelessly. Miss Rathbone was definitely the most vociferous of the three, for her high-pitched shrieks—quite unrehearsed this time, Sylvester was convinced—had caused the three elder ladies gathered around the picnic table to glance in her direction curiously.

At one point, the Beauty appeared on the point of swooning, and Sylvester noted with perverse satisfaction that the widow's expression became even more thunderous at the blatant way in which her rival clung to Peregrine's arm after her second scream. The wench had better take care not to overplay her role, the earl thought cynically. Peregrine might be an inexperienced puppy around females, but he was not entirely without common sense. He would drop a word of caution in his aunt's ear.

Their differences apparently settled, the group moved towards the entrance to the ruins, all but the Beauty carrying the oil lanterns provided by the footmen. Sylvester followed them with his eyes until the party disappeared into the Abbey. He did not envy Peregrine escorting three females through the dank passageways of the Abbey, and wished that he had not been obliged to put on this little farce to save his only son from the grasp of a fortune-hunting widow.

Actually, the rout of Mrs. Athena Standish was going according to plan, he thought, and within a few days, perhaps after another sennight, she would recognize her defeat, pack her bags, and return to London. Had she played her cards more wisely, Sylvester reminded himself cynically, the widow might have left St. Aubyn's three thousand pounds richer than when she arrived. But she had been greedy and held out for the big prize.

Greedy? Somehow the sin of greed did not fit Mrs. Athena Standish, and the idea made him uneasy. If she was not greedy, what could be her motive in coercing a boy almost young enough to be her son into matrimony? It could not be love. Sylvester had seen no sign of passion in either of them. His son was clearly infatuated with the widow; however, it was a boy's romantic infatuation for a charming woman. But now that the radiant Miss Rathbone had appeared upon the scene, perhaps Peregrine would be forced to recognize his relationship with the widow for what it was, mere puppy love.

But it would be up to Mrs. Standish to release Peregrine from his commitment. Sylvester knew that his son would never—even if he could be brought to see how mistaken his choice of bride had been—break his word once it had been given.

Sylvester grimaced. It must be his task to ensure that the delectable Athena Standish would be ready and willing to give up her claim on his son. A task he was beginning to look forward to with considerable relish. A task that would take his mind off the projected treatise on Ming porcelain he was writing for the Royal Historical Society. Two weeks ago the prospect of any delay in his work—particularly for such a frivolous reason—might have caused him no little annoyance. This afternoon, sitting at his ease beneath the ancient oak and listening with amusement to Mrs. Rathbone's thrilling voice relating some *on-dits* of an undeniably scandalous nature, Sylvester felt more alive than he had in years.

These pleasant ruminations came to an abrupt end when the earl heard a collective gasp of dismay from his three companions, and turned to witness his son emerging from the ruins, carrying a lady in blue clasped in his arms. Sylvester sprang to his feet as Perry approached, his gaze flying to the entrance of the Abbey.

There was no sign of Mrs. Standish or her daughter.

Sylvester felt a twinge of alarm.

"Oh, Perry," Mrs. Easton exclaimed in a tremulous voice, echoing his own alarm, "where is Athena? And our dear Penny? Never say you have left them alone in the dungeons?"

Peregrine deposited Miss Rathbone—who never ceased uttering pathetic little mewling sounds, and complaining about her broken ankle—in a chair beside the table. Sylvester noted that his son looked rather harried as the Beauty's arm clung tenaciously to his neck. After freeing himself from this stranglehold and assuring the young lady and her grandmother that her ankle could not be broken, but was in all likelihood merely strained, Perry mopped his face with his handkerchief and glanced apologetically at his father.

Had Perry stopped to think, the earl wondered curiously, what an entire lifetime with such an insipid creature would be like? He must really speak to his aunt about the young actress's penchant for melodrama. Ladies—at least none worthy of the name—simply did not hang upon a gentleman's neck as though they were drowning. Such behavior should be confined to the Green Room at Drury Lane, where standards were considerably more relaxed.

"Yes, indeed, Perry," Lady Sarah snapped, having risen to hover over the languishing Miss Rathbone, "what have you done with poor Mrs. Standish and her daughter? Answer me, boy."

"I have not done anything with Mrs. Standish," Perry replied in aggrieved tones. "She insisted upon going on without us—"

"You left the poor lady and her daughter to wander around by themselves in the dungeons?" Lady Sarah's voice rose to a pitch that rivaled Mrs. Rathbone's piercing soprano. "Have your wits gone begging, boy?"

"She will be paralyzed with terror, poor creature," Mrs. Rathbone remarked feelingly.

"What could you have been thinking of, Perry?" Mrs. Easton wailed, wringing her hands and looking as though she might swoon at any minute.

"Athena is not one of your silly ninnyhammers who go off into the fidgets over the least little thing," Perry said defiantly.

"Oh, yes, indeed," confirmed Miss Rathbone in a wavering voice. "I think she is *so* brave. Why, she is not even afraid of spiders. Can you credit it? Did she not say so herself, Peri—my lord?"

"There are no spiders in the dungeons," Peregrine said flatly. "And since I intend to return immediately to finish the tour I promised Penelope, there is nothing to get into a pother about."

"Then I suggest you do so without further delay," Sylvester said shortly. The Beauty's slip of the tongue in using his son's name had not gone unnoticed by any of those present, as he knew the sly minx had intended. But since his overriding concern at the moment was the safety of the intrepid widow, the Beauty's tricks failed to amuse him.

"Oh, do not leave me like this, my lord," Miss Rathbone wailed piteously, stretching up to grasp Peregrine's sleeve.

"You promised to escort me back to the house and have the doctor sent for. I cannot believe you can be so heartless—"

"Stuff and nonsense!" Mrs. Easton exclaimed loudly. "What fustian you do talk, girl. Get back in there this instant, Perry, and do not return until you bring Athena and Penny with you."

"But, his lordship promised—"

"Oh, do hush, Viviana," Mrs. Rathbone commanded sharply. "You are being very tiresome, child."

This unexpected reprimand produced an instant flood of tears from the Beauty, who managed—Sylvester noted irritably—to weep copious tears without in the least impairing the loveliness of her face.

Peregrine shot an anguished glance at his father, and Sylvester saw what had to be done.

"Take care of the ladies, Perry," he ordered tersely. "I shall go in search of Mrs. Standish and her daughter myself."

Picking up the viscount's discarded lantern, the earl strode down the slope and entered the dim labyrinths of the Abbey without a backward glance.

The moment Athena stepped into the dim interior of the Abbey, she felt the weight of a thousand years of history press in upon her. The rough-hewn stone walls that arched over her head to form the low ceiling seemed to exude a sense of other-worldliness that soothed her battered nerves. The sensation of having stepped into another era came over her, and for a moment Athena allowed herself to imagine what it must have been like to live thus sheltered from the harsh realities of the world.

But harsh realities had intruded even into this sacred place, she recalled, just as they had in her own life. Had not the Abbey been ransacked, pillaged, burned? Did it not stand, imposing relic that it still was, on St. Aubyn land, a stark reminder of power and prosperity laid low? Of the ephemeral nature of all things mortal?

Athena shuddered, her gaze settling on the slight figure of her daughter, skipping along in front of her, lantern swinging crazily.

"Penny," she called, brushing her maudlin fantasies aside, "do not get too far ahead, dear. I would not wish to lose you if you take the wrong turn."

"Pooh!" her daughter exclaimed with childish disregard for such fears. "Perry told me exactly which way to go, so trust me,

Mama. I can lead you straight through the dungeon to the torture chamber. Just follow me."

"Torture chamber?" Athena repeated, between alarm and amusement. "Perry said nothing of torture chambers, you silly minx. And I beg you will say nothing of the sort to Miss Rathbone; she will swoon for certain if you do."

"Miss Rathbone is a ninny," Penelope stated emphatically. "Fancy being scared of spiders. I cannot wait to hear her scream when she sees the rats."

"Rats?" Athena murmured in a faint voice. "Perry said nothing of rats, either, Penelope. I beg you will restrain your imagination, dear. I do not much care for rats myself."

"Oh, Perry says they will not hurt us," her daughter reported blithely, her voice carrying eerily in the cavernous passageway. "Unless they are hungry, of course. Then they might—"

"Enough!" Athena said sharply, aware of a tremor in her voice. "And I think we should wait here for Perry to catch up with us." She glanced uneasily over her shoulder at the dark tunnel behind her. "I cannot see any sign of his lantern."

"Oh, Mama, do come and see this!" Penelope cried excitedly, her lantern joggling wildly. "These must be the stairs down to the dungeons. Just as Perry said. You see, I do remember the way," she added proudly.

Athena stared dubiously at the narrow steps that led down into the darkness below. Suddenly the whole idea of exploring the lower regions of the Abbey did not sound quite so appealing as it had when Perry proposed it. She had never imagined that darkness could be so very intimidating.

Penelope seemed to be affected by no such fears, for she took a step down the stone stairs and glanced eagerly back at her mother. "Let us at least see what is down there, Mama," she begged. "Perry will be along directly. No doubt Miss Rathbone has swooned again, the silly creature."

Athena was never sure afterwards whether it was her daughter's eagerness to explore the stairs or her own reluctance to witness her betrothed fawning over the swooning Beauty that drove her to push onwards when common sense urged caution. Her only concession to prudence was to attach her handkerchief to an iron stave protruding from the wall at the head of the stairs. At least Perry would know where they were, she reasoned, stepping gingerly down the stone steps after Penny, who had danced ahead fearlessly.

Athena was not even sure how long they spent wandering

along the dim passageways, or arguing about which turns to take as the tunnels branched out every few feet along the way. It was a veritable rabbit warren of stone corridors, none of them straight, all of them dim, and cold, and foreboding.

She reckoned that it was pure chance rather than Penny's guidance that brought them ultimately to the central chamber, a vaulted cavern of a place with hand-hewn stone walls crouching around the huge open fireplace, large enough—Athena thought irrationally—to roast two oxen at once.

"So much for your torture chamber, Penny," she remarked, sinking down on a worn wooden bench beside a trestle table that seemed to have withstood the passage of time. The rough, uneven surface of the tunnel had left her feet aching, in spite of her sturdy half-boots, and Athena wondered how the Beauty was faring with her fragile slippers of pale blue leather.

"This must have been the monastery kitchen," she remarked, her eyes following the towering stone chimney that disappeared into the center of the ceiling. "That chimney must have been used to warm the upper rooms. And no doubt the monks gathered here to take their meals."

"Oh, no, Mama," Penny said patiently, as though talking to a child. "Perry says that the table here was used to chop off the monk's limbs when they refused to give up the Abbey's treasure. Cannot you see the dark stains in the wood?"

"Rubbish!" Athena exclaimed, annoyed that her sweet Penelope had revealed such bloodthirsty knowledge. "You are making this up, which is very naughty of you, dear." Nevertheless, she instinctively snatched her arm away from the table, noticing upon closer examination that the ancient refractory table did indeed have rather large dark stains embedded into the wood.

Athena shuddered and cast her eyes over to the far wall where several heavy crates were stacked. Her imagination, fired by Penelope's vivid explanation of the dark stains, immediately visualized the crates stuffed with tangled masses of pale limbs. Pulling herself together with a supreme effort, Athena was about to remind her daughter that ladies did not indulge in such hoydenish starts, when a movement between two of the crates caught her eye and froze her blood.

"Rats!" she exclaimed, her voice unnaturally high. She leapt to her feet and clutched her gown around her knees, quite as though she feared the rodents might take it into their heads to invade her petticoats.

Penelope giggled. "Never say you are going to swoon, Mama," she chortled. "And never mind the rats. They cannot be very hungry," she added cheerfully. "Perry said they only attack when they are starving, remember?"

Unconvinced by these brave words, Athena picked up her lantern. "I say we go back upstairs immediately," she said firmly, glancing around to find the entrance to the central chamber. It was then that she made an alarming discovery. There were six black passageways leading into the room, all exactly alike. Which was the one that would lead to the staircase up to the main floor?

"Are we not going to wait for Perry, Mama?" Penny sounded disappointed at their abrupt departure, but Athena was adamant.

"I suspect that Perry has been detained," she said flatly, a circumstance that had become more apparent as the minutes dragged by. They must have been wandering around in these tunnels for almost an hour, she thought. If Perry had not come, then he himself must also be lost. Lost in the company of that coy lady in blue. The notion made Athena feel suddenly quite sick.

A considerable time later, after exploring three of the tunnels leading off the central room and finding no staircase with a white handkerchief tied to a hook in the wall, Athena was feeling exhausted. Her feet were painfully sore, she was chilled to the bone, and it was all she could do to control the panic that fluttered around in her breast.

She sank down once more on the wooden bench, keeping her eyes averted from the mysterious dark stains on the table.

She felt an overwhelming desire to cry. She would never, *never* forgive Perry for this, she thought, fury at her betrothed's thoughtlessness momentarily obscuring her panic. He would pay dearly for abandoning her in this miserable place. Oh, yes, she mused wrathfully, Viscount Fairmont would be sorry he had ever suggested exploring the dungeons when she was finished with him. He deserved to have his ears boxed.

"Mama, I think this tunnel here might be the right one." Penelope's voice was still full of optimism, but Athena's had run out long ago.

"How can you be sure, dear?"

"I think I recall the table being on that side when we arrived." She waved to the right. "Let us try this one, Mama. I have a feeling we will be right this time."

Athena sighed. She was too tired to budge. The thought of

trudging down yet another dark tunnel depressed her. "Let me rest a few moments longer, love," she begged, reluctant to subject her poor feet to the rough stones again.

"I shall go a little way by myself, then," Penny suggested. "I just know this is the one."

Athena immediately objected. "I do not want you wandering off by yourself, Penny. We should stay here until someone comes for us. As Perry soon will, I am convinced of it."

"Only a little way, Mama. *Please*."

Too tired to argue, Athena at last consented, with the admonition not to go far.

Fifteen minutes later, when Penelope had not returned, Athena regretted sending her daughter off alone. She would follow her immediately, she thought, forcing herself to stand. A distinct rustling behind the crates made her turn towards them, thoroughly alarmed at the possibility of having to fight off hungry rodents. A sob broke from her as she clearly saw two small eyes reflected in the light of the lantern.

Blindly, Athena turned to escape the presence of the rats. There must be more than one of them, she realized in sudden panic, for she could clearly hear their high-pitched twittering. To make matters worse, the chamber seemed to be getting dimmer. Athena held the lantern aloft to adjust the wick, but noticed—her blood running cold in her veins—that it was almost out of oil.

She would be alone in the dark with the rats.

Athena was not normally squeamish about such things, considering herself a sensible female. But the events of the afternoon had undermined her reserves, and without conscious thought, she let out a piercing scream, which echoed through the tunnels in waves of sound. The echoes rattled her with their eerie reverberations, sounding to her fevered imagination like a host of ghostly monks—limbs mutilated, eyes blankly staring from beneath black cowls.

Paralyzed with terror, Athena watched the lantern flicker feebly and go out. She was about the scream again, when she thought she heard a shout. Could it be that Penny was coming back? Or that Perry had finally found her? She glanced anxiously in the direction Penelope had taken, but that tunnel yawned dark and forbidding. Then a light flickered in another passage, and as it approached, Athena saw that it was indeed the figure of a man.

Perry!

Tears sprang unbidden to her eyes. Without a moment's hesitation, Athena picked up her skirts and ran towards the tall figure. She had never been so glad to see anyone in her life. With a sob of relief, she threw herself into his arms and buried her face in his cravat.

"Oh, Perry," she sobbed, quite unable to control her tears, "I was so afraid here in the dark. How could you do this to me?"

An arm encircled her waist and held her firmly in place against the broad chest. It felt so wonderful that Athena nestled more closely against Perry's tall frame. They had never been this intimate before, and Athena wondered if perhaps she had misjudged her betrothed. Could it be that Perry was more mature than she had given him credit for?

She heard his breath expel close to her ear; then warm lips touched her cheek, trailing down to her neck. She knew she should draw away, but there was an hypnotic quality to the lingering kiss he placed in the curve of her neck, and to the warm fingers splayed against her back, holding her expertly in place.

"Perry," she murmured huskily, straining to see his expression in the flickering lamplight. But when a warm mouth caught her lips in the tenderest of kisses, Athena closed her eyes and gave herself up to the delight of being kissed by an expert. Where had Perry learned to kiss like this? she wondered fuzzily, opening her lips to the insistent probing of a hot tongue against her teeth. Why had she never allowed him to do so before? The few boyish pecks he had pressed upon her in London had given her no warning whatsoever that it could be like this.

The kiss deepened, until Athena's arms slipped up around his neck and pulled him even closer. Tentatively she touched him with her own tongue, and was enraptured by the fierce response. The lantern had been placed on the floor, and two strong arms now held her, caressed her, explored her as she had longed for years—ever since John had been taken from her—to be held, and touched, and kissed again. Athena opened her mouth more invitingly and was rewarded with a throaty male groan of desire that thrilled her beyond words.

This was so unlike Perry, her dizzy brain kept repeating.

So very unlike Perry.

It was gloriously seductive, promising delights beyond her wildest dreams, but so unlike Perry.

Unlike Perry? A core of fear shifted within her heart.

Perry was only a boy; surely he would not—could not—have kissed her like this. Suddenly she knew beyond a doubt that he had not done so. She pushed away and stared up at the man she had been kissing so recklessly.

No wonder he had felt so unlike Perry, she thought, her heart cringing in mortification and dropping down to the soles of her feet.

He was not Perry.

The Earl of St. Aubyn smiled down into her startled face, his blue-black eyes alight with the heat of desire she had undoubtedly kindled there.

Judging by the angry glitter in the lady's magnificent amber eyes, he was in serious trouble, Sylvester mused, watching outrage jostle with mortification in the widow's upturned face. He wondered idly if she might box his ears, and the notion amused him.

They were still standing close together, his hands on her waist, and Sylvester heard the agitation of her breath, matching his own. She was trembling again, he noticed. Not the distraught shuddering of her small body when she had flung herself into his astonished arms, but a sign of mental anguish, nevertheless.

Sylvester suddenly wanted—more than anything he had wanted in a long time—to pull her into his arms again and comfort her, but he dared not risk it. She would slap his face for him; he was sure of it. Yet would it not be well worth that slap, he wondered, to feel her sensuous body—far more voluptuous than he could ever have imagined—pressed against him again?

His eyes dropped to her lips. In the flickering light of the lantern he could see that they were soft, and full, and bruised-looking. From his kisses. The sight of them stirred him, and Sylvester tore his eyes away, knowing that if he did not take his hands off her, he would do what he was aching to do, and the devil fly away with the consequences.

Suddenly she sighed, and her head rolled back, exposing the tender column of her neck. For a delirious moment, Sylvester thought she had succumbed to the ardent yearning that had driven her to return his kiss with such unbridled passion. But as he groaned and bent to take possession of that sensuous mouth, he noticed that the widow's eyes were closed, her body a dead weight in his arms.

Athena Standish had swooned.

Sylvester paused, his heart racing, his lips poised inches from hers. The temptation to steal that kiss anyway was so strong, he actually shuddered with the need of it. He could feel her heart beating against his chest, and for the longest moment he just stood there, cradling the widow Standish in his arms with a fierce gentleness that surprised him.

He had no recollection afterwards of how long he stood there, listening to her breathing. Finally he shook himself out of the trance, reached for the lantern, swung Athena up into his arms, and strode back the way he had come, his mind a riot of unanswered questions.

That kiss had changed everything.

There was no way that either of them could pretend it had not happened. It had been too intense, too intimate, far too soul-wrenching to dismiss as an idle, flirtatious caress. What madness had driven him to accept that kiss from a female who considered herself betrothed to his son? Sylvester wondered. A female who imagined herself in Peregrine's arms even as she kissed his father?

The thought of Peregrine in Athena's arms, kissing her the way he had just kissed her, caused Sylvester to grit his teeth painfully. What kind of unnatural father was he to be lusting after his son's future bride? Of course, if he had his way—an eventuality that Sylvester did not for a moment doubt—the widow would not be Peregrine's bride at all. His son would be brought to see the error of his choice, and the seductive widow would be packed off to London.

She would be free again. The notion slipped unbidden into Sylvester's mind and skipped around there gleefully. The widow would be fair game, he told himself. Might she not be persuaded to consider another kind of arrangement? The idea was both titillating and faintly distasteful, and Sylvester put it resolutely out of his mind.

They were approaching the entrance by now, and the odd notion crossed the earl's mind that he might well be a modern Orpheus, bringing his dear Eurydice up from the dark realm of Hades. It was the kind of mythological parallel that would appeal to Athena, he thought wryly, with her love of the classics. Except, of course, that Orpheus had been warned not to look at his lady until they were well past the portals of darkness. The Greek bard had done so and lost her forever, according to the legend. Sylvester was no Orpheus, which was perhaps just as well, for he could not resist gazing down at the unconscious woman in his arms. Was she lost to him forever? he wondered, half embarrassed at his own superstition.

At that moment, the widow's eyelids fluttered and she opened her eyes, gazing up at Sylvester blankly. He saw recognition return and felt her stiffen in his arms.

"Put me down at once," she ordered, her voice unsteady. "How dare you touch me? Put me down instantly!"

"You fainted, my dear," Sylvester remarked, ignoring this request.

"I am *not* your dear," she spat out, struggling ineffectually in his grasp. "Put me down, I say. Are you deaf as well as depraved?" She seemed to remember something, and her expression changed to alarm. "Where is Penny?" she demanded. "My daughter is still down there in that dreadful place with the rats."

"Rats?" Sylvester raised an eyebrow. "Surely you mean a mouse or two? There are no rats that I know of."

"But I *saw* them," she insisted, her voice breaking. "I know I did. And now Penny is down there—"

"Your daughter is safe with your aunt, Athena," he told her gently. "I found her at the foot of the stairs and brought her out." He did not realize he had used her name until she glared at him.

"I did not give you leave to use my name, my lord," she said stiffly, her color high.

Sylvester looked deeply into her golden eyes and grinned crookedly. "After what has just passed between us, my dear, I wonder at such modesty."

The widow dropped her eyes, her cheeks flowering a deep pink. "That was unkind of you, my lord," she said through stiff lips. "I thought you were Peregrine."

"Did you indeed? I had no idea my son was such a man of the world. Does he always kiss you so enthusiastically?"

"Perry has never kissed me like that at all," she said, then bit her lip, evidently wishing she had not spoken so freely. "I merely thought that he . . . I t-thought he . . ." She stumbled to a halt, her eyes lowered.

"You thought a boy had suddenly turned into a man, is that it, my dear?" he said softly, watching the movement of her mouth, and feeling the need to kiss her again rising within him. He forced himself to look away. The world of sunlight beyond the Abbey doors seemed suddenly very far away. But it offered an escape from the lunacy they had committed together down there in the darkness. He must get her back there before anything worse happened.

"I think we had better join the others," he murmured after she made no reply.

"Please put me down." She sounded tired and perhaps frightened, like a little girl, Sylvester thought, oddly touched by her tone. He tightened his arms about her.

"Your nerves have suffered a great shock, my dear," he heard himself say gently. "Let me carry you back to your aunt."

She made no reply, but her head fell back against his shoulder again, a small sign of trust that gave Sylvester an inordinate amount of pleasure.

He was smiling to himself when he came out into the sunlight. He could not regret the kiss. But what would this new intimacy with Athena Standish do to his relationship with his son? he wondered. In a sense the kiss had placed her in his power, given him a weapon he could, if he chose, use against her with Peregrine.

He tried to push the other question aside, but it would not be stilled. Just how far, he wondered, had that kiss placed him in the widow's power?

CHAPTER SEVEN

The Riding Lesson

More distraught than she cared to admit, Athena retired to her chamber immediately upon their return from the Abbey. Unlike the Beauty, however, she did not enact a Cheltenham tragedy of major proportions, but simply slipped upstairs to nurse her wounds in solitude.

It did her self-esteem little good when Peregrine appeared not to notice her departure, so engrossed was he in assisting poor Miss Rathbone—as everyone insisted upon calling that languid lady—up to the Blue Dragon Saloon where she could, he assured her with more anxious attention than Athena deemed strictly necessary, rest her injured ankle.

The devil fly away with her injured ankle, Athena thought crossly as she continued up to the second floor. Her betrothed was acting like a love-sick swain. Could he not see that the Beauty was only pretending to be hurt? The wicked hussy had *wanted* to find herself in Perry's arms. She had planned it that way, but Perry was too innocent to see through this feminine deceit. He had not seen—as Athena had—the smug expression on the Beauty's lovely face when Perry had lifted her tenderly into the carriage for the drive home.

His father had seen it, too, Athena knew, for although she had avoided the earl's eyes from the moment he deposited her in the chair next to her anxious Aunt Mary, she had caught him looking at her during the little charade Miss Rathbone had enacted for them beside the carriage. Had that been disgust in his eyes? she wondered. Or amusement? Or had he been gloating at her discomfort?

Or had he been remembering what had passed between them down in the dungeon? Athena herself could not get the incident out of her mind. Try as she might, the heat of that forbidden kiss still made her stomach turn upside down. The earl's lips had burned their imprint of desire upon her poor heart that even now fluttered wildly at the memory of it.

With a sigh she pushed herself up from the bed and reached for the damp cloth she had used all evening to bathe her over-heated face. She had pleaded a megrim to avoid going down to dinner—she had yet to find the strength to pretend that nothing untoward had happened down there in the darkness—and the dinner tray Lady Sarah had sent up from the kitchen sat untouched on the dresser. How could she possibly eat anything when that sick feeling rose in her throat at the thought of her scandalous indiscretion?

Night had brought no rest and the following morning—still incapable of facing the cynicism in those blue-black eyes—Athena had stayed in bed, sleeping until noon. It had been a cowardly thing to do, she admitted, but she had managed to convince Aunt Mary that her nerves needed more time to recover from that terrible ordeal in the darkness with the rats. And with a man whose kiss had awakened all the unruly desires she had imagined long-ago buried with John.

"I wish John were still with us, Aunt," she said impulsively, as Mrs. Easton dipped the cloth into the fresh bowl of lemon water she had brought up from the kitchen.

"Now that is nonsensical, child," her aunt replied, bringing the cloth over to the windowseat where Athena had been sitting reading since nuncheon. "One should not wish for the impossible. Much better try for what is within our reach. You have Peregrine now, dear, but you must throw off this apathy, Athena, and make a push to keep his interest."

A cold hand clutched at Athena's heart, and she put down the book she had been reading, the latest novel by Mrs. Radcliffe that Perry himself had bought her as a surprise before they left London. "What exactly do you mean by that, Aunt?"

Mrs. Easton glanced at her sharply. "It cannot have escaped your notice, Athena, that Miss Rathbone has shown an extraordinary interest in our Peregrine. If you do not have a care, dear, the hussy will cut you out, and we shall find ourselves quite without a protector."

"Lord St. Aubyn has yet to sanction the betrothal, Aunt," Athena replied. "And since he has told me without roundaboutation that he does not approve of me, I fail to see that it signifies that Miss Rathbone does. I could never compete with that kind of beauty anyway," she added prosaically.

"Ah, but you forget that you have one vital card in your favor, dear," Aunt Mary said with a complaisant smile.

"And what is that, pray?"

"Peregrine is betrothed to you, dear, and I do wish you would consent to make this fact known to the Rathbone ladies."

"And you suppose that would dampen Miss Rathbone's interest do you, Aunt? I have no such confidence in that lady's scruples, let me tell you."

"But you do trust Perry's, I hope," her aunt said sharply.

Athena was given no opportunity to reply to her aunt's troubling question for at that moment there was a tap at the door and Lady Sarah entered, followed by a footman bearing a large vase of roses, evidently gathered from the Castle gardens.

"Ah, I see you are up, my dear Athena," she remarked, directing the footman to place the roses on the small table by the window. "My nephew will be glad to hear that you are feeling better, dear. He has ordered these roses to be brought up to you, and I thought I would come myself to make sure you have everything you require."

Athena stared at the beautiful pink blossoms in amazement. "That is exceptionally kind of you, my lady," she murmured, her mind racing around frantically searching for explanations, both for the earl's unusual courtesy and his aunt's sudden concern for their guest's well-being. "The roses are very beautiful indeed. Please convey my thanks to his lordship."

"Peregrine asked me to remind you that he promised to give your daughter her first riding lesson this afternoon," Lady Sarah continued, fixing her pale blue stare on her guest. "He hopes you will feel recovered enough to join them at the stables after tea." After a slight pause, she added smoothly, "It seems that Miss Rathbone will be there, too, my dear. It should be quite a merry party."

After this unlikely statement, Lady Sarah swept out of the room, leaving a heavy silence behind her.

"I told you that Rathbone hussy had designs on Perry, dearest. I strongly suggest that you get into your riding habit and sally forth to do battle with the insipid creature."

But Athena could not find the courage to take her aunt's advice. Her carefully laid plans to find security in a second marriage seemed to be crumbling around her ears. She was no longer sure of anything, not even her own sweet Perry, who had appeared so steadfast and devoted in London.

Not even the obnoxious Lord St. Aubyn, who had seemed so steadfast and immovable in his disapproval of her.

Not even her own heart, Athena thought miserably, her eyes

lingering on the perfect pink roses sent by a man whose motives she neither trusted nor understood.

Was this offering in the nature of a truce? she wondered fretfully. Or was it a cynical reminder of the shameful secret they shared? A secret that could destroy her betrothal to Peregrine as nothing else could.

That evening, Athena almost regretted her decision not to attend her daughter's first riding lesson. Penelope talked of nothing else when her mother came to tuck her in and tell her a bedtime story. That evening there was no need for Athena's story, for the child was bursting with tales of her own, which she insisted upon recounting several times in lurid detail.

"Buttercup is the best pony in the world!" her daughter assured her for perhaps the fifth time. "Perry says I may have her for my very own. If you approve, that is, Mama," she added as an afterthought, watching her mother intently from beneath her long lashes. So like John's, Athena thought with a twist of nostalgia.

She sighed. "I see no harm in it, darling. For as long as we stay at the Castle, of course. We have no place for a pony in London."

Penelope's eyes widened in horror. "But Perry promised we would never have to go back *there*," she cried, tears already forming in her blue eyes. "I thought you were going to marry him and stay here forever, Mama. I *want* to stay here. And Perry *promised*. Do say we may, Mama. Then Buttercup will be mine for always."

Athena gazed at her daughter's eager face, wishing she might assure her that yes, they would stay here forever and be happy together, the three of them, just as they had planned in London. But she did not like to lie to Penny. The child had a disconcerting way of seeing right through her mother's little deceptions and putting her small finger on the truth. But how could she bear to disappoint her by confessing that she might not be able to marry Perry after all?

One reckless kiss had changed everything.

If the earl chose to divulge their shameful secret, to tell his son that she had literally thrown herself into his arms and kissed him quite wantonly—which described exactly what she had done, not to put too fine a point to it—then Perry would surely demand that she release him from the engagement. And even if Perry stood by her—generous boy that he was—how could she marry him and remain at the Castle under the cynical eye of a man who had stirred her blood as her betrothed never had.

And never would, Athena saw with sudden clarity.

She sighed again and leaned forward to kiss her daughter. "I cannot answer any of those questions yet, darling," she murmured truthfully. "Perry's father is opposed to the match, and Perry and I have other things to work out before we can actually decide to marry."

"But you will come to see me ride tomorrow, will you not, Mama?" Penny exclaimed, her interest suddenly veering to something more tangible. "Perry promised you would if I asked you nicely."

Athena smiled. She wished Perry would not be forever making promises to please her daughter. "Of course, I will, dearest," she said, determined to make at least one of those good-natured promises come true.

And she had done so, wearing her new riding habit of deep blue, ordered—as a result of Perry's generosity—from Madame Lucille in London. She knew that shade of blue suited her, highlighting the rich auburn of her hair and deepening the amber of her eyes until they glowed a tawny gold.

"My dear Athena," Perry had exclaimed when he saw her, "you look absolutely regal. Does she not, Penny?" he added teasingly.

Regal? Athena would have preferred to be called beautiful, radiant, enchanting, even pretty. Regal sounded a shade too formal, too stiff, too mature. She submitted rather coolly to her betrothed's enthusiastic hug, thinking how very boyish he was with his golden hair in disarray and his face wreathed in smiles.

"I am glad to see you are feeling more yourself, Athena," he remarked with deplorable nonchalance, she thought. "We missed you yesterday. Did we not, Penny?"

"Of course," her daughter answered absently, her attention focused on the fat pony a stable-lad was leading out of the stalls. "Can I canter her today, Perry?" she demanded, her mother's ailment forgotten. "You promised that if I did not fall off, I could."

"Let us get your mother's mare saddled first, shall we? Then I want you to watch carefully as I saddle Buttercup. Every rider should know how to saddle a horse, my father always says."

Athena could not help but unbend towards her betrothed as she watched the patience and affection he displayed in going

over all the names of the saddle parts with her daughter, showing her not once but several times how to tighten the girth and
measure the length of the stirrups before mounting.

So absorbed was she in watching Penny listening in rapt attention to Peregrine's explanations that she did not realize they
had company until a deep voice spoke her name.

"Mrs. Standish," the earl remarked smoothly, coming to a
halt beside her, "I am delighted to see you once more among us.
I trust you have fully recovered from your indisposition?"

Athena felt that this double-edged remark was deliberately
phrased to fluster her, but she refused to rise to the bait. Favor-
ing him with a sweeping glance that did not meet his eyes, she
murmured a polite response and turned to greet his companion.

Miss Rathbone looked, if anything, Athena thought—a cold
stone settling in her stomach—more stunning than ever this afternoon. The Beauty was arrayed in a fanciful habit of the
palest primrose yellow, adorned with gold-braided epaulettes
and brass buttons on jacket and cuffs. It occurred to Athena that
it was vastly unfair for a blonde to look so ravishing in that
shade, but Miss Rathbone's abundant gold ringlets, topped by a
dashing military-style bonnet, had not only Peregrine but all the
stable-lads gawking in admiration.

The Beauty did not waste any time in demanding, in that lilting voice that grated on Athena's nerves, that Peregrine—the
fact that she made no bones about using his name was not lost
on the widow—immediately set her up in her saddle and review
the correct ways to hold the reins.

To Athena's everlasting chagrin, Perry seemed only too delighted to do so, leading the Beauty on her docile little bay mare
into the adjoining paddock to begin the lesson.

"What about me, Perry?" Penelope mumbled querulously,
and Athena felt a surge of anger at the viscount for abandoning
her daughter for a scheming hussy. She turned to assist Penny
herself, but the earl was there before her, swinging the child up
and settling her carefully in the saddle.

"Miss Rathbone must be addle-pated," Athena heard her
daughter confide innocently to the earl. "We learned all that
about the reins yesterday, and she seems to have forgotten already."

"Hush, Penny," Athena said hastily. "That is not at all polite
of you."

"But it is true," her daughter insisted, causing Lord St.

Aubyn to laugh aloud. "Now, lead Buttercup into the paddock if you please," Penny instructed the earl unself-consciously, much to Athena's amusement. "I wish to show Mama what I learned yesterday."

"You have a charming daughter, madam," the earl murmured as Penny trotted around the paddock to demonstrate her new abilities.

Athena kept her eyes fixed on her daughter, but she was very conscious of the man lounging beside her, one arm draped casually along the top of the fence. What had brought his lordship down to the stables this afternoon? she wondered. Should he not be in his study working on that treatise he had mentioned over dinner several evenings ago? And if he thought to draw her into idle conversation by praising her daughter, he would be disappointed, she thought. For there was nothing at all she had any wish to discuss with the wretch.

At that moment Penelope pulled her pony to a stop beside the fence. "What do you think, Mama?" she demanded, joy and excitement in every line of her little body. "Is Buttercup not the sweetest goer you have ever seen?"

Athena stared at the fat little pony seriously for a moment before nodding her head and trying not to smile at her daughter's enthusiasm and the cant expression she had doubtless picked up from Perry. "I believe you are right, dear. She is indeed a fancy pacer, and you handle her very well indeed."

"And what do you think, my lord?" the little girl demanded daringly, turning to the earl with a shy smile.

"I think you have the makings of a bruising rider, my dear," he drawled with obvious amusement.

Athena felt a glow of pleasure. She had not expected the earl to show any consideration at all for a little girl's feelings, but he had surprised her. Could it be that his lordship actually liked children? she wondered, stealing a glance at the man beside her. His smile was all for Penelope at the moment, and there was a touch of wistfulness in it that caught her off guard.

She was still staring when he looked at her, his blue-black eyes dark with a longing Athena could not identify. And then the look was gone, replaced by cynical amusement.

"A few more lessons and you will rival your mother, Penelope. What is Perry going to teach you today?"

"I shall learn how to canter," Penny said proudly. "And then to gallop. And then to jump over hedges, so I can join the hunt next spring."

"Whoa!" the earl exclaimed, his lips twitching with amusement. "I can see you are a fast learner, young lady, but you will need a larger mount before you can take to the fields with the hunt. I think you should learn everything you can from Buttercup first. Perry learned to ride on her when he was a lad, did he tell you? And look what a bruising rider he is. You wish to ride as well as Perry, do you not?"

"No," Penelope responded with a grin, which Athena noticed was mirrored on the earl's face. "I want to ride like Mama. She is a bruising rider, too, you know."

Athena was conscious of the earl's leisurely gaze moving over her face. "Yes, I know, my dear. Your Mama is certainly a good rider."

"My Mama is good at everything," her daughter announced innocently, turning her smile on Athena, who had tensed at the implications of Penny's words.

"Yes," the earl drawled after a short pause, his voice suddenly husky and oddly sensuous. "I can certainly vouch for that, young lady. Your Mama is an extraordinary woman indeed."

Athena froze, but before she could put a stop to her daughter's indiscreet chatter, Penny continued happily, seemingly unconscious of the undercurrents of tension her words had set off between the adults. "That is what Perry always says. I am glad you think so, too."

"And did Perry also tell you not to let your horse stand about, I wonder?" Athena put in quickly, not daring to look at the gentleman beside her.

"Of course, he did, Mama. Perry knows everything."

"Perhaps not quite everything," the earl's voice drawled *sotto voce*, and Athena imagined she heard the echo of a threat in his words.

"When you and Lord St. Aubyn come back from your ride, I shall show you how well I can canter, Mama."

Athena heard her daughter's happy voice through a fog of panic. No, she thought, she could not ride out alone with this man. She dreaded the threats he was bound to make. But more than that, she dreaded what he might do.

Her head seemed unnaturally light, and she wondered if she were about to embarrass herself by swooning again. Athena could remember swooning only once before in her entire life— when her father had come to tell her that her mother had finally succumbed to influenza. That was before she had encountered

Lord St. Aubyn, who had triggered this display of weakness two days ago, and appeared about to do so again unless she pulled herself together immediately.

"I think I shall forego my ride today," she heard herself murmur in a voice that sounded nothing like her own. "I do not feel quite the thing, darling."

"But Tom has already saddled Tarantella for you, Mama."

"I know, dear, but I do not think—"

"Nonsense, my dear Mrs. Standish," the earl said bracingly, a wicked light in his eyes. "A ride is just what you need to put the roses back in your cheeks."

Athena saw with alarm that the earl had waved to the groom who stood holding her mare. The mention of roses had convinced her that he was toying with her. It also reminded her that she had not yet thanked him for his thoughtfulness.

Thoughtfulness? Or was it perversity? she wondered.

"I would rather not, my lord," she protested, as he reached for her and lifted her into the saddle. To everyone who witnessed this normal courtesy, he must appear no more than the gracious host, Athena realized helplessly. And had his hands not lingered longer than necessary on her waist, and had they not slipped down imperceptibly to brush her hips; had he not guided her foot into the stirrup, his hand curled suggestively— and out of everyone's sight—around her booted ankle, Athena might have been able to persuade herself that he was nothing more than an attentive host.

But the pounding of her heart told her different.

"I think we should wait for Perry, my lord," she said, trying to sound reasonable, calm, collected, in control of her emotions.

"I am sure that Perry would urge you to enjoy yourself, Athena," he replied softly, his voice a caress that set her blood racing again, as it had in the darkness of the dungeon. And the fiend had used her name again, she noted, unable to still the trembling of her fingers as he handed her the reins.

She knew that the earl had spoken nothing but the truth. In his innocence, Perry would see nothing improper in his betrothed riding out with his father. Why should he? He trusted them both implicitly. How misplaced that trust, she thought miserably.

Athena forced herself to look down into the dark eyes of Lord St. Aubyn. The wicked glitter she saw there, and the even more wicked grin on his sensuous mouth, confirmed what she had already suspected.

Her prospective father-in-law was bent on seducing her.

Sylvester gazed up into the tawny golden eyes of his son's betrothed, and his grin slowly faded. She looked truly magnificent, he thought wryly, small chin raised defiantly, face pale with anger, eyes cool and challenging. But then he saw her mouth tremble, and Sylvester felt the sharp ache of desire. Behind that brave front, the little widow was afraid. And she had every reason to be, he mused cynically, watching in fascination as that sensuous mouth trembled more noticeably.

Resolutely, he dragged his gaze back to her eyes, and what he saw there gave him a perverse kind of pleasure. She had read his mind and knew exactly what he was about.

Well, so much the better, he thought. After what had happened in the dungeon, there was no room for pretense between them. He could hold that kiss as a threat over the widow's pretty head, and well she knew it. What she did not know—and Sylvester had no intention of letting her guess it—was that he would never run to his son with tales of his widow's peccadilloes. Causing Perry pain had never been a part of his plan to get rid of Mrs. Standish, and Sylvester could well imagine how crushed and hurt his son would be to discover that his own father had kissed his betrothed.

And worse yet, the widow had enjoyed that kiss. Sylvester could see it in her eyes even now. Her very reticence betrayed her. Had she not just attempted to escape riding out alone with him? And would it be too presumptuous of him to believe she was afraid of what he might do? Afraid of what she might *allow* him to do?

His grin returned, and he saw Athena's gaze slide away nervously. Sylvester had not felt so aroused by a female in years. The informal arrangement he had with a lady of relaxed morals over in Camelford had served him well enough for several years, but Betsy had never—even in the first months of their affair—made him feel ten years younger. Perry's widow had made his blood run hot again, and it was just as well that there would be no marriage between them. The prospect of living the remainder of his life under the same roof with this woman if she belonged irrevocably to his son was unthinkable.

Sylvester swung himself into the saddle and gentled the restive chestnut. In the paddock Perry was walking a very talkative Miss Rathbone slowly up and down, stopping every five paces to position the Beauty's hands more firmly on the reins. The lady's ploy was so transparent, Sylvester marveled that his son had not seen her drift. Sitting silently on her pony, Penelope watched the pantomime impatiently. Catching his glance, the child waved at him, a smile lighting her small face.

Sylvester waved back, feeling again the nostalgia tug at his heart for the daughter he and Adrienne had never had.

Pushing these mawkish thoughts to the back of his mind, Sylvester turned his horse to follow Mrs. Standish out of the stable-yard. Her back was ramrod-straight, and she did not glance his way as he brought Ajax abreast of her mare. As soon as they had left the house behind them, she urged Tarantella into a canter, choosing the open meadows rather than the bridle path through the Hanging Wood, as Sylvester had hoped she would. He needed to be private with the delectable Mrs. Standish. She must be prodded into accepting his more than generous offer to give up this idea of marrying his son, he mused, watching her lengthen the mare's stride as they approached a hedge.

The elegance with which the widow took the jump reminded him sharply of Adrienne, who had loved to ride. But his wife would have glanced teasingly at him over her shoulder, her blue eyes sparkling with excitement, daring him to chase her up the hill to the big oaks that had stood sentinel over St. Aubyn land for centuries. Daring him to catch her . . .

Athena Standish displayed no such playfulness, and it was pure coincidence that when she reached the top of the hill, she drew rein to admire the view. Spellbinding, Adrienne had always called it, and indeed it was, Sylvester thought, although words were a poor substitute for the grandeur of the prospect that lay before them.

As always, he was awestruck by the impassive majesty of a land that had harbored his family for so many generations. The blood of his forefathers had been spilled defending this plot of England, and every time he rode around the vast estate, Sylvester felt the pull of his blood linking him to the past.

He glanced at his companion and wondered what schemes and ambitions lay behind those amber eyes. It suddenly angered him to think of a fortune hunter daring to invade the patrimony his father had placed in his hands years ago.

"Magnificent, is it not?" he drawled.

"Oh, much much more than that," she whispered in a hushed voice. "It is simply breathtaking."

He allowed himself a cynical smile at the awe in her voice. "No doubt you are thinking that it would be no small thing to be mistress of all this," he said with deceptive softness, observing her closely.

He was unprepared for her look of astonishment and the flash of anger in her expressive eyes.

"You mistake the matter entirely, my lord, if you believe that is my ambition." She paused, meeting his gaze squarely. "We delude ourselves if we believe that we can be mistress—or master for that matter—of anything so enduring and grand as this." She made a sweeping gesture with her arm. "How impossibly arrogant you have grown, my lord, if you believe—as you appear to—that you can call this land yours. Do you imagine perchance that it will take note of your brief stewardship here? Other than adding your portrait to the Long Gallery and another headstone to the graveyard?"

She fell abruptly silent as though she had said more than she had intended, and Sylvester was struck by how precisely the widow's observations mirrored his own feelings. He had never put them into words quite so clearly before, and it seemed odd to him that a female should have understood so well his innermost thoughts. Either the widow was much wiser than he had given her credit for, or she was a clever trickster who thought to pull the wool over his eyes.

He cleared his throat. "Are you telling me that you do not aspire to be mistress here, madam?" he demanded, deliberately twisting her words. "If this is true, why not accept my offer and return to London? Three thousand pounds wisely invested will keep you in relative comfort."

The widow glanced at him pityingly. "London is no place to bring up a child, my lord. Would you raise your daughter there?" Her eyes dropped and she turned to gaze out at the peaceful fields and meadows around them. "I want Penelope to have a place where she can feel she belongs," Athena continued in a softer voice, "as I once belonged at Rothingham Manor. A place like Standish Park, her father's home, where she has every right to feel welcome. I cannot impose upon my aunt forever. We have been too long without a home of our own, and I intend to do everything in my power to see that she gets one."

"So you are refusing my offer, I take it?"

Again the pitying glance. "It is not wealth I crave, my lord. I do not expect you to understand, of course. You have belonged here at the Castle all your life, as has Perry. What do you know of being cast off by those upon whom you thought you had some claim?"

"And you think Perry will understand any better when he learns that his betrothed attempted to seduce his father?"

Her face paled, and Sylvester derived a perverse satisfaction from the trembling of her lips. "I did no such thing, my lord!" she exclaimed angrily. "It was a mistake, as you well know."

He laughed mirthlessly. "That all depends on your point of view, my dear," he said flatly.

"Perry would never believe you."

There was a brave defiance in her voice that Sylvester could not but applaud. He admired courage, and Athena had more than her fair share. If only his son had not offered marriage to the first female who caught his fancy, he thought. If only Athena Standish had been ten years younger and unwed. If only he did not find her so deuced attractive himself.

"We shall have to put that to the test, my dear, shall we not?" he responded with a grim smile.

Without a word, Athena whirled her mare and cantered back the way they had come, her defiance evident in every line of her body.

Yes, my dear, Sylvester mused as he put heels to Ajax and followed her at a distance. We shall have to see about that.

CHAPTER EIGHT

The Letter

Over the next few day, Athena found all sorts of excuses for avoiding the stable-yard at the hour set aide for the riding lessons. She regretted missing her daughter's progress, which—if Penny's excited recounting of her growing daring could be believed—was nothing short of miraculous. But she did not regret missing the earl's company. He had been present every afternoon, her daughter reported, and was so obliging as to help her mount Buttercup while Perry was occupied with Miss Rathbone.

Perhaps what disturbed Athena most, as she listened every evening to her daughter's happy chatter, was that her initial anger at Peregrine's besotted infatuation—for want of a better word—with Miss Rathbone had turned first to a numb resignation, then to something perilously close to disinterest. Despite her brave words to Lord St. Aubyn the other day, Athena felt increasingly disinclined to compete with the Beauty for the viscount's attention. If Perry insisted upon making a cake of himself over a female as brazen and ill-tempered as any Athena had ever encountered, even in London, then he deserved whatever he got.

Athena deliberately put the thorny question of her betrothal aside and set herself to find entertainment elsewhere. In this she found a willing ally in her hostess, who was turning out to be far less of a dragon than Athena had originally imagined. If anything, Lady Sarah leaned in the opposite direction, displaying an unexpected warmth and kindliness beneath her crusty exterior. Even Aunt Mary, gradually overcoming her initial fear of being labeled a Cit's daughter by their hostess, had remarked upon what she called Lady Sarah's subterfuge.

"Her ladyship merely pretends to be a dragon, my dear," she had told Athena only yesterday. "I do believe the old gel enjoys playacting. Did you know that she and Mrs. Rathbone ran away from their Seminary together to go on the stage?"

Athena gazed at her aunt in amazement. "What Banbury tale is this, Aunt?"

"It is quite true, dear. I do not believe her ladyship wished it to become public knowledge, of course, but Mrs. Rathbone does like to rattle on about the times they spent together as girls. And one afternoon it slipped out. Of course, I pretended not to notice, but her ladyship admitted it and regretted that she had been stopped by her angry Papa before she could realize her dreams of becoming an actress."

"Lady Sarah said that? And are you saying that Mrs. Rathbone *did* become an actress?" This notion was so startling that Athena could hardly credit her ears.

"Well, yes," her aunt replied, glancing over her shoulder conspiratorially. "Apparently she became quite famous, too."

"Did she tell you so herself?" Athena asked, amused in spite of herself.

"Oh, no! Lady Sarah said so. And you will never guess, dear, her stage name was Molly O'Neil. She has been retired for years, of course, but just think, Athena, I may have seen her at Drury Lane with my dear James and never known it!"

This revelation from Lady Sarah's past struck Athena as highly romantic, and her appreciation for the earl's aunt increased. The knowledge that the ever-so-proper Lady Sarah Steele had committed—or had intended to commit—the unpardonable sin of taking to the stage gave her an aura of rakishness that Athena found hard to ignore. So it was with considerable pleasure that she performed little tasks for her ladyship, one of which was the addressing of a pile of invitations for an informal ball Lady Sarah had planned for Peregrine's birthday the following week.

The sun shining in the open windows of the morning room had enticed Athena to choose to complete her task here rather than at the elegant French escritoire in her own sitting room upstairs. There was little chance of interruption, for Perry had driven off at dawn in his curricle to look at a horse at a neighboring farm, while Aunt Mary and Penelope had walked over to the estate lake to visit a new family of cygnets her daughter had learned about from the stable-lads. Miss Rathbone was still abed as was her custom, so Athena felt confident she could finish the invitations before nuncheon.

She was but halfway towards this goal when she heard the door open behind her. Thinking it was Jackson on some housekeeping errand, Athena did not acknowledge the intruder until he stood beside the desk, his buckskin breeches and dark blue coat announcing his identity as clearly as though he had spoken.

Reluctantly, Athena raised her eyes and stared coolly up at the earl.

"Good morning, Athena," he said caressingly, a slow smile teasing his sensuous lips.

"Good morning, my lord." Athena did not trust that smile, and the sight of it caused the blood to flutter wildly in her veins. "I believe I have asked you not to use my name, my lord," she said sharply, taking refuge in anger.

He merely laughed, and the sound of it brought the color to her cheeks. "Allow an old recluse his eccentricities, my dear," he murmured. "I have developed a fondness for your name, Athena. Unlike Mrs. Rathbone, I have a predilection for the classics, and the name fits you far better than you can imagine."

"Now you are being ridiculous, my lord." Athena dipped her quill in the ink-stand and reached for another invitation. "You must be the only person of my acquaintance who believes that."

"Perhaps they do not know you as well as I do, my dear."

"You do not know me at all, my lord, so do not deceive yourself," she replied sharply, all too uncomfortably aware that his lordship knew considerably more about her than was strictly proper.

Athena spoke impulsively, and the slow grin that spread over the earl's face told her that she had provoked the wolf in him. "Oh, I believe I do," he drawled, the blue of his eyes so dark that Athena was reminded of a deep pool at midnight.

Suppressing a flash of panic, Athena dropped her eyes to her work and reached for another invitation from the stack in front of her.

"Should you not be working on that treatise of yours, my lord?" she inquired, falling back on sarcasm to hide her uneasiness. "I was reading in the latest journal of the Royal Historical Society that it is eagerly awaited. Although I understand that Sir Thomas Harding is also preparing a series of lectures on Chinese porcelain which includes the early Ming dynasty."

The earl's expression sobered instantly. "Harding is a vulgar charlatan," he said dismissively. "And he is not sponsored by the Society. A mere dilettante. Two years ago he touted himself as an expert on Egyptian artifacts; this year it is Chinese pottery; next year it might well be Indian religious icons. Only the ignorant believe that getting one's name in the news makes a man an expert."

"I wondered why I had never heard of him before," Athena responded absently, dipping her quill in the ink-pot and addressing an invitation with her careful copperplate.

There was a slight pause. "And what do you know of Oriental pottery, my dear?" the earl asked in an amused voice. "It is not exactly a favorite topic of conversation among the ladies."

"Some ladies occasionally read something other than the latest romantic novels, my lord," Athena said dryly.

"And reading an article or two in an historical journal makes you an expert, I presume?"

This remark was so indicative of masculine superiority on the subject that Athena instantly bristled. "I would presume nothing if I were you, my lord." She raised her eyes from her task and glared at him. "And I do not recall claiming to be an expert. It does so happen, however, that I have read more than an article or two on the Ming Dynasty. Much more, in fact. My father, who never claimed to be an expert on the matter either," she added tartly, "has a small but rather select collection of vases. Or he did when last I was at Rothingham Manor."

Athena bowed her head over the invitations again. Why had she been provoked into mentioning her father to this insensitive oaf? she wondered. Remembering her dear Papa was still painful after all these years of silence. Although Athena still wrote for his birthday and Christmas, she had long since given up all hope of receiving a response. Her stepmother must be very insecure indeed if she had alienated the baronet so completely from his only daughter. And her Papa must be more infatuated with the blond widow than Athena had thought possible in a man of his years.

"Your father is a collector?" The earl's voice sounded sharp with disbelief. "I thought I was aware of every collector, large and small, on both sides of the Channel."

Once again Athena was struck by the arrogance of this assumption. She smiled condescendingly. "Evidently you were mistaken, my lord. My father's collection is small, insignificant almost when compared to yours, no more than twenty or twenty-five pieces. But he has been collecting for thirty years at least, and does have a few exceptional specimens."

"How can you be sure that these pieces are exceptional?" he demanded curiously.

Athena glanced at him pityingly. "Sir Joshua Carruthers—

whom I presume you *have* heard of, my lord," she added sar-castically—"used to take the waters in Bath when I was a girl, and Papa invited him out to Rothingham Manor to see the collection. Sir Joshua was so impressed he made my father a rather extravagant offer. He has been dead these ten years or more, so he cannot corroborate this story, of course. But it hardly matters to me what you believe, my lord. I would never have mentioned my father's collection at all had I known I would be subjected to this cross-examination."

She turned back to her task dismissively, but the earl did not take the hint. She could see his buckskin-clad thighs out of the corner of her eye, where he had perched on the corner of her desk.

"If you have no objection, my dear," he said after a considerable pause, during which Athena addressed another invitation, "I shall write to Sir Henry on the subject. Perhaps he can be prevailed upon to sell his collection."

Athena glanced up in surprise. "Whyever should I object, my lord?" she said. "But I doubt Father will sell."

"Perhaps you might help to persuade him, Athena?"

"Not if you insist upon using my name, my lord," she responded sharply, inexplicably annoyed that the earl continued to disregard her wishes. "Besides," she added truthfully, "I might actually hurt your cause. My father has not acknowledged a single one of my letters since I came back from the Peninsula. And now, my lord," she added when he did not reply, "I have promised your aunt that these invitations will be completed before nuncheon—"

"The invitations can wait, my dear," he interrupted brusquely. "It is too lovely a day to be cooped up inside. Come for a ride with me, Athena. I must go over to the village on an errand, and thought you might enjoy a view of our Cornish coast."

The invitation took her by surprise. She looked up at him and something in the depths of his midnight-blue eyes caused her heart to leap. If only things had been different, she mused, mesmerized by the slow smile that softened his harsh mouth. If only she might go with this man whose dark, angular face attracted her as Perry's fair perfection never had, whose eyes promised the passionate woman in her a sensuality she had been too long without.

Athena was so sorely tempted to reach out for what this man

offered that she forgot for a moment that she was betrothed to his son.

Long after the earl had gone, leaving the tantalizing male scent of shaving soap behind him, Athena sat staring blindly out of the open window, Lady Sarah's invitations forgotten.

After a solitary ride, during which his thoughts strayed with disconcerting frequency to the lady sitting at home in his morning room, Lord St. Aubyn made his way upstairs to his aunt's private sitting room.

His demeanor was more than usually troubled, a fact Lady Sarah was quick to remark upon.

"What ails you, lad?" she demanded as soon as Sylvester had taken up his stand before the empty hearth. "You look as though you had swallowed a spider."

Sylvester grinned. His aunt's penchant for sprinkling her speech with cant expressions never failed to amuse him. "You never heard that from me, Aunt. No doubt you have been listening to Perry again. I thought I told that boy to watch his language with the ladies."

"I am sure you did, dear," came the crisp reply, "but you might have saved your breath. Perry is still a sad rattle. His brief sojourn in London did not give him any town bronze at all as far as I can tell."

"Because he spent his entire stay sitting in the fair Athena's pocket, no doubt," Sylvester answered shortly. "That is what I want to talk to you about, Aunt—"

"Yes, I expect you do," Lady Sarah cut in, looking up from the needlework she had been engaged in. "That chit Augusta brought with her is a trollop, of course, but you must admit, Sylvester, that the gel knows her business. She has Perry dancing attendance like a puppet on a string. I do declare I feel quite sorry for the poor boy."

Sylvester was uncomfortably aware of the old lady's scrutiny, and glanced down at his ruby signet ring to collect his thoughts. During his ride he had felt the need for his aunt's sage advice on the apparent ease with which their plan had succeeded in separating Perry from his widow. Why, then, did he feel responsible for Athena Standish's plight?

"And Mrs., Standish?" he asked abruptly, absently twisting his ring on his finger. "Does your commiseration extend to her as well, Aunt?"

After an extended pause, Sylvester raised his eyes and saw

that his aunt was regarding him with an odd expression on her face.

"As far as I recall," she said slowly and distinctly, "feeling sorry for Athena was not part of our original plan, Sylvester. If I remember correctly, your goal was to rescue Perry from the nefarious clutches of a fortune hunter. Am I not correct?"

Much as he wished to do so, Sylvester could not deny it; but hearing his aunt speak so baldly of his plan to employ a younger female to wean Perry away from what he considered a disastrous marriage caused him to wince. Lady Sarah's words made him sound heartless, as indeed he was, he thought ruefully. The widow's feelings had not concerned him, if indeed he had considered them at all. Why had he suddenly developed a conscience? he wondered.

"And as far as I can see, we have succeeded admirably," his aunt continued, her sharp blue gaze never wavering. "Thanks to the ravishing Miss Rathbone's feminine charms, Perry's emotions are now hopelessly confused. Our darling Viviana is awakening the man in your son, Sylvester, and if she has not seduced him before he is much older, I shall be very much surprised."

"Seduced him?" Sylvester stared at his aunt in astonishment. Had he become so engrossed with his own less than honorable thoughts about Athena that he had failed to notice his son standing on the threshold of manhood?

"I had not intended it to come to that," he said harshly. "Surely you are mistaken, Aunt. After all, you—"

Lady Sarah chuckled. "I am only an unfortunate maiden lady who knows nothing of the ways of the flesh? Is that what you were about to say, Sylvester? Well, allow me to set your mind at rest, my dear boy," she said, a hint of defiance in her blue eyes. "Old I undoubtedly am, but not yet devoid of my powers of observation. You may take my word for it, lad, before much longer, our young Peregrine will know a good deal more about females than he does now. Believe you me."

When Sylvester made no reply, Lady Sarah picked up her needlework and continued in a softer voice, "If you are still reluctant to trust my observations, Sylvester, let me tell you that Augusta has noticed it, too. And she is hardly what you would call inexperienced," his aunt added with a sly smile. "Augusta has also noted—and remarked upon, I should add—your own assiduous pursuit of Mrs. Standish. In fact—and I am sure you will find this amusing, dear—Augusta is quite convinced that you hired Viviana to clear the way for your own designs upon the widow."

"*What* are you saying, madam?" Sylvester thundered, startled to hear himself shouting.

Lady Sarah glanced up at him, an innocent smile teasing the corners of her mouth. "Why, nothing at all, dear. And there is no need to shout. You and I both know that you are merely distracting Mrs. Standish to keep her mind off Perry's infatuation with the Beauty."

"Which was entirely your idea, if I recall, Aunt."

"Of course it was, dear," Lady Sarah murmured soothingly. "And you are doing a most convincing job of it. One might almost believe . . ." Her voice trailed off and she shrugged, applying herself once more to her embroidery.

"Believe *what*, Aunt?" Apprehension made his voice sharper than he intended.

"Why, nothing, dear. Except that Augusta seems to think that you are becoming as infatuated with our little widow as Peregrine is with the Beauty. She finds the whole plot of this melodrama highly entertaining, as you can well imagine."

"Your Mrs. Rathbone has an overwrought imagination," Sylvester snapped angrily. "And I can assure you, Aunt, that there is no truth whatsoever in her absurd allegations. I am merely following your suggestion—"

"Oh, I know that, dear," his aunt cut in gently. "And besides, it is not as though Athena might be deceived into taking your attentions seriously. It has not escaped my notice that she avoids you whenever possible. And as for the other kind of attention . . . well, I trust you will not deceive yourself into thinking Athena will accept anything less than an honorable alliance, dear. From what her aunt, Mrs. Easton, tells me, our widow is a romantic at heart, a characteristic she shares with you, Sylvester."

"Me?" he replied in a startled voice. "I am not a romantic, Aunt. You must have moonshine in your head to suggest it."

"Then why have you not taken a second wife, my dear?" Lady Sarah said gently. "It is now over five years since dear Adrienne left us, and yet—"

"I have no wish for a second wife," he responded shortly.

"I cannot imagine why not," his aunt murmured, almost to herself, setting a careful stitch in the colorful embroidery in her lap. "You are only two-and-forty, after all. Not yet in your dotage. It might be pleasant to have little ones running about this old castle again."

The earl uttered an impatient sound and strode over to stare down at the rose gardens. Unwillingly, his gaze was drawn to the lily-pond. Was it a flight of fancy, or was he only imagining that the scene appeared strangely forlorn without that slight figure in pink trailing her fingers in the still waters? Sylvester shook himself and turned back to his aunt.

"I did not come to seek your advice upon my improbable second nuptials, Aunt," he said brusquely. "But you are right about Perry. I believe he is ready to concede that his betrothal to Mrs. Standish was a mistake, and I am sure she will release him if we can offer her an acceptable alternative."

Lady Sarah looked up quickly, her blue eyes sparkling in anticipation. "Do not tell me that dear Augusta was right after all, Sylvester?"

The earl grinned humorlessly. "The only romantic here is you, my dear Aunt," he remarked affectionately. "I am sorry to disappoint you, but I think I have found a way to induce Mrs. Standish to remove herself from the Castle."

"I thought she had refused to accept your three thousand pounds. Will you offer her more, perchance?"

"No. But I did discover quite by accident this morning that her father, Sir Henry Rothingham, has a small collection of Oriental porcelain. Given my own interest in that area, it would be entirely unexceptional for me to write to him for information to include in my forthcoming lectures. If I were to mention his daughter's presence here and her desire to be reunited with him—"

"Oh, no!" Lady Sarah exclaimed hastily. "That would never do, dear. It never pays to interfere between parent and child. I suggest you merely mention that Athena is staying here as *my* guest—that should let the old reprobate know his daughter is not quite without friends in the world—and that she happened to mention her father's select collection."

The earl frowned. "That seems to be exactly what I proposed to do."

"Not quite, dear. I doubt Athena would wish you to intercede for her. She has too much pride for that. But if Sir Henry is really interested in seeing his daughter again, he will waste no time in writing to her here. Particularly if you mention something flattering about his granddaughter," she added with a smile.

An hour later, the Earl of St. Aubyn sat at his desk in a pensive mood, a half-written letter in front of him. His aunt's advice made perfect sense, and Sylvester had intended to follow it implicitly. However, halfway through his letter to Sir Henry Rothingham, it had suddenly dawned upon him that this same missive might set in motion a series of events that would take Athena Standish away from St. Aubyn Castle, perhaps forever.

The prospect did not bring him the satisfaction he had anticipated.

"We will not be living here at the Castle after all, will we, Mama?"

The question took Athena by surprise and brought home to her just how far she had allowed herself to drift apart from Peregrine. Had her disenchantment become so obvious to everyone? she wondered. And her betrothed? Had it become apparent to him, too?

She had been sitting beneath the old oaks with the other ladies watching the viscount engaged in a very lively game of croquet with Miss Rathbone and Penelope, when her daughter ran over to have her sash retied. She glanced around apprehensively, wondering which of the ladies might have overheard her daughter's question. Luckily, the earl had not yet joined the tea-party. Athena could well imagine his cynical smile had he heard Penny's words.

"Will we, Mama?"

Athena put an arm around her daughter and hugged her close. What was the use of lying to the child, to herself, any longer? she thought. But what could she say that might explain to her daughter the inconstancy of a gentleman's regard, the hollowness of his promises? What excuse could she give for her own lassitude? Had she not watched every one of the Beauty's flirtatious tricks to gain Perry's attention and never made the least push to keep what was hers?

Gently, she tucked one of Penny's stray ringlets into place, all too conscious of her daughter's relentless gaze. "Probably not," she murmured finally, wishing that there had been some other way of breaking the news.

"We will have to go back to London, then?"

"I am afraid so, darling. There is nowhere else to go."

"And Buttercup will stay here?"

"Yes." What else could she say? Athena asked herself, watching a tear roll down her daughter's cheek as the realization sank in. Quickly, Athena took a handkerchief from her sleeve and caught the arrant tear, but no sooner had she dried one than another took its place.

Stifling a sob, Penny pulled away. "Perry lied to us," she cried. "He promised we could—"

"Hush, dearest." Athena reached for her daughter, but the child whirled and ran away across the lawn.

"Whatever is the matter with Penelope?" Lady Sarah demanded, her blue eyes full of concern.

Athena rose to her feet. "She is a little tired, I think. She did not get her rest this afternoon."

"Let me go up to her, dear," Mrs. Easton offered.

"Thank you, Aunt," Athena responded with a grateful glance. "But I think this is something that needs my attention. Stay and enjoy your tea."

Thankful to escape further embarrassment, Athena hurried up the terrace steps and into the house. The time had come to have a serious talk with Penelope, she thought, not relishing the notion of shattering her daughter's dreams as well as her own.

Athena could hear Penelope's sobs from the landing above and quickened her pace. Then the deep voice of a man consoling the child made her pause. Lord St. Aubyn! That was all she needed, Athena thought disgustedly. That man gloating over her misfortune.

The sight that met her eyes on the landing caused Athena to experience a flurry of mixed emotions, the chief of which was anger. What did this odious creature think he was doing, down on one knee, his arm around her daughter, wiping her wet cheeks with his own handkerchief? Did he not know that Penny's distress was a direct result of his refusal to sanction her mother's marriage to his son? Had the earl not interfered, Athena might now have been firmly established at the Castle as Perry's viscountess. And he would not now be romping on the lawn with a notable Beauty.

Or would he? a little voice nagged at her. The thought of Perry behaving so cavalierly as her husband sent a chill down Athena's spine before she brushed the disturbing notion aside.

At least the earl would not have kissed his daughter-in-law in the dungeons, she told herself, and she would have been spared this odd racing of her pulses every time she heard his voice, or gazed into the enigmatic blue of his eyes.

Or would he have kissed her anyway?

And worse yet, would she have wanted him to?

Where this wicked notion came from, Athena did not dare to question, but she was honest enough to admit that the earl's clandestine kiss lay at the heart of her dilemma. She would not undo that kiss even had she the power to do so. It had been too precious, too all-consuming, too much of what was missing from her life. She had been ripe for such a kiss; she was ripe for so much more than a kiss that Athena trembled to think what irredeemable folly she might have committed had he asked for more.

But he had not done so . . . at least not yet. And she was not married, nor—if her premonitions could be trusted—was she in any danger of becoming a wife in the near future. Instead of the thought depressing her, Athena found comfort in it. Her aunt's small house in London suddenly offered a haven from the turmoil of emotions this dark, harsh-faced man had stirred within her heart. Now if only she might find the right words to console Penelope for the loss of that fanciful dream Peregrine had promised them both.

The earl raised his head at that moment and stared up into her eyes. Athena felt her breath catch in her throat.

"What has Perry done to make your daughter cry, madam?"

"I told you, sir," Penelope sobbed convulsively. "Perry lied to us. I *hate* him!"

"Hush, dear," Athena murmured, blushing at her daughter's straight talking. "It is not right to hate anybody."

"Well, I do hate him, Mama." Penelope gave a gasping sob, and the earl applied his handkerchief once more to her streaming cheeks.

"Come, darling," Athena pleaded. "Let us go upstairs and ask Jackson to send up a tea-tray with some of Mrs. Morton's lemon curd tarts, shall we? The ones you like so much, Penny."

"I do not *want* any tarts," her daughter wailed, clasping her arm more tightly round the earl's neck and hiding her damp face in his cravat.

"What do you want then, love?"

Athena had never heard the earl use that tone before, and it quite touched her heart. She had never imagined him as a patient man, and certainly not one to put himself out for a distraught child.

"I want Buttercup," Penny sobbed.

"Up in the nursery?" the earl asked in mock surprise. "Are you telling me that you want to invite Buttercup to take tea with you and your mother, brat?" The mocking amusement in his voice caused Penny to give a watery chuckle.

"Of course not, silly," she gurgled. "I want to have Buttercup for my very own. As Perry promised I might."

Athena watched in fascination as the earl pushed one of her daughter's wayward ringlets out of her eyes and smiled tenderly at her. "I thought she was your very own already, love."

"Mama says we have no room for Buttercup in London."

The earl looked up at her again, and Athena could see no sign of the triumph she had expected in his eyes.

"Then you will just have to stay here, my dear," he said softly, and Athena had the strangest sensation that the earl was talking to her, not to Penelope.

The effect of this suggestion was instantaneous. "Oh, may we, Mama?" Penny said, her tear forgotten. "*Please* say we may."

The sight of her daughter's sudden joy kindled her anger, and Athena turned on the earl, who had risen from his kneeling position to look down at her with an amused gleam in his eyes.

"That was quite unforgivable, my lord," she said, her voice low and husky with fury and unshed tears. "How *dare* you make such promises to a child when you must know they cannot be kept? Come, Penny," she said brusquely, fearing her emotions would betray her if she stayed in the earl's presence a moment longer. "Come, dear," she repeated, pushing Penelope towards the stairs. "Run up to the nursery this instant. And no argument," she added, noting the mulish look on her daughter's face.

"And you, my lord," she paused, one foot on the stair to look back at the earl, "let me warn you that we have endured quite enough deception in this house to last a lifetime."

Feeling the tears welling in her eyes, Athena turned and ran up the stairs after her daughter.

CHAPTER NINE

The Storm

Two mornings after this outburst, Athena sat at her dressing table staring at her reflection in the mirror and wondering how she could possibly bear to remain in this house until after Lady Sarah's ball. She had promised herself that she would not do anything impulsive. Much as she would have liked to pack her trunks and run away from the heartache of Peregrine's betrayal, the seductive intimacy of his father's gaze held her mesmerized, robbing her of the will to break away.

Besides, she told herself for the umpteenth time in the past week, Lady Sarah had come to depend upon her, consulting her on every detail of the approaching festivities in honor of her great-nephew's birthday. Almost as though her hostess had sanctioned the presence of Peregrine's betrothed at the Castle. Sanctioned their marriage. Although her ladyship's approval— if indeed her growing amiability denoted approval—had come too late, Athena mused, rising reluctantly from her silent contemplation. Since there would be no marriage—Athena had finally faced this unpleasant truth—it made no difference whether Lady Sarah approved of her or not.

Neither did it matter whether Lord St. Aubyn approved of her or not.

This conclusion should have cheered her, released her from the anxiety that had plagued her since her arrival in Cornwall. But all Athena felt was a great sadness. She had relinquished her dream. She should have realized back in London that her darling Perry, for all his generosity, attentiveness, and protests of undying adoration, had been in the throes of a boyish infatuation. Nothing more.

She should have recognized the signs and guided him, gently but firmly, through the troubled waters of puppy love. She had been so much older and wiser; she should have known better. But she had allowed herself to dream, and allowed Perry to take on responsibilities for which he was singularly unprepared.

She had accepted his offer of marriage.

She should have known that infatuations do not last. She *had* known it. Perry had imagined himself in love with her, and Athena had allowed him to believe it. Was she not therefore partially responsible for his subsequent disenchantment, his newly formed attachment to the ravishing Miss Rathbone? Much as she hated to admit it, Athena recognized every one of the signs of Perry's new infatuation with the Beauty. Had she not experienced each one herself in London? Every adoring glance, every touch of the hand, every tender smile and eager attention to her comfort? All those signs of infatuation now directed at Miss Rathbone?

Athena brushed the unpleasant thought aside and reviewed the tasks that still remained to be done before the formal dinner tomorrow. Cook had expressed some alarm that the lobsters might not arrive in time to make up the patties, and she must visit the estate hot-houses to confer with Turner, the head gardener, on which flowers should be brought up to the house in the morning.

Her thoughts were interrupted by Mrs. Easton, who came bustling into the room after a brief knock.

"What is all this nonsense I hear from Penny about returning to London, my dear?" Clearly agitated, her diminutive aunt advanced into the room, her blue eyes troubled.

Athena sighed. She had intended to inform her aunt of her decision to leave Cornwall once Perry's birthday celebration was over, but it appeared that the unpleasant task must be faced now.

"It must be clear to you by now, Aunt, that there will be no wedding between me and Perry," she said, opting for the direct approach. "So it behooves us to—"

"Has the rascal j-jilted you, dear?" Aunt Mary stammered, her eyes wide with shock.

"No, of course not," Athena responded quickly. "At least not in so many words. But since I have clearly been replaced in his regard by another, I intend to release him from his promise."

Her aunt opened her mouth as if to protest, but all she said was, "Oh, Athena! How dreadful for you, dear."

"Not at all, Aunt," Athena said, painfully aware that she spoke nothing but the truth. "I should have seen that Perry was too young for the role he wished to play. I should never have accepted his offer. His infatuation with Miss Rathbone is ample proof that he is not yet ready to settle down with a wife, much less one ten years his senior."

"That conniving hussy!" Aunt Mary hissed. "How very convenient for his lordship that she should appear just in time to distract Perry from his obligation to you, dear. And you are only eight years older than he is, not ten," she added inconsequentially.

"I might as well be a hundred," Athena murmured. "It was foolish beyond reason to imagine Perry had the maturity to give us the protection and security we need, Aunt. I have decided to return to London as soon as Lady Sarah can spare us. No doubt she may be persuaded to provide us with a carriage."

"Oh, dear."

Athena glanced at her aunt. "You think she may not?"

"Oh, no," Aunt Mary murmured, her brow furrowed. "I am sure her ladyship will be most glad . . ." Her voice trailed off. "The thing is, Athena . . . well, to tell the truth . . ." She paused, and Athena read indecision on her plump feature.

"I realize that it is not what we had planned, Aunt," she began.

"Lady Sarah has invited me to stay on indefinitely," Aunt Mary blurted out abruptly.

Athena stared at her aunt in utter amazement. Never in a hundred years had she imagined the possibility of Lady Sarah taking a liking to her mousy, unsophisticated aunt. A Cit's daughter, no less.

"As a paid companion?"

"Very handsomely paid, too," Aunt Mary confided with a grin. "You could have knocked me over with a feather, of course, but she insisted she was lonely here in this barn of a place."

"She called this beautiful place a barn?"

"Her very words, dear."

"And you accepted?" An uneasy sensation invaded Athena's stomach. This was a complication she had not counted upon.

Aunt Mary nodded and her frown reappeared. "Had I known how things stood between you and Perry, dear . . ."

"Nonsense!" Athena exclaimed with more assurance than she felt. "Of course, you must stay, Aunt. Penny and I will manage very well by ourselves—"

"I would not dream of such a thing," came the instant reply.

"We will all stick together as we have always done since you returned from Spain, dear."

Athena put her arms about her aunt and gave her an impulsive hug. "No," she said decisively. "You will do no such thing, dear."

And indeed, how could she deprive her dearest friend of the chance to augment her meager income? Athena thought as she accompanied her aunt down to the morning room. And of the obvious enjoyment Aunt Mary derived from her association with Lady Sarah. That would be selfish indeed.

Much as her aunt had protested her suggestion, Athena knew that she would allow herself to be persuaded to accept Lady Sarah's generous invitation.

And Athena would be once more on her own, she thought, alone but for the comfort her daughter might give her.

That afternoon, while Athena was in the kitchen making a few last-minute changes to the dinner menu with a flustered Mrs. Crompton, the summer skies clouded over and a sharp wind blew in from the coast.

The first inkling she had that the weather had turned was when the back door flew open to admit a wind-blown Jenny, the cook's helper, clasping to her bosom a large bunch of parsley from the herb garden.

"Lor' luv us, Mrs. Crompton," Jenny exclaimed between laughter and breathlessness, "there's a nasty squall brewing out there or my name ain't—oh! forgive me, ma'am," she said hastily, catching sight of Athena and bobbing a curtsy.

Athena walked to the window and looked out, her expression grave. "I trust that none of your menfolk are out in this weather, Jenny," she remarked.

Along that part of the Cornish coast, she had discovered in the first weeks of her arrival at St. Aubyn Castle, almost every one of the earl's staff had an intimate alliance with the sea. Fishing was a local tradition, and had been for hundreds of years, passed down from father to son. Hardly a family employed at the Castle had not lost a relative to the sea. Even the Steeles had paid the price of this strange fascination Cornishmen seemed to have with that infinite expanse of water that Athena had viewed from the safety of the clifftops. On one such expedition—before Miss Rathbone came upon the scene—Perry had told her the story of his great-uncle Gregory, whose yacht and all hands had been lost within sight of land during a summer storm.

Athena shivered. The sea scared her. One minute so calm and inviting, the next throwing up swells that rushed men to their deaths with frightening disregard for rank or fortune, for ambitions or dreams. There was a ruthlessness about the elements, storms in particular, that touched a core of primitive fear in her that Athena considered more appropriate to animals than to human beings. She repressed it vigorously, but whenever a storm threatened, she found entirely rational excuses to retire to her room and close the thick curtains to keep the elements at bay.

Gazing at the darkening sky and the branches of the elm trees responding erratically to the gusts of wind that blew in off the sea, Athena felt that familiar tremor of panic and gritted her teeth.

Abruptly another fear rose within her, and she forgot about her private dread of storms. Penny! She glanced at the kitchen clock and her heart sank. Her daughter was somewhere out there in the South Park, riding with Perry and Miss Rathbone.

She ran to the door and flung it open. A rush of damp air embraced her, pushing her backwards with its force. She grasped the doorframe to steady herself, then glanced back over her shoulder at the startled servants.

"My daughter is out there riding with the viscount," she cried, her voice rising against the noise of the wind. "I must go down to the stables to see if they have returned safely."

"Madam!" Mrs. Crompton exclaimed in shocked tones, moving to grasp Athena's arm. "Jenny here will run down there for you in a jiffy. There is no cause for alarm, I can assure you. His lordship will know what he is about."

The little maid stepped forward, tying a kerchief hastily over her cap and disordered curls. "Master Peregrine is a Cornishman, ma'am. 'E will 'ave seen the signs and no doubt is safe back in the stables. I'll just run down to make sure."

Athena was not entirely convinced that Perry was to be trusted, and when Jenny returned, her skirts tangled about her legs by the wind and her kerchief askew, Athena read the alarm in her eyes before she spoke.

"Old Bates tells me 'is lordship rode over to the lake with the lady and Miss Penny," she gasped, breathless from her exertions. "Would ye be wishing 'im to send one of the grooms after 'em, ma'am?"

Athena's heart chilled within her. "No," she responded sharply. "I shall go myself. Send down to have Tarantella saddled and brought up here, please."

Ten minutes later, after having donned her habit in record time, Athena found herself being tossed up onto her fidgety mare's back amid the garrulous protests of the head groom.

"There ain't no cause for alarm, ma'am," old Bates assured her, his shaggy eyebrows drawing together over the bridge of his large nose. "Master Peregrine ain't no fool. A tad rash at times, I'd 'ave to admit, but no fool. 'E'll be back with the ladies before ye get to Hanging Wood, ma'am. See if 'e ain't."

The old man appeared to be severely put out that she paid no heed to his advice, but Athena had ceased to care about anything except Penelope. Impatiently, she waved him away from the mare's head and urged her into a canter.

Once she was out of sight of the Castle, the sky seemed to become darker and the wind made an eerie moaning sound as Athena forced Tarantella into the Hanging Wood. It was even darker under the trees, and the mare became increasingly unmanageable, shying at every windswept leaf, snorting at every bramble that lashed across their path.

When she emerged from the wood, Athena felt the first heavy drops of rain on her cheeks. If only there was no lightning, she thought, urging the reluctant Tarantella past the elaborate summer house erected, according to Perry, by his great-great-grandfather. She spared hardly a glance for the clean marble columns of the classical structure, but kicked the mare into a faster gallop past the heavy growth of rhododendrons and up a sharp incline to the top of the hill. She paused for a moment, suddenly remembering that she had sat in this same spot with the earl, revealing to him more than she had intended about her need for a home.

Angry at herself for allowing Lord St. Aubyn even that brief confidence, Athena pushed on. She could not see the lake from here, but she knew it lay about two miles beyond the summer house on the estate lane, less than that if she could cut through the orderly plantings of apple trees laden with their ripening fruit.

Those first scattered drops became heavier and more frequent as she made her way through the estate orchards. Tarantella protested the rough ground, and Athena began to regret that she had not chosen the longer, more accessible lane that meandered past the tenant farms, the mill, and hot-houses before leading down to the lake.

Athena's exasperation grew as the minutes flew by and she realized that what she had imagined would be a short cut had turned into a confusing maze of fruit trees that obscured her view and distorted her sense of direction. After what must have been a full fifteen minutes of wandering through rows of fruit trees that stretched endlessly in all directions, Athena came across a wagon track that led her back to the lane.

By the time she forced the recalcitrant mare to push through a low hedge and scramble up a ditch, the rain had increased to a steady downpour, and Athena felt the panic fluttering in her stomach. She kicked Tarantella into a gallop, ignoring the rain that lashed into her face, almost obscuring her vision of the road ahead. She hardly noticed the mill as the mare raced past, and was only vaguely conscious of the startled faces of two laborers unhitching their team of plough horses in the shelter of an old barn.

And then the lake came suddenly into view over a crest in the grassy lane. Athena glanced nervously around, but saw no sign of riders along the banks. A family of swans sat stoically in the center of the lake, heedless of the gusts of rain rippling across the water around them. Athena turned the mare's head to the left, intending to follow the path towards the large boathouse at the farther end of the lake. Perhaps they had taken shelter there, she thought, urging the mare once more into a canter.

And then a bolt of blinding light flashed across the sky, followed by a roll of thunder that seemed to go on forever. Athena shuddered violently, and the mare, sensing her fear, reared up and twisted back towards the way they had come. Athena was only able to avoid a fall by grasping the saddle with both hands. Recovering instinctively, she pulled the mare around and forced her towards the boathouse.

Her spirits sank as she drew closer. They were not there, she thought, her fingers trembling as she clutched the reins to control the frightened mare. Then her heart lifted. A horse's rump was clearly visible in the dimness of the large shelter. Then another. Athena kicked the mare forward until she was out of the downpour. She wiped her eyes to clear her vision.

Yes, there were two horses—but neither of them was Buttercup. Her panic stirred again.

"Perry!" she cried, her voice shrill with rising hysteria.

A muttered oath came from the depths of the boathouse. Unable to see anything, Athena urged Tarantella further into the dim interior.

"Perry!" she called again. "Is Penny there with you?"

She peered into the dimness and suddenly froze. Perry had risen to his feet, his clothes in disarray. Behind him, on a bed of old sails and tarpaulins, Miss Rathbone sat with a smirk on her face. Leisurely, she tucked her bosom back into the bodice of her gown and drew her skirts down from where they had been bunched about her knees.

"La!" she trilled in lilting tones. "How ill-timed of you, my dear Mrs. Standish. I declare you have quite put me to the blush."

Athena ignored her and stared at Peregrine, refusing to believe the enormity of what he was about. But her brief, horrified glance at the Beauty had told her all she needed to know.

"The devil take it, Perry," she said with icy calm. "What have you done with my daughter?"

"She went home, Athena," he mumbled, tugging ineffectually at his crumpled cravat. "She is all right, I swear—"

"You allowed her to return by herself?" Athena did not want to believe it. "How dare you abandon my daughter to indulge in . . . indulge in your whoring?" she spat out, quite overcome with fury. "How could you be such a beast?"

"P-Penelope is p-perfectly safe, I c-can assure you," Perry stammered, abandoning his futile attempts to salvage his cravat and stepping forward.

"Do not come near me, you . . . you . . ." Words failed her.

"Penny is s-safe, I tell you," the viscount insisted.

"That is quite correct, my dear," a cool voice drawled so close behind her that Athena jerked the reins violently, causing the mare to rear wildly.

She fought to steady the frightened animal, but a firm hand on the bridle brought the mare abruptly under control. She snorted and rolled her eyes, trembling almost as much as her rider.

Athena glanced up into the earl's eyes. In the dimness of the old boathouse they were almost black, and his face as stern and humorless as that first day she had confronted him in the library. She felt a flicker of fear. Was he telling her the truth? she wondered. Or was this merely another of his deceptions to calm an hysterical female?

"I do not believe you." The words were no more than a whisper above the wind, barely moving her stiff lips.

"Nevertheless, it is quite true. I myself delivered your daughter safely to Mrs. Easton not ten minutes ago."

He was bare-headed, she noticed suddenly. His dark hair plastered to his head, curling damply about his ears and against his soaking cravat. His bottle-green coat was drenched, and the damp buckskin of his breeches clung revealingly to his powerful thighs. She could see the muscles ripple as Ajax moved restlessly beneath him. Athena quickly withdrew her gaze and found him watching her, a glitter in his eyes that had not been there before.

A drop of water ran down her cheek, and Athena dragged her mind back to her present predicament. Why had the Earl of St. Aubyn followed her through the storm? she wondered. And her daughter. Was Penny really all right as he insisted?

Needing to convince herself that Penny was truly safe, she edged the mare backwards, keeping her eyes averted from the dark recesses where Miss Rathbone still lurked. She felt Tarantella flinch as the mare's rump backed out into the rain.

"I suggest we remain here until the rain lets up a little," the earl remarked, quite as though it was an everyday affair to share a dark boathouse with a couple whose disarray proclaimed the nature of their assignation more clearly than words.

He did not look directly at either of the culprits as he spoke, but Athena could tell, from the hard line of his lips, that the earl was well aware of the impropriety of the situation.

"What a charming notion, my lord," the Beauty's voice murmured seductively from the dim interior, setting Athena's nerves on edge. "And how cozy, too," the voice purred.

She jerked the mare's reins, and Tarantella backed away from that sickly sweet voice until Athena felt the heavy rain envelop her again. All she wanted was to get away from that painful scene of Peregrine's ultimate betrayal. A sudden nausea threatened to undo her; she whirled the mare and urged her into a reckless gallop, a warning shout from Peregrine echoing in her ears.

Athena shut her ears to the sound of his traitorous voice and leaned forward over the mare's neck, clinging to the saddle with both hands, the reins flapping aimlessly. She could not wait to get back to her room and pack her trunks. There was no question of staying a moment longer under the same roof as her betrothed.

Her *former* betrothed.

There was no question after what she had witnessed in the

boathouse that her betrothal was at an end. She would give Perry back his ring—throw it in his face. No, she thought, closing her eyes against the driving rain, she would not give him the satisfaction of seeing how much she had been hurt by his thoughtless cruelty.

And how Lord St. Aubyn must have enjoyed her humiliation. Athena grimaced as she realized the implications of that strange glitter in the earl's eyes. He had been amused! He had been gloating over her defeat at the hands of that frivolous chit, Miss Rathbone. It did not bear thinking about.

A flash of lightning erased all these uncomfortable thoughts from her mind. She braced for the inevitable thunder, her teeth chattering as she clung desperately to the saddle, the reins entirely abandoned. She knew that tears were running down her cheeks, but she could not feel them, lost in the rivers of water that lashed her face. Another clap of thunder, so close it made her cringe with terror, drove all but the most primitive fears from her distraught mind.

Abruptly the mare swerved crazily off the lane and plunged through a hedge. Athena felt thorns tear at the skirt of her habit, low branches brush her knees as Tarantella careened through what must have been the apple orchard. Soaked by the downpour, the ground was soft and made heavy going. The mare slowed her runaway pace, her flanks heaving. Athena dared to glance up and realized that the sky was now so dark it might well have been evening instead of midafternoon.

Once clear of the orchard, the mare picked up speed and bolted up a slope, ears laid back in terror. Before they reached the crest, another flash of lightning caused Tarantella to shy violently. Athena clung desperately, the wet surface of her gloved hands slipping on the mare's streaming mane and the wet saddle pommel. Feeling her hands slip, Athena cried out in panic, knowing that she was falling.

Then she felt a hard jolt, and she was on the ground, her face buried in the wet grass, the sky darkening, descending, enveloping her in its cloak of oblivion.

CHAPTER TEN

The Rescue

Sylvester cursed under his breath when he saw the mare swerve from the lane and plunge through the hedge. The beast was obviously out of control, and he wondered why a consummate horsewoman like Athena Standish had allowed this to happen. She appeared to make no effort to regain control of her mount.

He hesitated for a second, then set Ajax at the hedge, which the chestnut cleared easily. The ground in the orchard was soggy and his heavy horse sank up to his hocks in the mud. The mare was lighter and made better time. Sylvester lost sight of her among the wind-lashed apple trees.

When he emerged onto the grassy slope, the runaway mare was nowhere in sight. Sylvester spurred Ajax impatiently. He had intended to catch up with Athena long before this, but she had surged ahead with such reckless disregard for her own safety that he had hesitated to urge Ajax to his full speed. As it was, the great chestnut had come close to falling twice, and now his hooves faltered on the wet grass, sliding dangerously as he pounded up the gentle incline.

The earl brushed ineffectually at the driving rain that almost blinded him. He might well have missed the still form in dark green lying near the top of the slope had not Ajax pricked his ears nervously.

With another curse on his lips, Sylvester pulled the chestnut to a slithering halt and threw himself from the saddle. The stillness of the woman in the grass sent a tingle of panic snaking up his spine. Dear Lord, he thought, let her not be hurt. The intensity of this plea surprised him, but he did not stop to examine it.

He went down on his knees beside the body and gently placed a hand on her shoulder. There was no response. The jacket of her riding habit was soaked and the drenching rain had loosened the neat auburn chignon she usually wore into a tangled mass of curls spread around her on the grass in delightful disarray. At least under different circumstances it would be delightful, Sylvester corrected himself, his thoughts shying away from the inappropriate direction they had taken of their own accord.

He ran his hands over her shoulders and down her arms. Nothing seemed to be broken, but the lady's stillness alarmed him. Gently he let his hands roam over her ribs and hips, then down her legs, firm and rounded beneath the soggy habit. He paused, curling his hand around her ankle in its leather half-boot, slim and cool beneath his fingers.

She made no move, lying there completely passive under his questing hands. In spite of himself, the thought titillated him. What if, he thought . . . allowing the idea to trail off uncompleted.

Then he heard a low moan and felt her shudder.

"Athena," he said urgently, touching her cold cheek with his fingers. She moaned again, moving her head restlessly.

"Athena," he said again, squeezing her shoulder. "Are you all right, love?"

There was no answer except for another deep shudder. Sylvester gently took her by the shoulders and turned her over on her back. She did not protest, so he assumed that no bones were broken. The discovery that she was not seriously hurt brought a sudden rush of pleasure.

"Oh, no," she murmured incoherently, moving her head from side to side as if to escape from the pelting rain.

Sylvester reached out and brushed a soggy strand of auburn hair from her cheek, marveling at the smoothness of her pale skin. She murmured something he could not hear, so he leaned over her, straining to catch her words. He felt the rain beating on his back, running in rivulets down his face, the back of his neck.

Suddenly impatient with his crouching position, Sylvester impulsively gathered the limp form in his arms, attempting to shelter her body from the force of the rain. She moaned again and cringed against him, seeking—or so it seemed to him—shelter from the downpour. He cupped her face, edging it close to his shoulder.

"Athena," he murmured close to her ear. "Athena, my dear, we should get you out of these wet clothes before you catch your death, love." He grinned briefly at the visions conjured by his words. "Do you feel well enough for me to put you up on Ajax?"

She made no reply, but one gloved hand came up to grasp his lapel, clinging to it as though her life depended upon it. Gently, he unclenched her fingers and kissed the cold flesh of her wrist.

Without warning a bolt of jagged lightning slashed across the sky, and Sylvester felt the woman in his arms shudder violently. The thunder that followed caused her to cry out in terror and grasp frantically at his coat.

He leaned down to soothe her, laying his cheek against hers, listening to her ragged breathing, and feeling anger at his helplessness. "There, there," he murmured against her cold lips.

Her mouth was wet with rain, as was his own; rivulets of water ran down his nose and cheeks and dripped onto her upturned face. Instead of protecting her from the downpour, he thought irrationally, he appeared to be adding to the wetness that cascaded over them both. There was a puddle of it collecting in the hollow of her throat, trembling with her breathing. Sylvester found it oddly erotic, and could not stop himself from kissing her there, displacing the small pool of water, sucking up the rest in an impulsive, amorous gesture. It was faintly tepid from her body warmth and he felt instantly aroused.

This would never do, he told himself abruptly. If he were not careful, he would find himself making love to an unconscious woman in the middle of a rainstorm. The possibility only excited him further, a feeling he repressed with difficulty. He braced himself to get up when another flash of lightning slit the sky, followed instantly by a clap of thunder that made the ground beneath them shudder.

Before Sylvester could react, he felt two arms grasp him in a stranglehold, and a female body press itself frantically against him with such force that he clearly distinguished every curve and valley of her. His reaction was automatic and instantaneous. His right arm tightened around her shoulders, and then his hand ran down the trembling length of her, molding her more closely—if such a thing were possible—to his own body.

Athena moaned into his ear, and for a delirious moment, Sylvester allowed himself to imagine she was in the throes of love. And then her trembling began to subside, and his caress became more comforting than seductive. She relaxed her arms, and when he looked at her, he saw two pools of dark amber looking back at him, glazed with fear. Even as he stared, he saw realization flood back and the fear turn to shock, then to horror and finally mortification.

Mrs. Standish had regained her consciousness, he thought with a stab of regret.

Sylvester grinned at her, allowing his amusement to show.

He saw her close her eyes tightly, screwing them up and then popping them open, as though willing herself to be somewhere else, anything but lying there with him in the wet grass.

"Yes, it is indeed me, my dear," he drawled. "And I have no intention of going away. You are not dreaming. I found you here on the grass—"

"What are you doing sitting down here?" she demanding in a weak voice, her eyes dangerous.

He grinned wolfishly. "I should think that must be pretty obvious, my dear," he said, deliberately provoking her. "And since I am quite as wet as you are, Athena, I did not think it would signify."

Athena struggled to sit up, and Sylvester immediately rose to his feet and lifted her—under muttered protests—to stand beside him.

She looked around, evidently unaware that she still rested in the circle of his arm for support. "My horse appears to have disappeared."

"I shall take you up in front of me." He turned to whistle to Ajax, who ambled up to stand beside them, his head lowered under the deluge of water that still fell.

"No," she said sharply. "Thank you, my lord. I shall walk."

Sylvester laughed. "No, you will ride with me, Athena."

"I am quite able to—"

"I said you will ride with me."

Without waiting for further argument, he put his hands around her waist and lifted her up onto Ajax, swinging up behind her before she had a chance to protest.

Settling one arm about her rigid shoulders, Sylvester turned Ajax towards home.

Much later that evening, Athena curled up under her covers wishing that she might remain hidden in the warm cocoon for the rest of her life. She had no desire to remember anything that had occurred on that dreadful afternoon. She wanted to put Peregrine and his disgusting behavior completely out of her mind.

Least of all she wished to recall that Lord St. Aubyn had witnessed her humiliation. He most assuredly had glimpsed Miss Rathbone's naked bosom—full and pink and curved to perfection—rising saucily above the bodice of her riding habit, pulled down around her hips. Athena had the niggling suspicion that the Beauty had intended the earl to see it, but she suppressed this ungenerous thought.

The earl must have seen the disarray of Peregrine's clothing, too, yet—now that she thought about it—he had said not a word to his son. He had not even looked at Perry. Only at her, his face grim, that odd glitter in his eyes.

Had he been amused? she wondered. Had he gloated at the definitive destruction of her betrothal to his son? That was what the earl had wanted, was it not? It was what she herself had wanted, Athena reminded herself bluntly. But never had she expected it would occur so publicly, so painfully.

There was a tap at the door, which opened to reveal her Aunt Mary, bearing a tray of covered dishes.

"His lordship is asking about you, Athena, love," she said in a stage whisper, setting the tray down on the small table beside the bed. "He ordered Jackson to bring up your dinner tray, but I wanted to bring it myself. His lordship wants a full report on your condition, my dear. I believe he would have come up himself had not Lady Sarah pointed out the impropriety of such a visit."

Athena shuddered and snuggled deeper under the covers. "I am not hungry, Aunt. Truly I am not."

Aunt Mary made disapproving noises and uncovered one of the dishes. "It is your favorite, dear. Fricassée of veal with fresh green peas from the garden. His lordship ordered it particularly."

"You may tell his lordship," Athena responded tartly, "that my well-being is none of his concern. And after tomorrow I hope never to set eyes upon him or his son again."

"Never say you will leave the Castle tomorrow, dear?" Her aunt sounded dismayed. "Lady Sarah is anxious that we should stay for Perry's ball, at least."

"You may stay as long as you choose, Aunt," Athena said firmly. "But I intend to leave tomorrow, come rain or shine."

"Very well, dear," Aunt Mary replied, her blue eyes twinkling mischievously. "But I should warn you that you will have to share a coach with Mrs. Rathbone and her granddaughter. They are returning to London tomorrow at first light, and you can hardly expect his lordship to provide a separate carriage for you, dear."

With that parting shot, her aunt left her, promising to bring Penelope in later to say good night.

Since the notion of sharing a coach with the Rathbone ladies was clearly out of the question, Athena reconciled herself to staying on at the Castle for at least another day. This would allow her the opportunity to release Perry from his commitment, she thought, and to return his ring personally rather than enclosing it in the curt little note she had planned.

The abrupt departure of the Rathbones must be Lord St. Aubyn's doing, Athena reasoned. No doubt his lordship objected to Miss Rathbone for his son's bride as much as he had to her, although obviously on different grounds. It struck her as rather odd that the earl had not insisted upon his son's providing immediate reparation to the Beauty by offering her marriage. Peregrine had certainly compromised the young lady beyond any hope of salvaging her reputation by any other means. Unless, of course . . . But Athena's mind shied away from the unpleasant thought that had intruded there.

Inexplicably, her appetite seemed to have returned, and after savoring the fricasséed veal, she curled up again, her mind in a turmoil.

The earl had been correct about her daughter. Penny had returned quite safely and Lord St. Aubyn had delivered her personally to Mrs. Easton before setting out to find her mother.

But why had he done so? Athena wondered, quite unable to imagine his lordship's motives. Had he perhaps been concerned about his son falling into the clutches of Miss Rathbone? If so, he had arrived far too late to prevent a scandal. But there had been no scandal. And now the Rathbones were leaving . . .

It was all very perplexing, Athena thought. And the most disturbing fact of all was Lord St. Aubyn's behavior with her.

She could clearly hear the patter of rain on her window, but the fury of the storm had passed, leaving her with memories she would much rather not examine too closely.

Resolutely, she turned over and closed her eyes, but the memories persisted. The earl's warm lips on the hollow of her throat, the rain dripping from his face onto hers, the tenderness of his hands cradling her head against his shoulder, his futile attempt to shelter her with his body from the pelting rain, his strong arm about her trembling shoulders as they rode back to the Castle. But perhaps most vividly, the warmth of his body as she curled against him, shuddering uncontrollably every time the heavens opened above them with another flash of lightning.

For some inexplicable reason known only to himself, the earl had treated her as though she were precious to him. He had cradled her and comforted her as John would have done. He had carried her in the kitchen door and up the back stairs to her room—ignoring the startled glances of the servants—and laid her on her bed, removing her boots and chafing her cold feet until her horrified aunt had banished him.

None of this made any sense. Tomorrow she would find a logical explanation for Lord St. Aubyn's odd behavior, Athena told herself drowsily, but tonight she would only remember the tenderness and dream impossible dreams.

Athena came awake slowly, languorously, luxuriating in the warmth of the feather bed. Betsy, the maid Lady Sarah had assigned to attend her, must have already been in to draw the curtains, because the room was filled with sunlight, and Athena could hear the starlings' shrill cries in the eves. The sky was blue and cloudless, and it would have been so easy to blot out yesterday's storm from her mind and pretend it had never happened. That nothing out of the ordinary had happened yesterday at all.

But did she really wish to erase yesterday afternoon from her mind? Athena wondered. Last night she might have said yes, but this morning she was not certain. She could well dispense with the shocking sight of Miss Rathbone's exposed bosom, of course, and with her coarse comments; but catching her sweet Perry *in flagrante* in the arms of another woman had opened her eyes to a reality she had been unable or unwilling to admit even to herself.

The feelings she had for her betrothed were those of a mother, not a lover.

A sobering thought indeed, Athena thought, slipping out of the warm bed and into her robe and slippers. One that explained why she had felt no jealousy for the Beauty yesterday, no real animosity for the female who had made it her business to entangle Perry in a rather sordid seduction. All she had felt was anger at Perry for his thoughtless treatment of Penelope. There had been no outrage at the discovery of Perry's tryst with another woman, and now she understood why.

Her love for Peregrine had been as much an illusion as his

was for her. She had *wanted* to be in love with Perry. She had
needed to believe herself in love in order to accept his offer of
marriage. To make her dreams come true. But what good were
dreams if they were based on make-believe?

She had been a hypocrite!

Unlike Perry, who had at least been honest in his infatuation,
she had deliberately woven an illusion of love around her heart
so that she might become a wife again.

The memory of Perry's startled face, awash with guilt and
shame, flashed before her eyes, and Athena knew exactly what
she must do. She would break their betrothal—that was now
more imperative than ever—but she would not heap the contempt of a jilted woman upon his handsome head. She would be
honest with him, perhaps for the first time since they had met.
She would take her full share of the blame for what had occurred yesterday. After all, she had never even kissed the poor
boy, not as a woman kisses a man she loves. Athena had felt no
desire to kiss Perry, she realized with new honesty, because she
had not loved him.

So she would definitely not wish to erase yesterday afternoon from her memory, Athena decided resolutely, at least not
that part of it that concerned Perry. It had forced her to face an
unplatable truth about herself.

As for the other part . . . She paused, conscious of the quick-
ening of her pulse. The part that concerned his father. No, if she
were honest with herself, she would not wish to lose that memory either. It was something she could hold on to in the days
ahead. Memories of tenderness, of warm male skin against her
cheek, of a man's body pressed close to hers with the urgency
of a lover, of his kisses in the hollow of her throat, but perhaps
more than anything else, the comfort of his arms around her as
they rode back home together.

"Good morning, ma'am. A right lovely day it is outside,
ma'am. Master Peregrine will have a good day for his birthday
celebration tonight." Betsy's cheery greeting distracted Athena
from her daydreaming as the little maid brought in a steaming
cup of chocolate and set it down.

"Thank you, Betsy," she said with a smile.

"Will you be wishing to dress now, ma'am?"

"Yes, Betsy. The blue lustring, I think. But before we start,
be a good girl and ask the viscount's man if Lord Fairmont will
grant me a few minutes in the morning room after breakfast."

The sound of Perry's title felt odd on her lips, and Athena

was reminded of his father's recent accusation. The earl had imagined—quite understandably under the circumstances— that she aspired to Perry's title. How wrong he had been! Athena Standish had wanted a man in her life again, a second husband to give her the home she dreamed of. An exciting, virile man like Lord St. Aubyn himself, she thought, admitting— with her newly acquired honesty—what she had suspected all along but had not dared to confess, even to herself.

She loved Perry's father.

"Sylvester Steele." Athena savored the whispered sound of his name on her lips and smiled, the vision of the earl's darkly handsome features and brooding blue-black eyes rising unbidden in her mind. At least now she knew where she stood. This was one dream that would never come true.

He imagined her a fortune hunter. She could still remember the contempt in his voice that first morning when he had accused her. He had considered her unworthy of his son; how much more unsuitable must she be for a man like himself. If he thought of her that way at all, Athena mused with painful honesty. She knew he desired her; she had seen it in his eyes, felt it in his touch. At most St. Aubyn might offer her *carte blanche*; she was surprised he had not already done so.

But marriage? No, that was a dream that would certainly not come true. She would be foolish indeed to entertain such impossible fantasies.

Athena smiled at her own foolishness as she came downstairs shortly before ten o'clock. She was pleased with the new understanding she had reached concerning her own heart, and knew exactly what she would say to Perry in the morning room.

As for his father, the man she could never have, Athena was determined to cast him out of her life the minute she left St. Aubyn's Castle behind her.

He would still possess her heart, of course, but Athena would eventually learn to live with that. She had no choice.

"But whatever shall I *say*, Father?"

Lord St. Aubyn glanced unsmilingly at his son, wondering if he had ever been so desperately naive and unsure of himself.

"I suggest you tell Mrs. Standish the truth," he said coldly.

"And just what is the truth, Father?" Sylvester heard the despair in Perry's voice and his expression softened.

"You will admit that you behaved abominably and are not worthy of her regard."

"But what if Athena insists upon releasing me from our betrothal?" Perry demanded in a voice that shook. "She was counting on me to give her and Penelope a home, Father, and I have betrayed them both. I feel like an absolute cad."

Sylvester laughed shortly but said nothing, since Peregrine's words conveyed only the truth.

"It is no laughing matter, Father," Perry said stiffly. "I swear I cannot imagine how I ever got myself into this pickle. How could I have compromised a lady's virtue like that? And the worst part is that Athena saw it all, Father. She must believe me the veriest libertine. How can I ever face her again?"

His father suppressed a cynical smile at his son's claim to libertine tendencies. "I rather suspect that Miss Rathbone has very little virtue worthy of the name, Perry," he said gently. "So disabuse yourself of the notion that you are the villain of this Canterbury farce."

Perry looked shocked at this plain speaking. "How can you say so, Father?" he muttered. "She was so very, very beautiful."

His son's voice was wistful, and Sylvester felt a pang of regret that Perry had to learn about the fickleness of women from one such as the counterfeit Miss Rathbone. Worse yet was the guilt he felt for his own selfish part in the Cheltenham tragedy that had played itself out here at St. Aubyn Castle, touching so many lives, his own included.

"Beauty and virtue are two separate things, Perry," he said softly. "Often unrelated, I am sorry to say." He paused, his thoughts troubled. "How simple life would be if beautiful women were all virtuous. Unfortunately, it is more often the exception than the rule."

"Athena is both, Father," Peregrine said defensively. "I cannot imagine so far forgetting myself as to . . ." He hesitated, and Sylvester saw his son's face color hotly. "As to . . ." he tried again, but could not say the words.

Sylvester could not suppress a cynical smile. "As to roll her in the hay, lad? Is that what you are trying to say?"

"Father!" Perry exclaimed in shocked accents. "How can you even imagine such a thing about Athena, much less *say* it?" His blush deepened.

Very easily indeed, Sylvester thought to himself, feeling suddenly rather sorry for this son of his who still had so much to learn about females. He himself had little difficulty at all imagining the delectable widow in all sorts of delicious poses, her small, delicately rounded body warm and pliable under his hands. But he could hardly admit as much to Perry. He should not even be thinking along these lines himself, although since yesterday afternoon, the widow had rarely been out of his mind.

She had felt so right in his arms, her body warm against his thighs, head burrowing into his shoulder, streaming hair smelling of wet grass and violets. With every clap of thunder, Athena had curled more tightly into his lap, setting off delicious tremors of anticipation in his own body that had required all his moral fortitude to control. The trembling of her slight frame at every new flash of lightning had aroused conflicting emotions—both sensuous and tender—in his chest, and the way she clung to him, mindless of propriety, had moved him as no other woman had since Adrienne.

"You are right, Perry," he murmured contritely. "Forgive me. Athena is indeed special."

His son beamed with joy. "I am glad you finally admit it, Father. I have known it all along. But," he paused uncertainly, his smile vanishing abruptly, "do you think I can make everything right with her again, Father?"

Sylvester smiled thinly and shrugged his shoulders. "I would not count on it, Perry." He hoped that his son's betrothal was definitely at an end, but he could not say so. He also hoped that Athena had come to her senses since yesterday afternoon. Surely she must be ready to admit—after what had passed between them out there on the grass—that Perry was not the man she needed.

Peregrine looked downcast. "You believe that Athena wishes to break our betrothal, Father? Is there nothing I might to do change her mind?"

"That is indeed what I believe, Perry," Sylvester admitted reluctantly. "I never did consider you well matched, remember?" He had no wish to hurt his son, but a marriage between Perry and Athena could bring nothing but misery to them all. And it would be intolerable for him, Sylvester thought. After yesterday afternoon he did not believe he could relinquish her to anyone, even to his own son.

The realization stunned him. Before he had a chance to consider the implications of this discovery, the doors swung open and the woman who had the power to make Sylvester feel like a raw youth again stepped into the room.

The sight of her triggered something within the innermost core of Sylvester's being. Something so primitive and powerful that he felt the hairs on the back of his neck stand erect.

It took every ounce of will power he had to suppress the growl of pleasure, of passion, and anticipated possession that rose in his throat.

CHAPTER ELEVEN

Double Deception

Athena stood poised on the threshold of the morning room, disconcerted to find herself the object of two pairs of very different eyes. Her own gaze was drawn, as if by some invisible magnet, to the earl, who stood before the empty hearth, one elbow propped on the mantel. The predatory stare she encountered in his dark, hooded gaze made her flinch and glance away.

Peregrine had been standing at the open window, but when he saw her, he came across the Oriental carpet towards her, stopping abruptly several feet away, his blue eyes troubled.

"Athena," he stammered, his face pale and drawn. "You have every right to think me the worst villain in England, but—"

"I had hoped to have a few words with you in private, Perry," Athena cut in gently, touched by the anguish in his eyes.

Peregrine glanced nervously at his father. "I have asked Father for his advice, Athena. You see I did not—"

"Advice?" Athena stared at him in astonishment.

"Yes," Perry continued hastily, his face turning a bright pink. "I thought he could advise me . . ." His voice trailed off uncertainly. "I thought he might tell me what to say to avoid . . . what I might do to persuade you not to . . . how I could explain to you . . ." He stopped abruptly and rubbed his face nervously with both hands. "Dash it all, Athena . . ."

Any vestige of resentment Athena might have harbored in her heart against this boy evaporated instantly. She smiled gently, feeling only a deep sorrow for the way life had treated both of them.

"Then I trust your father has advised you well, Perry," she interrupted him, steeling herself against the flash of hope that flickered in those cornflower-blue eyes that had held such promise for her future. Hers and Penelope's. "That is what I wish to talk to you about, my dear," she added, knowing that sooner or later she would have to break away from this boy she held in such deep affection.

Impulsively, Peregrine stepped forward and grasped her two hands in his, carrying them to his lips and kissing them wildly. Athena was acutely conscious of the earl's cynical gaze upon her, but she refused to pull away.

"Tell me you will forgive me, Athena," he mumbled incoherently, his blond head bent, his agitated breath warm on her fingers.

Her heart went out to him.

"Of course, I forgive you, darling," she whispered softly. Then in a stronger voice, she added, "But surely your father has told you that we cannot marry, Perry." Gently, she pulled her hands away from his grasp.

He raised his face and stared at her, eyes miserable. "You are still angry with me, then?"

"No, I have indeed forgiven you, my dear. But your father was right, you know. We will not suit at all. So I wish to return this." She brought his ring out of her pocket and held it in her palm.

Peregrine stared at the modest opal ring in silence, and for a terrible moment Athena thought he was going to cry.

"Please keep it, Athena," he said at last, in a thick voice she hardly recognized as the happy-go-lucky boy she knew so well. "Or let me buy you a bigger one. Would that make you happy, Athena? A monstrous diamond ring? Will that make things right again between us?"

Athena's heart constricted within her. Never had her beloved Perry appeared so young and naive as at this instant. She wanted more than anything to put her arms around him and comfort him, but she knew such an action would be misconstrued.

"No, darling," she said as gently as she could. "The size of the ring has nothing to do with anything. At least not for me. I treasured your opal because *you* gave it to me, Perry. I thought it the most beautiful ring in the world. That is why I must give it back. You know that I must, my dear."

"I know nothing of the sort," Perry answered petulantly, quite as though she were denying him a special treat he had counted on. "Are you forgetting that tomorrow is my birthday, Athena, and I come into a small bequest from my grandmother? I swear I will spend every shilling on you, my love. Ask me for anything your heart desires and it is yours."

Athena shook her head in disbelief, not daring to glance at the silent man by the hearth. "I am sure your father never advised you to make such a rash offer, Perry," she remarked, wondering what the foolish boy would think of next. "One that I cannot accept, of course. But I thank you for your generosity, Perry. Truly I do."

She held out the ring, but he turned aside, pacing over to the window and back. Coming to a stop before her, he gazed at her pleadingly. "Let me do *something* for you, Athena," he begged. "Let me buy you a house. You have always wanted a house, have you not?" His expression became eager. "A house with a garden where Penny can play. I shall settle a comfortable sum on you . . ."

Athena had been struck speechless by this bizarre announcement, and was all too aware of an impatient movement from the earl. She could feel his disapproval reach out to touch her; the air in the small room was thick with it.

"Perry," she said severely, when she had recovered her voice, "you really must be more careful what you say, dear. Only consider how such an arrangement would appear to your family and friends. And to your father, Perry," she could not resist adding. "Surely you cannot mean to brand me before all the world as your—"

"No!" Perry shouted before she could say the damning word. He had turned bright red again, and looked so embarrassed that Athena could only pity him. "I intended no such thing, Athena," he stammered, glancing nervously at his father. "You must believe me. I would not dream of insulting you thus. I merely wished to take care of you. As I promised," he added, rather forlornly she thought.

"I know, Perry," she replied in a choked voice. If she were not careful, Athena thought, she would burst into tears herself and give Lord St. Aubyn something else to amuse him. "I know you are kind and generous to a fault. But it will not do, Perry." She smiled a little tremulously. "Here," she took his hand and pressed the ring into it, closing his fingers around it. "I shall always remember you with great affection, as will Penelope."

"Is there nothing I can do? Nothing at all?"

Athena shook her head and turned to go, quite unable to utter a single word. Before she reached the door, there was a discreet knock and Jackson appeared with a pale blue letter on his silver salver.

"Excuse me, milord." He addressed the earl, then turned to Mrs. Standish. "I beg your pardon, madam," he said stiffly. "I was instructed to deliver this to you the moment you came downstairs. I apologize for the delay, madam."

"Thank you, Jackson," Athena murmured, taking the missive from the butler's tray.

Jackson coughed discreetly. "I was instructed to ask you to open the letter in the presence of his lordship, madam. Those were my orders, madam. I understand the contents are rather urgent."

Athena stared at him in surprise. "I shall do so, Jackson. Thank you." He bowed and withdrew, leaving a heavy silence behind him.

Athena glanced at the two men. Which lord had the mysterious instructions referred to? she wondered, intrigued in spite of herself.

Before she could open the letter, the earl moved away from the hearth and spoke to his son. "You may be excused, Perry," he said brusquely. "I imagine this note concerns me."

"How can you be sure, Father?" Perry responded. "For all we know, it may well concern me."

Lord St. Aubyn made an impatient gesture, but Athena cut short any argument he may have contemplated. "It may well concern both of you, my lords," she said, breaking the seal and opening the thick sheet of expensive paper. She immediately recognized the St. Aubyn seal at the top of the note, but the handwriting was unfamiliar.

Athena perused the untidy scrawl quickly. Then she read it through again more slowly. No, she thought, this could not be true. But deep in her heart she knew that it was. The signs had been there for her to see all along. She marveled at her lack of perception. Everything was so clear now. Everything was explained. She felt as though she had been pushed by ruthless hands into the deepest, darkest pit imaginable.

She looked straight at Perry, ignoring the earl. "Would you leave us, please, Perry," she said in a voice that sounded as though it came from somewhere far away. "I wish to have a few words with his lordship."

The door closed behind the viscount; then, and only then, did she turn to look up at the earl. So, she thought, strangely aloof from the sense of betrayal that seeped into her heart, he had deceived her right from the start.

"Perhaps you would care to explain this, my lord?"

Athena handed him the blue sheet with fingers that had turned to ice.

*   *   *

Lord St. Aubyn gazed at her for an endless moment before he took the letter from her stiff fingers. He wished he could erase that expression of shock and hurt clouding her marvelous amber eyes, but if the mysterious letter was what he imagined it must be, Sylvester feared that his own deceptions were about to catch up with him.

The earl perused the letter slowly; it was not long, only enough to damn him completely and utterly. Intensely aware of the woman beside him, he sensed that she was willing him to deny everything. It pleased him immeasurably that Athena wanted to believe in his innocence. Pleased him and saddened him, too, for his guilt hung heavily upon him. Sylvester wished that he could deny it; he wanted fervently to deny the truth that Miss Rathbone—or whatever the vindictive chit's real name was—had so baldly scrawled on the blue paper.

But when he raised his eyes he knew she saw the truth in them even before he spoke.

"What would you have me explain, Athena?" he asked in an expressionless voice.

In truth, there was nothing to add to what was written there so damningly. Miss Rathbone's style was less than polished, and her spelling left much to be desired, but she had gone right to the heart of the matter. Had he known she was such a despicable little bitch, he would have given her the extra few pounds she had demanded last night.

He had summoned Miss Rathbone to the library after dinner, and told her bluntly that her services were no longer required at St. Aubyn Castle. He suggested an early morning departure would be appropriate, and had paid her the promised two hundred pounds for her acting skills in the little deception he had planned weeks ago.

But she had turned suddenly quite nasty. Dropping all pretense at refinement, the Beauty—and Sylvester had to admit that she was indeed that—had twined her arms about his neck and simperingly offered to warm his bed before she left. For an additional fifty pounds. His son had turned out to be quite a disappointment, she confessed, and deprived her of the romp she had been led to expect from him. She had been left in quite a lather, she had explained—in much cruder terms, Sylvester recalled with a grimace of distaste—and it was only fair that he compensate her for Peregrine's poor performance.

He had made the mistake of allowing his revulsion to show,

and Miss Rathbone's sultry voice had turned ugly. "Think yerself too good for the likes of me, do ye?" she had snarled at him, her lovely face contorted with fury. "But not too high and mighty to go sniffing after your own son's mort, are ye now? Took yer fancy, did she, milord? Well, ye can forget about that starched-up bitch, milord. Believe me, ye'll get no pleasure out of her."

As suddenly as she had turned ugly, the Beauty had flashed her seductive smile again. "Now for an extra pony or two—call it appreciation for a job well done, if ye like—I could make ye forget that dowdy old Tabby, m'dear."

He had turned down her offer, perhaps not as diplomatically as he should have, and Miss Rathbone had flounced out of the library. The letter he held in his hand was her revenge for his rejection. It had been shortsighted of him not to have seen it coming.

Yes, his deceptions had indeed caught up with him, Sylvester thought bitterly, and he could tell from the bleakness in the widow's eyes that he had burned his bridges with her as surely as Perry had done. The irony of it was that, like his son, Sylvester wanted her forgiveness above anything. Unlike Perry, however, whom Athena had forgiven with a rare demonstration of genuine affection, he could hope for nothing but contempt from this female who had stirred his heart again after too many years of loneliness.

He saw her take a shuddering breath. "Are you telling me that this is true, my lord?" she demanded in a whisper. "That you did indeed pay Miss Rathbone two hundred pounds to seduce your son away from me? And that you yourself . . ." She paused, seeming overwhelmed by the enormity of his deception. ". . . That you deliberately set out to seduce me away from Perry?"

Her eyes were luminous with unshed tears, and Sylvester wanted desperately to take her in his arms, as he had yesterday afternoon, and kiss her fears away.

"Is that what you believe I did, Athena?"

The note of pleading in his voice reminded him of Perry, who had pleaded with her and been forgiven. She had forgiven his son with a generosity that had moved him deeply. Now if only she could find it in her heart to . . . But no, he thought with a sinking feeling, his guilt was far greater than Perry's. He had laid siege to her heart without a thought for the damage he might do.

"What I believe appears to have no relation at all to reality, my lord," she replied, so softly he could hardly hear her. "You have made complete fools out of both of us. I suppose I should congratulate you," she said with evident difficulty. "You have achieved your wish. Perry is free of me. I hope that he never finds out the double deception his father devised to obtain that freedom."

Her words, so softly spoken, seemed to brand themselves in his mind. Sylvester winced. "Before you condemn me entirely, at least allow me to speak in my defense," he said, wondering what he could possibly say to mitigate his guilt in her eyes.

"That will not be necessary, my lord," she said coolly. With a moue of distaste, she picked up the blue paper from the round table where he had thrown it. "You have refused to deny it, so I must assume . . ." Her voice suddenly quavered out of control, and Athena turned and fled.

Sylvester listened to her rushing footsteps disappearing in the direction of the stairs. His heart cringed at the sound of her door closing in the hall above.

By the time Athena reached the safety of her room, the tears ran unchecked down her face. Casting herself upon her bed, she let her misery pour out in great gulping sobs, her shoulders shaking uncontrollably with each fresh wave of tears. She could not remember being so overwhelmed by grief since her mother died, leaving her bereft of the protective warmth Lady Rotherham had woven around her only daughter.

Athena moaned into the damp pillow. Today she felt the same sense of abandonment she had felt then. Her world, unstable at best but at last under nominal control, had fallen apart beneath her feet. Her tenuous illusions had blown up in her face, leaving her with nothing to hold on to in the dark days ahead.

She curled herself into a ball, her face turned from the window through which the rays of sunlight bespoke a glorious summer day. But not for her, she thought disconsolately. Not for her the warmth of the summer breeze, the perfume of the flowers, the starlit sky under which Castle guests would dance and make merry this evening in honor of Perry's twentieth birthday. She would see none of it.

Suddenly, Athena felt very very old indeed. Her throat constricted but the healing tears would not come. She closed her swollen eyes and gradually sleep took her into an uneasy rest.

"My dear girl, whatever is the matter?"

Athena opened her eyes to see the anxious face of Aunt Mary leaning over her.

"It is nearly one, dearest, and the family is gathering for nuncheon. I thought we could go down together, love." Her aunt regarded her with sharp blue eyes. "But I see you are not feeling quite the thing, dear," she continued gently, pushing a strand of Athena's hair off her face. "Perhaps we can have a tray sent up, and you can tell me what has upset you so."

Athena struggled to sit up, feeling sluggish and exhausted with grief. "I am not hungry, Aunt. And I would rather be alone, if you please."

It seemed quite impossible to speak about her recent humiliation to anyone, much less her aunt, whose sympathy would only bring more tears.

"Nonsense, dear," Aunt Mary chided her. "You cannot dawdle in bed, today of all days. Have you forgotten Perry's ball? Lady Sarah is counting on you to arrange the flowers, dear. And no doubt she will have a dozen other tasks for us. Here," she continued briskly, "let me put this cool cloth on your forehead, dear. You look quite dreadful, I must say."

The cool lavender water felt good on her heated brow, and Athena felt herself relax under her aunt's ministrations.

"Her ladyship will have to get along without me today," she said firmly. "I shall stay here in my room until I can arrange for transport back to London. I hope I never seen another Steele for as long as I live."

"You have broken with Perry, I take it?"

"Indeed I have. And his father may go straight to the devil for all I care," she added viciously.

Quite suddenly, the tears started again, accompanied by great shudders that Athena seemed unable to control.

Her aunt sat down on the bed and gathered her niece into her arms. "There, there, my pet," she crooned, stroking Athena's tangled hair until she relaxed against her aunt's ample bosom. "Tell your old auntie all about it, dearie. What has that scoundrel done to my little girl?"

Quite undone by such genuine affection, Athena opened her heart and poured out her misery as her aunt rocked her gently and murmured soothing nothings in her ear.

"And here is the proof of his infamy," she said at last, feeling considerably restored after her confession. She thrust the incriminating letter—somewhat crushed and smeared with tears—into her aunt's hands.

Mrs. Easton read it in silence.

"Well," she said after a lengthy pause, "this settles it. We shall all depart tomorrow as soon as I can find out when the London stage leaves Camelford. This," she shook the crumpled blue sheet of paper in the air, "is the outside of enough. We shall go back to Mount Street, my dear, and everything will be the way it was before."

Athena's spirits, which had risen as she unburdened herself to her aunt, sank again. In spite of Aunt Mary's optimism, nothing would ever be the same again. To believe that was to disregard the ugly reality of the earl's deception that would leave its mark on all of them. When they left the Castle, they would all abandon something they had treasured, something that would scar their hearts and minds.

Particularly her heart, Athena thought. Whereas Aunt Mary would be deprived of the comfortable position of companion to Lady Sarah, and Penelope would have to give up her pony Buttercup, Athena herself would leave behind her heart, a foolish heart to be sure, but the only one she had. It would remain in the possession of a thorough scoundrel, a man who had used it as a plaything to bring about the downfall of her dreams.

Those dreams she had brought with her to St. Aubyn Castle had been foolish, too, she had to admit. The earl had proved beyond a doubt that her heart had never belonged to Peregrine, and never would. He had prevented her from making a disastrous mistake. But why had he led her to believe . . . ? Why had he been so tender? Had she imagined his concern? Had that all been pretense, too?

"No," she exclaimed, suddenly determined that her aunt, at least, would not be deprived of the position Lady Sarah offered her. "Penelope and I will leave, Aunt. You have already accepted the position of companion to Lady Sarah. I would not have you give that up, dear."

"Fiddle!" her aunt exclaimed. "I shall do no such thing. In fact, I intend to inform her ladyship this very instant that I cannot stay under the same roof as that lying rogue."

And before Athena could stop her, she had whisked out of the room, carrying the blue letter with her.

Athena knew she must have dozed off after Aunt Mary left her, for when she again opened her eyes, the room was dim as though someone had drawn the curtains to shut out the sun. Her pillow was damp beneath her cheek, and her hair was miserably tangled over her face. Her favorite blue lustring must be horribly creased, she thought, wishing she had taken it off before abandoning herself to her paroxysm of grief.

She stretched her cramped legs, which had been curled up against her chest, and discovered that her stockinged feet were cold.

And there was someone standing beside her bed.

Some second sense warned Athena that the intruder was not her aunt, and she became suddenly still. Gingerly, she moved her head and her hair fell away, revealing a stalwart pair of masculine thighs encased in buckskin.

Quickly, she closed her eyes again, squeezing them shut and willing the apparition to disappear. She was obviously still asleep and dreaming, she told herself. There could not possibly be a man in her bedchamber.

But there was, of course. And Athena knew instantly who the intruder was. There was only one man who had the unmitigated gall to imagine he could accost her in the privacy of her own room. Only one man who would dare to assume he had the right to badger her.

"Athena," Lord St. Aubyn murmured softly, dispelling any doubt as to the reality of his presence, "I need to talk to you urgently, my dear."

Athena reared up, suddenly angry. She pushed her tangled hair out of her eyes and glared at him, "Well, I have nothing to say to you, my lord, so you may leave at once. You should not even be here."

"Do you think I am not conscious of that fact, Athena? But you will not come downstairs, so I had to come to you."

"I do not *wish* to see you."

"But I had to see you, my dear. Please believe me." There was something in his voice Athena had never heard before. A note of urgency, of sincerity, perhaps. She disregarded it instantly. This man had never been sincere with her; why should he change now?

"I shall never believe you again," she said curtly. "I am amazed that you would imagine that possible. I may be a fool, but I am not stupid."

"I never imagined for a moment that you were either foolish or stupid, my dear."

His voice curled about her insidiously, causing her heart to flutter uncomfortably, although it must know by now how adept the rogue was at lying.

"Please go," she said, furious at the quaver in her voice.

"Athena," he said, moving closer until his thighs touched the bed, "please do not make me out to be more of a villain than I am, love."

The endearment caused Athena to bury her face in the damp pillow again, willing him to go away before she committed an act of irreparable foolishness. She felt him touch her shoulder with gentle fingers and flinched, shaking him away.

"I confess I have made a terrible muddle of this whole affair. But believe me, I never intended it to end this way."

"Please leave," Athena muttered from the depths of the pillow. She did not want to hear any of this. She did not want to forgive the terrible deceit this man had practiced upon her. She wanted to learn to hate him for breaking her heart.

He appeared not to hear. "I merely wanted to distract Perry," he continued. "To make him realize that . . . that his infatuation with an older woman was not enough to sustain a lifetime of marriage."

"That she was not good enough for him, I think you mean," she cut in sharply. "I was a fortune hunter, remember?"

He was silent for a moment. The she heard him sigh. "That was a natural assumption, my dear, although foolish, as it turned out. And I apologize for it. I never intended it to be more than a distraction. That was foolish of me, too, of course. I did not anticipate seduction."

He paused again, and Athena wondered which seduction he was referring to, Perry's or her own.

"That was not in the plan at all, Athena. It is important that you believe me. I never imagined that you would witness . . . well, witness what you did, my dear. I wish there was some way I might make it up to you."

"There is," she muttered harshly into the pillow. "You may leave at once, and never come near me again."

"Athena, my dear," and suddenly she felt the unnerving touch of his hand caressing her back, "you cannot mean to be so cruel to me—"

"Sylvester!" came a shocked exclamation from the door, and the caress ended abruptly, leaving her—despite her resolution to hate this man—aching for the tenderness of his fingers again.

"What on *earth* do you think you are doing here, boy? How

dare you intrude upon dear Athena like this? Have you taken leave of your senses?"

She heard the earl step away from the bed. "I was attempting to persuade Mrs. Standish to come down to Perry's ball tonight, Aunt. The lad will be quite cast down if she is not there."

"It is not your place to do so, as you must know, Sylvester," Lady Sarah retorted in icy tones. "Now, leave at once, if you please."

Athena heard his footsteps grow fainter and the door close with a sharp click.

There was an uncomfortable silence broken by Aunt Mary, who came over to help Athena sit up and pull her gown down over her ankles.

Lady Sarah cleared her throat rather noisily. "I do apologize for my nephew's improper behavior, my dear Athena," she said finally, with something less than her usual *sang froid*. "I cannot imagine what has come over him. He is not usually so inconsiderate of his guests, I can assure you."

Athena said nothing. There was much that she might have said, much that the poor lady was probably better off not knowing, including the earl's deliberate deceptions regarding Miss Rathbone.

Miss Rathbone! Athena suddenly went rigid. If Mrs. Rathbone was a bosom bow of Lady Sarah's from the days of their youth, surely the earl's aunt must know that the Beauty was not her granddaughter. Had she been duped by the old lady as well as by her scheming nephew?

Before she could open her mouth to demand an answer to this uncomfortable question, Lady Sarah came across the room and took Athena's cold hands in hers.

"You have been grossly misused, child," she murmured in a strangely subdued voice. "And I must bear part of the blame, for it was I who invited Augusta to St. Aubyn Castle."

"Miss Rathbone is not your friend's granddaughter at all, is she?"

Lady Sarah gave a snort of derision. "I should hope not, my dear. For all her unconventional choices in life, Augusta is a lady. I cannot say the same for that blond hussy. But they are both gone now, my dear, and for Perry's sake I would like to restore a little sanity to the Castle on his special day. I have come to ask your help, child."

Athena gazed at the old lady in astonishment. "I cannot

imagine why you are telling me this, my lady," she said. "I am at a loss to know how I might help you."

"Would you if you could, my dear?"

Both her aunt and Lady Sarah seemed to be regarding her with some trepidation, a circumstance that made Athena wary.

"Of course, she will, Sarah," Aunt Mary assured her hostess, her eyes darting a silent message to her niece. "Will you not, dear?"

"Let the gel speak for herself, Mary," the old lady said. "Let us ring for tea," she added unexpectedly. "Tidy yourself a little my dear, and come along to my sitting room. I think it is time you knew the whole story behind Sylvester's foolish plan."

Sylvester's plan? Athena mused, at a loss to know what to think of Lady Sarah's participation in her nephew's deception.

"Come along, child," the old lady commanded, her tone indicating that she had recuperated her spirits considerably. "There is much to do this afternoon if Perry's birthday is to be a success."

Although she still did not see how Perry's ball had anything to do with her, Athena followed the two elder ladies down the hall without further protest.

CHAPTER TWELVE

The Birthday Ball

Lord St. Aubyn curbed his impatience as he stood beside Lady Sarah Steele and Viscount Fairmont at the top of the gently curving stairs, welcoming those of their guests who had not attended his son's intimate birthday dinner. Taking advantage of a pause in the flow of guests up to the ballroom on the first floor, Sylvester glanced over at the narrower stairs leading up to the private chambers above.

They were empty.

"Athena came down ten minutes ago, while you were complimenting Squire Mason on his prize Jersey," his aunt remarked in an undertone. "I presume she is whom you are watching for, Sylvester."

The earl wished his aunt had not such sharp eyes, which saw far more than he found comfortable. Her blue gaze softened as he grinned ruefully.

"You promised you would not pester the poor child, dear," she added softly, after greeting old Sir James and Lady Potter, the latter dressed as always in her purple velvet ball gown and favorite turban with its huge spray of tattered ostrich feathers. "It took Mary and me an hour to persuade her to come down at all this evening."

"Perry will appreciate your efforts, Aunt," he growled under his breath, watching the weighty Mrs. Rowellen and her two stringy daughters ascend the stairs slowly. "He is anxious to request a dance with the lady."

As the garrulous Mrs. Rowellen and her tongue-tied daughters paused to greet Peregrine, Lady Sarah turned to murmur gently in his ear. "You will keep your distance from Athena, my boy, if you know what is good for you. The poor gel has had enough to stomach for one day."

"We cannot allow her to take the Mail Coach back to London, Aunt," he whispered back. "Particularly if Mrs. Easton is to remain here with you."

"I hope she may be persuaded to delay her departure for a day or two, dear. Mary has promised to lend her entreaties to mine, but Athena is sorely put out with you, Sylvester. And I would not be at all surprised if you deliberately set out to seduce the poor gel."

"I did not such thing, Aunt," he growled under his breath. But his aunt had already turned away to greet another noisy group of arrivals.

He was glad his aunt had not heard his denial, because it was patently untrue. He *had* set out to seduce the lovely widow. Not at the beginning, perhaps, but after that feverish kiss in the dungeons there had been little doubt in his mind about his own intentions. His own desires. He had *wanted* to seduce Athena Standish. He *still* wanted to seduce her.

Who could have predicted that Sylvester Steele, renowned collector of Oriental art, would be drawn out of his comfortable shell by a diminutive, auburn-haired widow of undistinguished lineage and no fortune? It had been those eyes, of course. He was sure of it. Those two pools of molten amber that had tempted him, set him on fire, consumed him with a passion Sylvester had thought safely behind him.

And now she was going to leave Cornwall. How was he ever going to settle back into his sedentary scholarly life again? he wondered. During the past week he had hardly spared a thought for Oriental pottery, much less the completion of his treatise. He had not written a single word in all that time.

Life at the Castle would never be the same again, he thought regretfully, offering his arm to Lady Sarah and leading her into the ballroom, where the musicians had started to tune their instruments. They moved among the throng of guests, and Sylvester glanced around the gaily decorated room, illuminated by hundreds of candles suspended in the huge crystal chandeliers and set in elaborate sconces on the walls.

And then he saw her. She had taken refuge among the elderly matrons at the far end of the hall with her aunt.

Sylvester felt himself smile. The mere sight of her sent shivers of delight through his body. It had been a long time since a woman had managed to do that, he mused, feasting his eyes upon her small frame swathed in deep blue silk, momentarily oblivious of where he was.

"Who is she?" a deep, amused voice inquired beside him, and Sylvester turned to meet the laughing gaze of his longtime friend and contemporary, Martin Douglas, the Earl of Ridgeway.

His smile became wry. "None of your damned business, Ridgeway," he answered casually. "And if you dare to show any interest in that direction, I shall have you out behind the stables at dawn, my lad."

"Do not say that you are already misbehaving, Martin?"

Sylvester turned to encounter the intelligent gaze of the new Countess of Ridgeway. Old Martin—who must be Sylvester's age, if not older—had quite surprised them all when he suddenly married the Earl of Weston's eldest daughter a scant two months ago. Lady Jane Sutherland had never been a Beauty as far as Sylvester could remember, but she was elegantly tall, possessed of a quite luscious bosom, and a pair of eyes that were almost the exact shade of Athena's.

She was also quite obviously enamored of her new husband, and Martin seemed to be equally besotted with the tall redhead. Sylvester smiled, although their obvious happiness with each other reminded him painfully of his own disconsolate state.

Martin Douglas had been his best man when he had wed Adrienne so many years ago. He had been at the funeral, too, when Sylvester had lost her. Full of their own happiness, he and Adrienne had paraded many a young beauty for Martin's benefit, but the young Viscount Hammond, as he had been then, merely laughed at the efforts to entangle him in matrimonial webs and gone back to London where he had acquired, over the years, the reputation of a consummate rake.

And now Rogue Martin, as he had been called back then, had succumbed to the least likely of females, but Sylvester could not doubt that his friend's joy was deep and sincere.

An uncomfortable twinge of envy snaked through him as Sylvester watched his friend smile seductively at his countess and slip an arm about her trim waist. Had he and Adrienne been this obvious about their love for each other? he wondered. No wonder poor Martin's visits to Cornwall had so often ended in abrupt departures for the glittering, seductive life he led in London.

It was no fun watching the happiness of others from the outside.

Lady Ridgeway met his eyes and blushed. Sylvester thought her quite enchanting, but her amber eyes reminded him so vividly of Athena's that he glanced towards the far end of the room.

"You really must tell us who the delightful creature is," Ridgeway insisted. "I trust it is more than a summer dalliance, old man. It is high time you brought another bride to the Castle."

Sylvester stared at his friend in alarm. Martin had given shape to the illusive notion that had invaded his mind recently and which as yet he had not dared to identify. He looked over at Athena again, his heart beating unnaturally fast.

"Put that notion out of your head, Martin," he said, conscious of the regret in his voice. "The lady has taken a deep dislike to me. With good reason, I might add."

"Then you must change her mind, my lad," Ridgeway said jovially. "You have no idea the lengths I went to in order to persuade this lass of mine that she could not live without me." He grinned down fatuously at his blushing countess. "I am living proof that old bachelors do not have to sleep in cold beds."

"I imagine you were proof of that long before you wrecked your curricle in front of Lark Manor, my lord," Lady Ridgeway said tartly, and was rewarded with another hug from her doting husband.

"You are making a spectacle of yourself, Martin," the countess hissed, her blushes deepening.

"Come to think on it, lass," Ridgeway murmured in a husky voice, "I fear I am not much in the mood for dancing tonight." He winked at her suggestively. "What do you say if we escape upstairs—"

"Martin!" Lady Ridgeway exclaimed, quite sharply. "You are putting me to the blush. What will Lord St. Aubyn think?"

"Nothing that he has not known these twenty years or more, love," her unrepentant husband remarked, letting his arms fall with obvious reluctance. "But for your sake, sweetheart, I shall try to behave."

"I am glad to hear it," Sylvester remarked dryly. "I had hoped to persuade Lady Ridgeway to open the ball with my son, while you, Martin, do the honors with my aunt."

"I would prefer the lady in blue," the earl teased, his black eyes fixed on his host's face. "Or are you reserving that pleasure for yourself, old man?"

Sylvester was saved from having to reply to this leading remark by the sounds of the musicians signaling the opening of the ball. Perry detached himself from a group of young friends and came across to claim Martin's countess, with whom he was to open the festivities. Martin himself went off in search of Lady Sarah, who, in spite of her advanced age, delighted in the more sedate dances.

He himself was obliged by strict protocol to lead out the plump Marchioness of Oldham, a distant relative, who would doubtless fill his ear with salacious stories from her recent sojourn in the Metropolis.

His eyes were drawn again to the low settee shared by Athena, her aunt, and Lady Potter, whose purple plumes bounced restlessly as the old Tabby chattered with her two companions.

Sylvester willed Athena to raise her eyes from her lap. She looked rather wan and forlorn to his anxious gaze, and he wondered what measures he might take to convince the lady that—to borrow Martin's expression—she could not live without him.

For Sylvester had already convinced himself—again like his outspoken friend—that he had no wish to sleep in a cold bed for the rest of his life.

The opening strains of the first set caused Athena to glance up at the crowded dance floor. She saw Perry, looking as fine as fivepence in his new blue satin coat and white knee-breeches, leading out a tall redhead in shimmering gold brocade. The lady's smile was wide and generous and Athena wondered who she was. She had not come downstairs all day and had missed meeting the dozen or so dinner guests and those special friends who had arrived throughout the afternoon to spend the night at the Castle.

She had broken a vow to herself in coming down at all, but Lady Sarah's entreaties, joined to those of Aunt Mary's, had weakened Athena's resolve. Even her determination to wear her plainest gown had been overridden by her maid, who had been shocked that her charge had decided to forego the deep-blue shot silk in favor of a sober dove-gray confection left over from her period of mourning. Very inappropriate for Master Peregrine's birthday, Betsy had declared, shaking her head in disapproval.

So she had worn the shimmering blue gown, knowing that it made her conspicuous, drawing attention as it did to her slim but shapely form, and emphasizing the expanse of ivory skin above her low neckline. The extravagant gown was one that

Perry had insisted upon having made up for her in London. He had also purchased her pale blue gloves and the beaded reticule she held limply in her lap.

She wished that she had at least been permitted to wear the lace cap she had tried to borrow from Aunt Mary. But even that attempt to appear inconspicuous had been denied her, and Athena had been obliged to sit silently as Lady Sarah's own hairdresser skillfully teased her auburn curls into an elegant cluster, held in place by a sapphire clip that her ladyship insisted was just the thing to set off her gown.

Athena listened with half an ear to the endless chatter of Lady Potter, a female of uncertain age garbed in a purple velvet gown of dubious vintage. In the short time since she had slipped into the ballroom to join her aunt on one of the settees placed strategically for the elder guests, Athena had learned more than she cared to know of the effusive though obviously kind-hearted Lady Potter. Aunt Mary had diverted the bulk of the lady's questions, but it was obvious that Lady Potter was possessed of an insatiable curiosity about the ladies presently sojourning as guests at the Castle.

Finally Lady Potter had resorted to direct questioning. "And how long have you been acquainted with the Steeles, my dear?" she shot at Athena, taking her by surprise.

Athena blinked, but before she had a chance to think up a sufficiently ambiguous answer, she was interrupted by Perry's voice at her elbow.

"Athena," he said in his eager way, "Lady Ridgeway has begged me to make you known to her, my dear. May we escort you to the refreshment room?"

Had she not been so sorely accosted by Lady Potter, it is doubtful that Athena would have accepted this invitation. As it was, she was glad to escape the impertinent questions and rose instantly, murmuring her excuses, and placed her fingers on Perry's proffered arm.

"We could see you needed saving from that dreadful old quiz, Athena," Perry remarked flippantly. "Could we not, Lady Ridgeway?"

"Oh, that is true enough, you shameless rogue," the red-haired countess laughed. "But it is also true that I have been wishing to meet you, Mrs. Standish. St. Aubyn speaks very highly of you."

Athena felt herself blush and stared at the countess in alarm, but the redhead's smile was guileless. What had the earl told his guests about her? she wondered.

"Athena and her daughter are spending the summer as guests of my great-aunt," Perry informed the countess quickly, letting Athena know indirectly that their brief betrothal had not been mentioned.

"You have a daughter, Mrs. Standish?" Lady Ridgeway exclaimed, her intelligent eyes lighting up. "I hope we may meet her tomorrow, my dear," she added impulsively. "I do adore children."

"I wager you will have one of your own before another year is out, my lady," Perry remarked with paralyzing candor. "Penelope is a great gun. I am teaching her to ride. Perhaps you would care to accompany us tomorrow afternoon, Lady Ridgeway?"

"Perry!" Athena exclaimed in a shocked voice. "You really must watch what you say. You are putting Lady Ridgeway to the blush."

"Oh, pray do not consider it," the countess said, her face flushed and smiling. "And the outing sounds quite delightful. I shall look forward to the opportunity of a quiet coze with Mrs. Standish."

Flattered by the countess's interest, Athena nevertheless shook her head. "I doubt I shall have time to join you my lady," she said with sincere regret. "I must supervise our packing."

"Do not say so, my dear," the countess exclaimed. "I had thought we might become friends. But I see I am to be deprived of that pleasure." Her smile was so warm and friendly that Athena wished things had been different.

Perry handed glasses of punch to both ladies and then addressed himself to Athena. "Aunt Sarah tells me you might be persuaded to stay a few more days, Athena. I trust that was not all a hum."

Athena wished she could reassure him, but the presence of his father was an uncomfortable reminder of things she would rather forget. No, she thought, that was not strictly true. She would remember the earl's kisses, the pressure of his lean body against hers, the heat of his blue-black eyes as long as she lived. She could not forget this man even had she wished to. Part of her cried out for him, while the other part cringed at the deception he had practiced upon her.

"You are very kind, my lady—"

"Please call me Jane, my dear," the countess said, a perfectly irresistible smile transforming her unremarkable face into quiet beauty. "And I hope you may be persuaded to ride with us tomorrow, Athena. I hope I may call you Athena? I fear I am hopelessly informal."

"Of course." Athena returned the countess's radiant smile, suddenly tempted to prolong her acquaintance with this charming female. "And perhaps I will join you tomorrow after all. Penelope has been badgering me to do so."

"Has my wife been badgering you already, Mrs. Standish?" a deep baritone murmured behind her.

Athena looked up at the gentleman standing at her elbow and blinked. Sleepy gray eyes regarded her with deceptive blandness. He took her fingers lightly in his and raised them to his lips, managing to infuse the simple gesture with a world of sensuality.

"Ridgeway, at your service, madam," he drawled, his gaze raking her face. Then he grinned and the impression of dissipation on his face disappeared instantly, and Lord Ridgeway appeared as he must have been in his youth, an utterly charming rascal.

Athena could not resist smiling back. "Lady Ridgeway is doing no such thing, my lord," she retorted. "We were merely planning a ride together if the weather is fine tomorrow."

"Are we gentlemen invited?" The gray eyes slid past her to the countess, and Athena blushed at the depth of passion she saw in them. The countess seemed unable to tear her gaze away from her husband's, and her cheeks flushed enchantingly. Athena felt a deep stab of longing at the obvious affection between them.

She quickly lowered her eyes, intensely conscious of the tall dark man beside her, so similar in looks and bearing to that other gentleman she had sworn to put out of her mind.

"I see no reason why we should exclude you, Martin," the countess said rather breathlessly. "Do you, Athena?"

Unable to find a plausible reason to disagree with Lady Ridgeway, Athena assented, wondering if she were not once again breaking her vow to avoid Lord St. Aubyn.

Perhaps deep in her heart she really did not wish to stay away from him, she thought, as the evening progressed. She danced twice each with Perry and Lord Ridgeway, and then with several other gentlemen of the neighborhood, some of whom had visited at the Castle during her stay. But the Earl of St. Aubyn did not approach her. Lady Sarah had informed Athena that her nephew had promised not do so, since she found his presence so distasteful.

Unhappily, Athena soon discovered that it was not the earl's presence that she found distasteful but his deliberate avoidance of her company. She could find no rational explanation for this ironic development. And what her heart whispered every time she caught his deep blue gaze fixed upon her during the course of the evening was clearly irrational on all counts.

But what would she do if her heart was right? a little voice murmured persistently.

Long after the last guest had left and the family retired for the night, Sylvester sat moodily before the library fire idly swirling his brandy around in his glass and gazing into the flames.

"If I had not seen this with my own eyes," the Earl of Ridgeway remarked in his rich baritone, "I never would have believed it. You are behaving like the veriest slowtop, Sylvester. Why the devil did you not dance with the chit, lad, and then take her out on the terrace and kiss some sense into her?"

Sylvester grimaced at his friend's blunt advice. "Lady Sarah promised Athena that I would not come near her, that is why."

"Since when do you allow a female to make promises for you, old man?"

"Athena would not have come downstairs otherwise," Sylvester said, a hint of frustration in his voice. "She has taken me in extreme dislike."

He relapsed into silence again.

Ridgeway rose to pour himself another brandy, then looked down at his friend, an amused light in his gray eyes. "Having just gone through a similar experience with my dear Jane," he remarked languidly, "I can tell you that a frontal attack will eventually carry the day. None of this shilly-shallying around, lad. That is for callow youths and moonlings. Men our age have no time to waste on frivolous courting rituals, old man. Nor do females past what society considers *marketable age* wish to be treated like chits in their first Season. They like a man to be forceful. They may pretend they are outraged, of course. My Jane certainly gave me the sharp edge of her tongue on various occasions, but women are secretly delighted when we men confess we cannot live without them."

Sylvester took a long gulp of brandy and grinned wryly. "And was that true in your case, Martin? I confess I find it hard to believe that you are actually leg-shackled after all these years on the Town."

Ridgeway reached for the decanter and filled his friend's glass. "I can scarce believe it myself, if you must know the truth, lad. Sometimes I wake up in a cold sweat just thinking about it; but then my Jane opens her eyes and smiles at me, and I wonder why in blue blazes I waited so long."

"You could have had your pick of the Marriage Mart any time these twenty years," Sylvester pointed out. "And you cannot say Adrienne and I did not produce our share of eligibles for your benefit."

Ridgeway laughed. "How could I forget it. I remember spending a good part of my stays at the Castle dodging mealy-mouthed little ninnyhammers without two thoughts in their heads to rub together." His face became suddenly serious. "It took that firebrand Jane to show me that all females are not either Haymarket ware or insipid chits with more hair than wit. It was a rude awakening, let me tell you." His expression softened into a fatuous grin.

"How can you be sure this is not an aberrant start brought on by advancing years?" Sylvester wanted to know. "You are over forty, after all, Martin. As am I," he added pensively.

This was the main reservation he had about his sudden attraction to Athena Standish. Sylvester had firmly believed that he would never get over Adrienne's death, and had been unprepared for the intensity of his desire for the diminutive widow. At first he had believed it to be merely lust for her shapely body. He might be forty-two, he told himself wryly, but he was certainly not past the enjoyments of the flesh. But then came the storm, and he had found her out there in the grass so helpless and inviting, so vulnerable. She had needed him, he realized. Needed his arms around her to protect her from the storm that obviously terrified her. It had been a long time since Sylvester had felt needed. And when Athena had put her arms around his neck and trembled against him, something inside him had cracked wide open. It was only after he had carried her up to her room and laid her on the bed that he began to understand that he had lost part of himself in that storm. Part of himself that would be forever lost to him unless . . .

Abruptly, he dragged his thoughts back to listen to his friend's self-conscious laugh.

"There is no mistaking it when it hits you, old man," Ridgeway said, his deep baritone vibrating with feeling. "It took me ten days after I left her to realize that I had lost something of myself back at Lark Manor." He gave an embarrassed laugh and paused to stare into the flames. "I would not admit this to anyone but you, Sylvester," he continued at last. "It took me days to admit it to myself. But I finally realized that I was fed up with bedding other men's wives, and spending fortunes on lady-birds who cared not a fig for plain Martin Douglas, and that it might be nice, rather delightful in fact, to have a wife of my own to bed. A female who would be mine alone . . ." He broke off abruptly, grinning self-consciously. "But here I am running on like a moon-struck halfling."

The two men sat silently regarding the flames until Ridgeway spoke again. "If you feel any of this for your widow, old man, my advice is to waste no more time in fixing your interest with her."

"It is not quite that simple, Martin," Sylvester murmured, wishing he had half his friend's experience with females.

"Your problem, old chap," Ridgeway explained patiently, "is that you have lost touch with reality. All these years with your nose stuck in musty old tomes of Chinese antiquity have atrophied your wits, lad. It looks to me as though you have forgotten how to deal with females."

"You may be right, Martin, but let me warn you that Athena Standish had more than enough cause to wish me in Hades."

Ridgeway's dark eyebrows rose quizzically. "Then you obviously have not told me the whole, Sylvester," he said quietly. "Perhaps you had better do so before I waste any more of my considerable expertise on you. Your case may indeed be hopeless after all."

The thought that he might lost Athena forever shook Sylvester out of his apathy. Putting all his reservations aside, he launched into his tale, spilling out the whole sordid deception he had woven around the unsuspecting widow and his innocent son. When he mentioned Perry's former betrothal to Athena Standish, Ridgeway raised an eyebrow and whistled softly.

"Now I understand why you are in such a pother, lad," he said compassionately. "Betrothed to your son was she? But if she broke if off herself, that should have cleared the way—"

"No such luck," Sylvester cut in sourly, and told of the disastrous scene in the boathouse and his subsequent wild ride through the storm with Athena.

"It appears to me that catching Perry with that doxy—what was the wench's name? Viviana? Well, catching Perry with Viviana might well have been the excuse your Mrs. Standish was looking for to break off the engagement. From what you tell me, she is more than a little partial to you, lad."

"Not anymore," Sylvester responded harshly. "The whole thing blew up in my face after I sent Viviana back to London yesterday. The greedy little bitch made quite sure of that."

At Martin's prompting, he related the contents of Miss Rathbone's letter detailing her part in the deception and making much of Sylvester's role in the double seduction.

When he had finished the sordid tale, Sylvester felt little of the relief he had expected. If anything, his actions, though not strictly as deliberate as Miss Rathbone had implied, appeared as coldly damning as ever.

"Is that the way it really happened?" Ridgeway's voice was carefully noncommittal.

Sylvester sighed and took another mouthful of brandy. "Athena believes it to be so," he said heavily. "I did not set out deliberately to seduce her, of course, although it certainly appears that way. Actually, it was Aunt Sarah who suggested that while Viviana was distracting Perry, it might facilitate matters if I set myself to keep the widow entertained."

"And I take it you found that task very much to your liking?"

Sylvester glanced at his friend and saw that Ridgeway was wearing a sardonic grin on his handsome face.

"It is no laughing matter, Martin," he said shortly. "But you are right, of course. I did not anticipate actually enjoying Athena's company. She made me feel . . ." He paused to swirl his brandy around the glass. "I cannot say exactly, but I felt—"

"Young and foolish again," Ridgeway broke in with a laugh. "I know, old chap, because that is precisely how I feel with Jane. It beats feeling ancient and bored, let me tell you. I had the devil of a time convincing Jane that I was serious, you know. She had this misguided notion that I was some kind of a dissipated rakehell." He laughed again, and drained his glass.

"Athena believes I am a cold-hearted seducer," Sylvester said heavily. And since she would not talk to him, he thought bitterly, how was he to convince her that although the seducer part may be close to the truth, there was nothing cold about his heart.

Ridgeway stretched and yawned. "I have been away from my

Jane quite long enough, even for a good friend like you, Sylvester," he said dryly. "But one last piece of advice from a happily married man, old chap. If a woman is worth fighting for, then fight for her. Fight like the very devil. You may not get a second chance."

Martin's words rang in Sylvester's ears long after his friend had gone up to bed.

CHAPTER THIRTEEN

The Boat Ride

The morning after the ball dawned calm and sunny, a perfect English summer day. As Athena sipped her hot chocolate curled up in the windowseat, she allowed herself—in a moment of pure self-indulgence she did not often permit—to pretend that this wonderful old house with its century-old Park, its vast expanse of lawns, its well-tended flowerbeds, its Oriental pond full of fat orange fish, its grape arbors, its rose-covered trellised paths, was really her home. That she belonged here in this haven of peace and comfort, safe from the vicissitudes of life, safe from want, and pain, and loneliness. Safe in the arms of a man she could never have.

The dream dissipated, and Athena drained her cup and set it down beside her. At least she had one more day, she thought, suddenly glad that she had agreed to go riding with Lady Ridgeway this morning. One more day to enjoy the illusion of belonging here at the Castle, part of a heritage stretching back to the days of the Conqueror.

She shook herself impatiently and reached for the bell pull. She would enjoy her last ride on Tarantella this morning, attend to the packing in the afternoon, and be gone by tomorrow before the family had breakfasted.

Betsy came into the room with Athena's blue habit, freshly pressed, over her arm.

"Molly says that her ladyship is up already and intends to take her breakfast downstairs, ma'am," the little abigail reported, laying the garment down on the bed. "Lord Ridgeway went out with the master nearly an hour ago," she added. "Something about inspecting the site for the new mill his lordship plans to build, Jackson says."

"Thank you, Betsy." It never ceased to amaze Athena how little of what their masters did escaped the notice of the servants. She had known this to be true at her aunt's little house on Mount Street with its staff of four, but here at the Castle, with its army of servants, there were eyes everywhere to record the comings and goings of the family and guests.

Without the fear of encountering Lord St. Aubyn at the breakfast table, Athena enjoyed both a hearty meal and the very lively company of Lady Ridgeway. How pleasant it would be, she thought, as the two ladies strolled down to the stables where Perry was seeing to the saddling of their mounts, to have a friend like the countess.

Penelope was with him, her small face alight with enthusiasm and her tongue going thirteen to the dozen. She ran to meet her mother, bubbling with news. "Perry says I really am to have Buttercup for my very own, Mama. He will take care of her for me until I can visit again. When will that be, Mama?" she demanded. "Perry says perhaps for Christmas?" Her voice rose questioningly, and Athena wondered just what unrealistic promises Perry had made to the child.

"Perhaps, dear," she responded absently. "But now I want you to meet Lady Ridgeway, who is come to ride with us."

"Do you have a daughter, too, my lady?" Penny asked after sketching a brief curtsy.

"Where is Perry taking us this morning?" Athena broke in hastily to cover her daughter's improper remark.

As it happened, Peregrine had, with the assistance of Lady Sarah, he confessed sheepishly, organized a picnic for the guests at the lake. Athena stared at him in astonishment when he mentioned the lake. Had he so soon forgotten the scandalous goings-on in the boathouse? she wondered.

"There is an Oriental Folly built by my great-grandfather on the east side of the lake," he explained hastily, catching her eye and blushing furiously. "It is one of Aunt Sarah's favorite picnic sites."

"You should have invited your great-aunt to join us, Peregrine," Lady Ridgeway remarked. "And Mrs. Easton, too. It is too fine a day to sit inside doing needlework."

"Aunt Sarah said she may drive out later," Perry said, lifting Penny up onto Buttercup's fat back. "I have had Rosebud saddled for you, Lady Ridgeway," he added, motioning to a pretty little roan mare who seemed unable to stand still. "A silly name, of course, for the prime goer she is, but Aunt Sarah gave it to her when she was born. She was so pink and soft." He eyed Lady Ridgeway uneasily. "The mare has become rather a handful, I must confess. But Lord Ridgeway assured me that you are the best horsewoman in Dorset, and left instructions not to mount you on a sluggard under pain of death."

Lady Ridgeway grinned broadly. "She is a pretty little thing," she said, stroking the mare's velvet muzzle with her gloved fingers and motioning to the groom to help her mount.

After Perry tossed Athena up on Tarantella, he mounted his own hack and the party trotted out of the stable-yard, Penny cantering ahead.

The ride to the lake was very diffcrent from the wild race through the rain that Athena remembered, and she tried not to think of that day, which brought back so many confusing memories.

The Folly, located as Perry had indicated on the east bank of the lake, was indeed an ideal spot for a picnic. Constructed in the Oriental style, its pagoda roof resting upon five white marble columns entwined with ferocious-looking dragons, and situated on a slight rise, it presented a pleasing vista of the lake.

Perry had evidently expended considerable effort on providing for the amusement of his guests, for Athena noticed three flat boats tied to a giant willow that trailed its branches in the still waters of the lake.

"Oh, Perry," her daughter cried in delight as soon as they dismounted, "will you take me for a boat ride? Please, Perry," she added, catching Athena's sharp glance.

"Can you swim, brat?"

"Of course I can swim," Penny responded with alacrity. "Papa taught me in Spain."

Memories flooded back to Athena as she listened to her daughter describe in great detail the fun she had had with her beloved Papa during the all-too-brief time they had shared on the Peninsula. There had been so much hardship during those years they had spent as a family. Athena remembered them well, but mercifully, her daughter seemed to recall only the happy times. John had sheltered them from the worst discomforts as best he could, but there had been many times when he had not been there, and Athena had been forced to cope with the rigors of traveling with the motley assortment of humanity that made up the baggage train of a huge army.

"Then you and I shall go punting before our picnic baskets arrive," Perry exclaimed. "That is, if you approve, Athena?" he added, turning to where she sat on a marble bench beside Lady Ridgeway.

Half an hour later, amid much laughter, squealing, and

splashing, Perry had poled her daughter to the middle of the lake and was proceeding to instruct her on the fine art of fly-fishing. Athena regarded them affectionately, glad that she had delayed their departure for another day. Penny would have little enough chance for such adventures when they returned to London.

The peaceful scene was interrupted by the arrival of the gig driven by Tom, the undergroom, accompanied by two footmen sent by Lady Sarah to ensure that the feast was served according to rigid etiquette.

Lady Ridgeway's eyes became round as she watched the lengthy process of unloading the gig and setting the round marble table with white linen and delicate china. One of the footmen opened a bottle of champagne and offered the ladies a glass.

"I propose a toast to Lady Sarah," the countess exclaimed in an awed voice. "One could easily become addicted to picnics served with such élan. There is a little Grecian Folly at Ridgeway Park, situated on a hill overlooking the valley near Shaftsbury, that would make an admirable picnic site. I must suggest it to Martin." She glanced conspiratorially at her companion. "I do hope you may visit us there very soon, Athena," she said. "Perhaps we might try it out if the weather is good."

Athena felt a rush of affection for this outspoken female who gave such evident signs of wishing to further their friendship. She smiled. Friends had always been precious to her; she had so few of them.

"That is very generous of you, Jane," she began.

"Oh, fiddlesticks!" the countess exclaimed gaily. "Actually, I am being very selfish, since I find your company so enjoyable, Athena. 'Tis a pity you feel you must leave so soon. Martin is bound to stay on a few days with St. Aubyn. They have known each other since they were lads together, or so I gather." She paused, glancing at Athena before adding, "Martin tells me that Sylvester has been mourning his wife for over five years. Now that is what I call true devotion."

"Yes," Athena murmured, wondering what Lady Ridgeway would think of the earl if she knew about his disgraceful behavior in the dungeon. And would Jane invite her to Ridgeway Park if she learned of Athena's own wantonness in kissing a man she hardly knew and did not even like?

Her musings were interrupted by a delighted cry from the

countess, and Athena turned her head in time to see two riders emerge from the trees and canter towards the Folly.

One of the riders was the Earl of St. Aubyn, and her heart gave a peculiar little lurch.

Athena watched the gentlemen approach with some trepidation. They were well worth watching, she admitted silently, quite unable to drag her eyes away. Lord St. Aubyn was riding Ajax, and the chestnut gelding's coat fairly gleamed with vitality. Lord Ridgeway was mounted on a powerful bay with a white blaze on its face. Horse and rider were well matched, she thought appreciatively, the gentleman's muscled thighs firmly outlined beneath his pale corduroy breeches, and his broad shoulders straining the seams of his wine-colored hunting jacket.

Almost reluctantly, Athena turned her gaze to her host and found his eyes fixed upon her. They were intensely blue this morning in the bright sunlight and held none of the cynical, half-seductive amusement she had come to expect from him. Had she not known better, Athena might even have supposed the earl to be feeling apprehensive about intruding upon her like this. Had he not promised Lady Sarah that he would not do so?

Her thoughts were abruptly interrupted when she felt a warm hand squeeze her own, clasped nervously in her lap. She turned to see Lady Ridgeway smiling at her. "Do not poker up so, my dear," the countess whispered as the gentlemen dismounted under the trees. "He is not going to bite you."

Athena looked at her, round-eyed with amazement.

"St. Aubyn," the countess added with a sly wink. "He cannot seem to take his eyes off you, my dear. I noticed it last night, too. Martin thinks his friend is about ready to give up his single state again. Would it not be wonderful if—"

"No!" The sound was little more than a gasp, and Athena felt herself blush. "The notion is absurd, Jane," she mumbled, wishing the countess had not chosen that precise moment to make her unthinkable suggestion. "You do not know the whole of it. And you are mistaken, you know; there is no way I would even consider . . ."

Her voice trailed into silence as the gentlemen mounted the steps into the Folly.

Lady Ridgeway smiled up at her husband encouragingly, and he promptly bent to place a kiss on her upturned face. She flushed and protested this improper display of intimacy, but Athena thought Jane looked thoroughly delighted with this public acknowledgment of her lord's regard.

Athena had avoided St. Aubyn's eyes, but she could not very well disregard the civil greeting he directed to both ladies. The quick glance she did permit herself confirmed her original unlikely assessment. His lordship appeared troubled and—for the first time since she had met him—unsure of himself.

She listened in silence as Lady Ridgeway bandied words with the two gentlemen, envying her friend the easy intimacy she shared with her new husband. Her eyes wandered out onto the surface of the lake, where Perry and Penelope appeared to have turned the fishing lesson into a riotous experience, punctuated by happy shrieks from her daughter countered by Perry's loud bursts of laughter.

"What a marvelous idea, Martin!" she heard Jane exclaim enthusiastically, shattering her train of thought. "Do you not agree, Athena?"

"Of course, Mrs. Standish agrees, you silly goose," Lord Ridgeway chided his wife tenderly. "No female can resist the lure of a boat ride on a summer afternoon."

Lady Ridgeway glared at her husband with feigned indignation. "How is it that you know so much about the lure of boat rides, sirrah?"

"I· have taken a few of them myself, that is why," he responded with an affectionate grin. "Come, my dear." He stood up and pulled his wife to her feet. "Let me show you exactly what I mean. What do you say, Mrs. Standish?" he added, staring down at Athena with those lazy gray eyes that seemed to see everything she was most anxious to hide. "I know Sylvester is too bookish to appreciate the aesthetic pleasure to be derived from poling a beautiful woman about in a punt, but I can guarantee he will not overturn you, my dear. Trust me on that."

Athena felt her blood freeze. She glanced desperately at Lady Ridgeway, but much to her chagrin that lady gave her another knowing wink.

"Do say you will, Athena," she begged. "And pay no attention to Martin; he was only teasing. I am sure Lord St. Aubyn is an expert punter. Are you not, my lord?" she demanded, turning to her host, who was looking more bemused than overjoyed at the prospect of the boating expedition.

Athena sat in awkward silence, watching as Lord Ridgeway lifted his lady into the punt and settled her solicitously among the cushions. She was uncomfortably aware of the earl leaning negligently against one of the dragon pillars, a wry smile on his face as he watched his friend push off from the bank.

"I trust Martin has not discouraged you with his raillery," he remarked after a while. He turned to look at her directly. "He is right about one thing, however; you can trust me not to overturn you, Athena."

The sound of her name on his lips disconcerted her. One would think the wretch would have realized by now, she thought crossly, that such pointless intimacies between them must end. Had indeed ended as far as she was concerned the moment she laid eyes on that dreadful letter from Miss Rathbone, or whatever her name was. The memory of that humiliating moment when she had discovered the true nature of the earl's flattering attention came rushing back, and Athena kept her eyes firmly focused on the punt that moved lazily out onto the lake.

Lady Ridgeway raised an arm and waved encouragingly. "Do come on, Athena," she called, her voice floating gaily across the water. "It is glorious out here."

Athena lifted a hand to acknowledge her friend's invitation, but she could not share the countess's enthusiasm. The countess had a doting husband in attendance. Was it surprising she found the experience enjoyable? She knew she should not feel envious of the other woman's happiness, but Athena could not stop the despair that constricted her throat and made her want to weep.

"May I tempt you to take a chance with me, Athena?"

The earl had moved to stand beside her, his hand outstretched. Athena looked into his eyes and felt her resolution falter. Tempt her? she thought disgustedly. Had he not already tempted her beyond the bounds of what was proper? Had he not turned her head and touched her heart? And now the wretch wished to tempt her into further dalliance. What kind of a simpleton did he think she was?

She shook her head. "I do not think . . ."

He grinned engagingly, and his eyes caressed her. "It is cool on the water, my dear," he said softly, his hand still reaching for her.

Without quite knowing how it happened, Athena found her hand firmly clasped in his. Then she was standing on the small wooden jetty, while Lord St. Aubyn poled the boat over and reached up for her. She lowered her eyes as his hands encircled her waist and lifted her into the punt. The flat boat rocked gently beneath them as the earl guided her, one hand still on her waist, to settle comfortably on the nest of cushions. And then they were moving slowly, almost sensuously Athena thought, across the unruffled water.

Peregrine and her daughter had settled down to some serious fishing in the middle of the lake, she noted, surrounded by a family of swans looking for crumbs. She could clearly hear Penny's childish voice asking one of her interminable questions. The swans reminded Athena vividly of the first time she had met Peregrine at Lady Hereford's alfresco gathering on the banks of the Thames. He had saved her from the attack of another family of hungry, bad-tempered birds, she remembered. Had she but known the complications and heartache that innocent meeting by the river would bring, she might have reacted differently to the viscount's charming invitation to drive out with him.

Or perhaps not, she thought, glancing up at the earl from under her lashes. Perhaps the whole disastrous affair of her misguided betrothal to the viscount had been worth the pain it had caused her. How else would she have met his father, and discovered that her heart had not died with John on the battlefields of Spain as she had imagined during those first dreadful months back in England?

She was distracted from these morbid thoughts by a willow branch trailing beside her in the water. She glanced up and found that the earl had guided the punt under the mottled shade of the huge willows that lined the bank. He was looking down at her, his eyes inscrutable, but the faint smile on his lips disconcerted her.

"Is it not pleasant out here, my dear?"

In the semi penumbra beneath the willows, his muted baritone resonated seductively, setting off warning signals in Athena's head. They were alone, she thought with sudden alarm, isolated from the other boaters by a wall of greenery that created a soft, enchanted aura around them.

He plied the pole with languid grace, the muscles of his arms bunching under the sleeve of his brown jacket with a smooth regularity that was almost hypnotic. Athena felt herself falling under the spell of his masculine presence and dragged her eyes away. The light twilled bombazine of her riding habit suddenly felt warm and constricting on her skin, even without the usual high-buttoned neckline. Her palms were damp and she leaned over to trail one hand in the water to cool it.

The shock of the water on her fingertips carried her back instantly to the Rothingham Manor of her childhood. Her father had a small artificial lake on the estate, which was strictly out of bounds for swimming. But of course she had not resisted the temptation of that cool water on those lazy summer afternoons. Athena smiled at the memory of those glorious days when she managed to slip out of the nursery, leaving Miss Pettygrew, her governess, snoring gently in her easy chair. Accompanied by her father's two old spaniels, Paris and Juno, Athena would run all the way to the lake and throw herself down on the bank to look for minnows.

The dogs would run straight into the water, yapping joyously as they splashed around hunting frogs and the occasional garter snake. One day she had pulled off her shoes and stockings and waded in after them. She could still recall vividly the thrill of the cool water lapping at her knees, creeping up her thighs. Not long after that, she had dared to throw off her muslin gown and join the dogs in the shallow water where frogs and minnows lurked. Inevitably, her shift had become soaked when she tripped and fell full length among the water lilies, and after that she had always carried an extra shift with her on those unforgettable adventures in the lake.

"Will you not share those pleasant memories with me?" The earl's voice broke into her reverie, and Athena looked up, startled, to find him regarding her quizzically.

She sighed audibly. "I was thinking of home," she confessed reluctantly. "Or what used to be my home. At Rothingham there was a lake, too. Nothing like this," she swept an arm around her, "but a wonderland for the child I was then. I used to slip away from my governess on hot afternoons and take my father's spaniels down there for a stolen hour or two." She smiled sadly. "They must both be dead by now, but I will never forget them. They taught me to hunt frogs, catch minnows, even to swim."

"To swim?" His dark brows rose in surprise. "That sounds rather dangerous to me." He had ceased his poling and the punt moved sluggishly in the water.

"I supposed it was," she replied, "but I trusted the dogs. They pulled me out by my shift one time when I got in too deep. And even after I learned to swim, they trailed me about like two shaggy guardian angels." She glanced up at him, but the intense

look in his eyes made her shudder, whether from fear or anticipation she could not tell.

"I was never afraid in those days," she added in a low voice,
listening to the distant laughter of her daughter, so carefree, so
innocent, so unprotected from the trials she herself had been
forced to face after her return to England. Trials she would have
to face again once they returned to London, she thought.

"And now are you?" His voice cut into her memories and
Athena turned back to him questioningly.

"Afraid, I mean."

She smiled. "Not of drowning, my lord," she replied, evad-
ing the real question. "I am still a strong swimmer. And you
promised not to overturn me, remember?"

"I was not talking of drowning, Athena."

She looked at him for a long moment before answering.
"Everybody is afraid of something, my lord," she said with
more calm than she felt. "Some with more reason than others,
perhaps. I am certainly no exception."

When he did not answer, Athena sat up and dried her fingers
on her handkerchief. It had seemed for a moment as though
Lord St. Aubyn was about to say something about the deception
that hung like a bleak cloud between them. But what difference
would that have made? she wondered with a return of her old
bitterness. How could she ever again trust a man who admit-
tedly had tried to seduce her to further his own ends? What
good would it do to listen to his excuses—and she was sure his
lordship would be dangerously convincing—if her heart could
no longer trust him?

"I would like to go back now, my lord," she said, quite suddenly tired of the cat-and-mouse game the earl seemed to be enjoying at her expense.

Without a word, he swung the punt around and headed out
into the sunlight.

CHAPTER FOURTEEN

The Visitor

"I gather that your suit was not entirely successful, old chap?"

Sylvester grimaced. He had been dreading this question, but no amount of reflection on his part had enabled him to place the blame anywhere but squarely on his own shoulders. He had behaved like a raw youth, tongue-tied at the prospect of revealing his sentiments to his first love.

Except that Athena was not his first love, of course, and for the life of him Sylvester could not remember experiencing this wrenching agony of uncertainty when he had spoken of love to Adrienne. Everything had seemed so much simpler twenty years ago. He had known long before he made his formal offer that Adrienne returned his regard. There had been no question of rejection. He had not felt like some illiterate rudesby who could not find the right words to express his feelings.

He had felt both awkward and incoherent this morning with Athena. The fear of rejection had paralyzed him, and the words he had wanted to speak turned to ashes in his mouth. She had sat in her cushioned isolation, cool and remote in the shaded bower of the willow branches, and spoken of her childhood with a haunting nostalgia that seared his heart and made him yearn to take her in his arms again. He had wanted to kiss her, but he had lacked the resolve, the courage, the foolhardiness—he knew not which—to break through the wall of reserve she had thrown up between them since reading that infernal letter. Since learning the partial truth of what he had done.

That kiss he had anticipated, had actually needed more than anything he could recall, had escaped him. With Adrienne, there had been no uncertainty at all. She had blushed adorably and stepped into his arms without hesitation, lifting her sweet face for their first kiss. They had fit together like two halves of a marvelous whole, and there had never been any doubt in his mind that they would spend the rest of their lives in that loving harmony he had taken for granted.

With Athena, there had been no harmony at all. From the moment of their first kiss, which had stirred emotions he did not know he possessed and turned his life into a maelstrom of uncertainties, Sylvester had tried to convince himself that the delightful Mrs. Standish had merely aroused the dormant male in him. His cynical self suggested an obvious remedy for this uncomfortable state of affairs, but Athena had suddenly revealed herself in all her vulnerability, and he had been unable and unwilling to push his attraction for the widow to its logical conclusion.

Encouraged by Ridgeway's example and advice, Sylvester had been ready to pursue a more honorable course. But contrary to what Martin had promised, the boat ride had been neither romantic nor propitious. Athena had clearly wished to have nothing to do with him. His declaration had died on his lips.

Sylvester found himself at *point-non-plus*.

"Well?" Ridgeway prodded him. "What went wrong, old man?"

"Everything," Sylvester growled. "She wanted nothing to do with me."

"She said that?"

"She did not have to," Sylvester muttered. "It was as clear as a bloody pikestaff that she despises me."

Lord Ridgeway sighed audibly. "You did not even ask her, did you?"

"How *could* I?" Sylvester protested in an aggrieved voice. "We were in that damned boat, and I could not get near her. I felt like a bloody fool standing there with the pole in my hand, trying to make an offer. How the hell was I supposed to kiss her without dumping us both in the lake? Can you tell me that?"

He was taking his frustration out on his friend, Sylvester realized, but it had been Martin's idea to maneuver Athena into the punt alone with him. That part had succeeded admirably, in spite of Athena's initial reluctance. But once he had her to himself in that magical green world under the willows, the proper words had not come. He had made a mull of the whole affair.

And by tomorrow, Athena would be gone.

"I gave you credit for a little imagination, old man," Martin remarked, his shoulders shaking with repressed laughter. "Jane and I were quite prepared to act surprised and wish you both happy, but when we saw those long faces . . ." He paused, glancing at the two women who rode ahead deep in conversation. "They make a splendid pair, do they not?" he said with obvious appreciation. "Jane is very taken with her, you know," he added. "We shall just have to think of something else."

"You can save yourself the trouble," Sylvester growled harshly. "She will have none of me."

Ridgeway merely laughed again. "We shall see about that," he said with a confidence Sylvester was far from sharing.

The more he considered the matter, the less likely it appeared to Sylvester that Athena could be brought to believe that what had started out as a mild deception—never as the deliberate seduction of Viviana's accusation—had turned into a real attachment on his part. He would be lying, of course, if he failed to admit that the thought of intimacy had not crossed his mind, but recently that primitive urge had been mitigated by other, less tangible emotions that had caused Sylvester to change his intentions towards the widow.

None of it signified anything, he thought dispiritedly, if Athena would not listen to him, would not forgive him, or believe that he spoke nothing but the truth when he confessed that the mere thought of spending the rest of his life without her was unbearable. In that, at least, Martin had been right on the mark. Life without Athena loomed like a dark lonely tunnel before him. He must do something drastic before it was too late.

The sight of one of his footmen in the stable-yard chatting with the grooms distracted him. But after he learned that a gentleman had arrived from Bath to see him, Sylvester saw a ray of hope in that dark future.

Perhaps all was not yet lost.

Athena closed her chamber door behind her and rang for the abigail. Throwing off her plumed riding bonnet she took the pins out of her hair, letting it fall in auburn waves over her shoulders. She was tired, frustrated, and deeply miserable. The picnic at the lake had promised a respite for her battered nerves, and at first it had been pleasantly relaxing. Lady Ridgeway had proved to be every bit as friendly as Athena had hoped, and she had relished the female companionship.

But then the gentlemen had intruded.

Athena sighed audibly. From the moment her eyes had encountered Lord St. Aubyn's, her peace of mind had been shattered. It had taken every ounce of her fortitude to remain calm in the face of his smile. She had had to remind herself several times that this charming rogue had deceived her in the most callous way, deliberately setting out to seduce her—if Miss Rathbone could be believed—with no regard for anything but his own selfish ends.

She took up her silver-backed brush and was about to untangle her hair when a startling thought struck her. One that had not crossed her mind before.

What if Miss Rathbone could *not* be believed?

Slowly, Athena laid the brush back on the dresser and stared into the mirror, her mind working feverishly. If the Beauty had lied, or even distorted the truth to suit her own purposes, then perhaps, just perhaps, the earl was not so black a villain as she had supposed. And now that she came to think of it, she had not allowed the earl the chance to explain. She had been only too ready to believe him guilty.

Her heart gave a painful lurch. The ramifications of such a novel idea made her suddenly dizzy with emotion. Perhaps Lord St. Aubyn had *not* intended to seduce her, a little voice whispered encouragingly. Could it be that she herself had put the idea into his head when she had kissed him so brazenly in the dungeon the afternoon of that first picnic? she wondered.

For the first time Athena began to see the possibility of such a misunderstanding. In truth, she had behaved quite immodestly. Had subsequent attempts to avoid him also been misunderstood? Was it possible that he saw her as nothing but a tease?

These and similar disturbing thoughts occupied her while Betsy helped her out of her riding habit and into a primrose-yellow muslin gown. By rights, she should be supervising the packing this afternoon, but she felt a strange reluctance to take that first step that would lead her away from the Castle forever. Perhaps as a result of this hesitancy, she had promised to stroll in the rose-gardens with Lady Ridgeway, who must even now be waiting for her. Athena put on her wide-brimmed straw bonnet and picked up her parasol. A visit to the fish pond was just what she needed to restore her sanity.

Twenty minutes later, strolling arm-in-arm with Lady Ridgeway through the multicolored beds of roses, Athena had been cajoled into confiding some of her fears to the countess.

"I can well imagine your mortification upon reading that little hussy's letter, my dear Athena," Lady Ridgeway remarked, after Athena had shown her ladyship the missive that had caused her present unhappiness. "My own chagrin would have been enormous had Martin been the object of this accusation. But then, let us not forget—much as I hate to admit it—that my dear husband is—or was—a rake of some notoriety." She paused and glanced at Athena with a wry smile. "I should not tell you this, my dear," she continued hesitantly, "but Martin tried to seduce me just as this wretched female describes in her letter. He wanted me to run off with him to some love-nest by the sea."

Athena stared at the countess, wondering how her friend had resisted the immoral proposal of such a dashing gentleman. "I gather you did not go, Jane," she remarked after a pause.

"No, I did not," her ladyship admitted with a sigh. "But I do not scruple to admit I was sorely tempted. And now, of course, it is a moot point. Martin came back to put his neck in the noose, as he likes to refer to his tumble into matrimony."

"He appears to be very reconciled to this noose," Athena said with a smile. "I quite envy you, Jane."

"Oh, he is, indeed," Jane acknowledged gaily, "but the point I wished to make is that while my Martin might well have been capable of a casual seduction—I know for a fact he has had a dozen liaisons or more—Lord St. Aubyn is a very different kind of man."

Athena wished her friend might be right, but something prompted her to argue. "They seem so alike to me; they even look alike, except for their eyes."

"Ah, but you are mistaken, my dear Athena," exclaimed the countess. "That similarity is entirely superficial. Underneath all that aristocratic breeding, Martin is a notorious rake, a reformed one I hope, but a rake nevertheless. Sylvester, on the other hand, married young, had an idyllic marriage, and has led an almost monkish existence since Adrienne died. No, St. Aubyn is no seducer, Athena. Your Miss Rathbone must have wished to cause trouble for him. And for you, too, most likely."

"But he would not deny it," Athena said in a distressed voice.

"And you assumed the worst, naturally?"

"What else was I to do?" Athena felt like weeping, and her distress must have been apparent, for Lady Ridgeway took her hand in a firm grasp.

"I would give him a chance to explain, my dear. Perhaps that is what he wished to do this morning on the lake. Perhaps not. In any case, you will never know unless you give the poor man a chance to speak his mind."

"I do not know . . ." Athena began.

"Fiddlesticks!" Lady Ridgeway exclaimed sharply. "You do welcome St. Aubyn's addresses, I presume?"

"Yes," Athena whispered, wishing she had half her friend's strength of character.

"Of course, you do," her ladyship said bracingly. "I wonder he has not seen it for himself. Martin remarked upon it right away, naturally. But then my husband has more experience with females. St. Aubyn is a monk by comparison, and blind into the bargain." She smiled encouragingly. "You must help him out of his quandary, Athena."

Athena stared at her in horror. "You cannot be serious, Jane," she murmured faintly. "Whatever can I do?"

"Do not run away from him," the countess answered bluntly.

"I am *not* running away."

Lady Ridgeway smiled complacently. "You know you are, my dear." She paused and regarded Athena speculatively. "I would wager twenty pounds that if I were to leave you here sitting by the pond . . ." The countess paused to gaze at a footman hurrying across the lawn. "Ah, what have we here? Perhaps he cannot wait for me to leave and has sent to demand your presence, Athena." She laughed gaily at her own jest.

When the footman delivered his message, however, Athena was alarmed at the accuracy of her friend's prediction.

She had, indeed, been summoned to the library.

Her heart racing uncomfortably, Athena made her way across the wide lawn and up the terrace steps. At the threshold of the open glass doors of the morning room, she glanced over her shoulder. Lady Ridgeway sat where Athena had left her beside the fish pond, and as she watched, her friend raised a hand and waved, a conspiratorial smile on her face.

Athena smiled back and stepped into the house. Her smile faded as she made her way out into the hall and turned towards the library. To tell the truth, she was more than a little alarmed at the notion of a private tête-à-tête with Lord St. Aubyn. Her fingers trembled visibly as she reached for the doorknob.

The memory of their first encounter in this very room returned with such vividness that she shuddered. But thrusting such unpleasant thoughts aside, she knocked resolutely, and heard his voice telling her to enter.

Taking her courage in both hands, Athena opened the door and stepped inside. The sight that met her eyes was so reminiscent of that first painful encounter that she almost gasped.

"You wished to speak with me, my lord?" she murmured to the man standing—as he had that other time—behind the huge mahogany desk. She moved over to stand before it, searching his darkly handsome face for any sign of that softening, that change of heart that Lady Ridgeway had spoken of.

She could find no sign of it in the blue-black eyes that regarded her enigmatically, nor in the harsh lines of the sensual mouth. And then the earl smiled, and Athena felt her heart skip a beat.

"Yes, indeed I did, my dear," he said. "I have quite a surprise in store for you." He held her gaze for several moments before gesturing towards the hearth.

Athena swung round and saw a gentleman standing there, unnoticed in his sober clothes. She stared for what seemed like an eternity, then took an involuntary step toward him.

"Papa?" Her voice sounded breathless. "Is it really you, Papa?"

The man by the mantel coughed nervously. " 'Tis I all right, Athena." He paused for a fraction of a second, then added with strained joviality, "You are looking well, child."

The intervening years seemed to slip miraculously away as Athena stared avidly at her father's dear face. He appeared untouched by time, except for the increased scattering of gray at his temples and the uncertainty in his still-piercing blue eyes.

"Oh, Papa," she choked, taking another uncertain step towards him.

"I have missed you, child," Sir Henry Rothingham said gruffly, opening his arms.

That was all the encouragement Athena needed. With a cry of joy she ran into her father's arms and clung to him, her eyes blurred with emotion. "I have missed you, too, Papa," she murmured, her voice a sob. "I wrote and wrote, but when you never answered, I thought . . ."

"I wrote, too, child," he interrupted brusquely. "How could you imagine I would not? I wrote to Standish Park, then to your Aunt Mary's in London, then to Spain, but I never received any word of you until St. Aubyn mentioned, quite by accident, that you were staying here in Cornwall as his aunt's guest."

Athena abruptly recalled that they were not alone. She glanced over her shoulder at the earl, who had not moved from behind his desk. There was a strange smile on his face, and Athena knew, with a flash of sudden intuition, that the mention of her presence at the Castle had been no accident.

"I asked Sir Henry for his assistance in authenticating a vase I purchased in London last year," the earl said evenly. "When your daughter told me that her father was a collector of long standing," he continued, addressing the baronet, "and that you had an identical piece in your collection, I could not resist the temptation of inviting you to the Castle to help me verify the provenance of the piece." He paused and smiled ruefully. "But enough of this talk. I expect that Sir Henry is anxious to have you to himself for an hour or two, Athena. I shall meet you again, sir, in the garden over tea."

In the silence that followed the earl's departure from the library, Sir Henry examined his daughter's face avidly. "You have not aged a day since I saw you last, my dear," he said at length, tracing her cheek gently with his fingers. "But I trust that I will never again have to spend so many long years without a glimpse of you, my pet. It makes my heart break to think that I have a granddaughter I have yet to meet. Where is she, Athena? Does she take after you, my love?"

Athena smiled up at him mistily. "I believe you will find that Penelope takes after Mother, Papa. And after John, too, of course."

"Where is Standish, by the way?" Sir Henry asked suddenly, catching Athena quite unprepared. "I look forward to renewing my acquaintance with the lad."

Athena opened her mouth but no sound came. She had forgotten that, not having received any of her letters, her father was unaware of John's death.

"Oh, Papa," she moaned softly, laying her head on Sir Henry's comfortable chest. "John is no longer with me. That is to say," she faltered, "he was lost at Talavera nearly two years ago."

"My poor darling girl," Sir Henry murmured hoarsely, enveloping Athena in another bone-shattering hug. "And I was not with you to help you bear that terrible burden, child. How can I ever forgive myself? I should have known you had written, and would never leave my letters unanswered. That woman shall pay dearly for this, love. I promise you."

Athena raised her head and wiped her eyes. "Whatever are you talking about, Papa?" she demanded.

She saw there was pain in his eyes as he looked down at her. "Your stepmother, Athena. I have a feeling she is behind this, and I shall get to the bottom of it, mark my words."

"Gracie?" Athena had never been close to her father's second wife, but she had difficulty believing evil of her. "Surely you are mistaken, Papa?"

"I hope you are right, love, but let us not waste time on that now. There is so much I want to know about your life in the past years. But first of all, I want to meet my granddaughter."

"And Aunt Mary?"

"Yes, and your Aunt Mary, too, dear. It is time this family came together again, would you not agree?"

Athena agreed whole-heartedly, but at the back of her mind, she could not rid herself of the notion that, had it not been for the Earl of St. Aubyn, this family reunion might never had happened at all.

CHAPTER FIFTEEN

Confessions

The rest of the day passed in a blur of contentment for Athena. She could not remember experiencing such happiness since she had lost John, and as she watched her daughter's unrestrained joy in her newly discovered grandfather, Athena could not contain the surge of gratitude she felt for the man who had made this reunion possible.

She knew she should thank him, but had been too shy—after that strange interlude they had shared under the willows—to approach him when the family dispersed after taking tea in the garden. When they gathered before dinner in the Blue Dragon Saloon, the earl and Lord Ridgeway had talked politics with her father, and Athena knew better than to interrupt gentlemen while they debated the fate of their country.

So she sat on the imposing dragon-footed settee with Lady Ridgeway and Lady Sarah, basking in her newly acquired bliss, and wondering why she was not quite as delighted as she should have been at her father's insistence that she make her home at Rothingham Manor with him. She had accepted, of course. Her dream had been for Penny to grow up in her childhood home, with the dogs—Papa had told her that Paris and Juno had left numerous progeny when they passed on—the lake with its new generations of frogs and minnows to tempt a young girl's sense of adventure, and the pony Buttercup, which Lord St. Aubyn had insisted belonged to Penny, to have for her very own.

Her life had suddenly changed dramatically for the better. Dreams that she had never expected to achieve now seemed within reach. Not all of them, perhaps, but enough to assure that Penny's future was as secure and happy as Athena could make it.

But what about her own future? she wondered. She would be secure enough in her father's house, but would she be happy?

Lady Ridgeway reached over to squeeze her clasped hands.

It was uncanny, Athena thought, how this woman could tell when her mind was troubled. She smiled at the countess and was not surprised when she received a sly wink in response.

After dinner, the ladies removed to the Blue Dragon Saloon again, and Athena was persuaded to play a duet with Lady Ridgeway. It amused her to discover that they were entirely compatible on the pianoforte and later in singing old country ballads that Lady Sarah played for them.

"We are destined to be bosom bows in our old age," Jane remarked jokingly. "I wager you are a rotten card player, too, Athena, and that you do not like needlework."

"She is that all right," Aunt Mary remarked with a laugh. "I tremble every time I partner my niece. She has no guile whatsoever, which is what a successful gambler needs."

"Who is talking of gambling?" Sir Henry boomed out heartily as the gentlemen sauntered into the room. "Still up to your old tricks, are you, Mary?" he teased.

After a cheerful amount of badinage with the baronet, Lady Sarah—whose passion for cards matched Aunt Mary's—organized a game of whist with Sir Henry and Mrs. Easton. Perry was persuaded to make up the fourth, on the condition that Lady Sarah cover his losses.

As soon as the card players were absorbed in their game, Lady Ridgeway linked her arm in Athena's and led her friend down to the morning room and out onto the long brick terrace overlooking the rose-garden.

"It is cooler out here," the countess remarked. "And I do so enjoy the summer twilight. I think it the most romantic part of the day."

Athena took a deep breath, savoring the perfume of roses in the still air. A splash from the pond told her that one of the fat fish had bestirred himself enough to jump for his dinner. And from a distant hedgerow, a nightingale sent up its first liquid trill of the evening.

As they strolled in comfortable silence, Athena felt her heart swell with happiness. She needed to share her joy with her new friend, and speak of the shadow that troubled her heart.

As if divining her intent again, Lady Ridgeway spoke first. "Tell me all about Rothingham Manor," she said. "Will you be happy there, Athena?"

Ah! that was the rub, Athena thought. At Rothingham there would be Gracie to deal with. If her stepmother was indeed guilty of destroying all communication between Sir Henry and his daughter, how could Athena forgive her?

"It will not be easy, my dear," the countess agreed, after Athena had confided in her. "But it might be that Lady Rothingham acted out of love for your father. And if this is the case, then how can you not forgive her?"

"Love?" Athena exclaimed in astonishment. "How can you say so, Jane? What she did was irrational and unkind."

"And do you suppose love is always rational and kind, Athena?" Lady Jane laughed softly. "Nothing could be farther from the truth. The things we do in the name of love are often hurtful and selfish."

Athena stopped abruptly and stared at her, an uncomfortable thought crossing her mind.

"Yes, exactly, my dear," Lady Jane said gently. "Only consider your own love for your daughter, Athena. Was it not that love that moved you to accept an offer from a man you did not love?"

"But I merely wished the very best for Penny," she protested weakly. "Is that so very wrong?"

The countess smiled. "No more so than St. Aubyn's wish to save his son, whom he obviously loves very much, from an unsuitable marriage."

"Are you suggesting that I tricked Perry into making me an offer?"

"No, of course, not," Lady Jane responded soothingly. "But if you are honest with yourself, you must admit that St. Aubyn was right. It would have been an unsuitable match for both of you."

Since this was not the first time such a thought had crossed her mind, Athena did not respond immediately. Jane was right, of course. How could she deny that marriage to Perry, sweet boy that he was, would have fallen far short of fulfilling her own needs as a woman? Such considerations had not entered into her decision to accept his offer. All she had seen—in her blind love for her daughter—had been the immediate solution to their straightened circumstances. Had she really been so unconcerned about Perry's needs, and her own? The answer was so obvious now that Athena felt deeply shamed at her own callousness.

Lord St. Aubyn had seen the betrothal for what it was. She realized with painful clarity that he had also seen her for what she was. He had called her a fortune hunter, and in a sense he was right. She had accepted Perry under false pretenses, not for rank or fortune as the earl had supposed, but for something her heart had yearned for and imagined within her grasp.

"Yes," she murmured after a while, "he was indeed right. The betrothal was a mistake. *My* mistake, if you will. But it was a shabby trick to use seduction as a weapon against me, do you not agree?"

"Seduction is always a weapon, my dear Athena," Lady Ridgeway said with a knowing smile. "A weapon as old as the world itself. But even when used innocently, as your St. Aubyn seems to have done—"

"There is nothing innocent about that rogue," Athena broke in heatedly, her mind flying back to the searing kiss she had shared with the earl in the dungeon.

Lady Ridgeway laughed outright at this protestation, and Athena felt herself blush at the wicked light that danced in her friend's tawny eyes. "Well, now," the countess murmured complacently, "that is a good sign, my dear. Our seducer is not such a slowtop as I had feared."

"*Our* seducer?" Athena repeated incredulously. "You must have windmills in your head, Jane," she added severely. "This is no laughing matter, I can assure you."

"Well, *your* seducer, if you insist, my dear," Jane corrected herself teasingly. "I should warn you, Athena, that seduction can be unpredictable. All too often the unwary seducer becomes the seduced, as Martin found out to his surprise. I cannot wait to see what St. Aubyn does when he discovers he has been seduced."

Athena stared at the countess, a horrible suspicion coiling inside her. "Seduced?" she repeated vaguely. "By whom, pray?"

"By you, of course, you silly goose." Lady Ridgeway laughed delightedly as Athena's hands flew to cover her mouth.

"How absurd you are, Jane," Athena managed to choke out after a fit of coughing. "I am not the least bit interested in seducing anyone."

"How cruel of you to say so, Mrs. Standish," an amused baritone murmured behind her. "Are we gentlemen so devoid of all manly appeal that you can cast us aside without a quiver of regret? What a lowering thought. Would you not agree, Sylvester, old chap?"

Both ladies had swung around at the sound of Lord Ridgeway's voice, and now Athena noticed that he was not alone.

Lord St. Aubyn, his face enigmatic in the deepening twilight, stood beside his friend, his eyes fixed on Athena.

Lady Ridgeway must have sensed Athena's shock, for she slipped her arm through her husband's and smiled up at him with immoderate pleasure. "You are a sad tease, my lord," she murmured. "You will have Athena thinking you are the veriest libertine. Come, let us stroll through the gardens for a while before we go up to bed."

"Anything your heart desires, my love," Ridgeway murmured huskily.

Lady Ridgeway's words were spoken softly, but Athena caught the hint of anticipated pleasure in her friend's voice and blushed hotly. Before she could think of an excuse to prevent Jane's desertion, the couple had turned away and descended the shallow steps into the twilight.

Athena was left standing beside Lord St. Aubyn in the gathering dusk of the warm summer evening, her heart beating furiously.

In the sudden silence, Sylvester heard the soft splash of a fish jumping in the pond. The air was redolent with the scent of roses, and in the distance a night bird cut through the dusk with a burst of sweet song.

Sylvester's heart felt like singing, too. Thanks to his ingenious friend, Ridgeway, he was finally alone in the warm summer evening with a female who made his pulses race like a young man's. It amused him how deftly Martin had arranged the scene, separating his countess from Athena with just the right hint of intimacy in his voice to deter others from joining them in their amorous tête-à-tête. Even now the randy devil must be kissing his wife, Sylvester thought enviously, gazing down at the woman beside him.

Athena's expressive eyes were lowered, her hands clasped tightly, and for a delirious moment Sylvester wished he were Martin, who would undoubtedly have pulled her into his arms without further ado and kissed her soundly. But Sylvester was not Ridgeway; indeed, they were so different in this respect that he often wondered why they had developed a lasting friendship over so many years. Martin would not be a loss for words, he thought, chafing at his own lack of initiative. There was so much he needed to tell this woman, so much he wanted to share with her, but aside from his beloved Adrienne, he had never been adept at expressing his intimate feelings to any woman. Much less to one who still seemed to hold him in dislike.

Athena moved restlessly and suddenly raised her eyes. "I should not have waited so long, my lord," she said softly, her voice unsteady, "but I want to thank you for inviting my father to the Castle. He is delighted and flattered that you chose to consult him about his collection. But you mentioned me in your letter, and he confessed that was what brought him down to Cornwall so quickly. For that I thank you from the bottom of my heart."

"I wanted to make sure that Sir Henry would accept my invitation," he said quickly, blurting out the first thing that came to mind. Almost before the words left his mouth, he cringed at his foolishness, because that was a lie. He had originally written to Sir Henry to induce Perry's widow to leave the Castle. How many little deceptions would he be forced to practice on this unsuspecting woman before he could clear the air between them? he wondered.

"Oh, I see," she murmured, and Sylvester could have sworn she sounded disappointed. "I thought that perhaps . . ." She paused, her eyes dark and mysterious in the failing light. "But never mind. I shall always be deeply grateful that you did tell Father we were here. You have helped to heal a breach that might have dragged on forever. Our letters were never delivered, you see—and Father says he wrote often. He seems to be convinced that my stepmother had something to do with it. I hope not, for his sake, for Father is very fond of her. Lady Ridgeway says . . ." Her voice trailed off into silence, and she turned to stare out into the gathering darkness.

"What does Lady Ridgeway say?" he prodded gently.

She sighed audibly. "Jane says I must learn to forgive. I shall certainly try to do so. If Gracie and I are at odds, Father will be unhappy. And I do so want to go home again," she said huskily, her voice full of longing that tore at his heart. "Father has begged me to make Rothingham my home, and naturally I have accepted. Rothingham has always been home to me, even while I was in Spain. John and I never had a home of our own, you see. The earl, his father, cut him off without anything when he married me."

"But he had the good sense to marry you anyway, Athena."

Sylvester felt a surge of irrational jealousy for this unknown soldier who had enjoyed the youth and innocence, the love and loyalty of this woman who seemed determined to ignore his own growing need to make her a permanent part of his life.

She laughed lightly. "John was young and foolish, as was I. We did not believe that the earl would actually carry out his threat." She stopped and glanced up at him. "You were right, my lord. I must confess it."

"Right?" He was momentarily confused. How could he be right, when he felt that everything he had done to this woman was so wrong? Rather than bridging the chasm between them, everything he said seemed to make that chasm deeper. "Right about what, my dear?"

"About my betrothal to your son, my lord." She glanced at him from beneath her lashes. "I am glad you made me see how disastrous it would have been for him."

"And for you, too, Athena," he said softly, wishing she would give him some sign that she no longer blamed him for the part he had played in breaking her betrothal. "May I hope that you can one day forgive me for the role I played, deliberately I must confess, in ending that betrothal? Miss Rathbone's letter was partially true. I did pay her to come here and flirt with Perry. As for the other accusation, I promise you it was never my intention to—"

"Oh, I can well believe *that*," Athena interrupted quite sharply, causing Sylvester to wish he had phrased his denial somewhat differently. "After I had time to consider it more carefully," she continued in a cool voice, "I realized that Miss Rathbone sounded very put out with you, my lord, and that her words quite possibly lacked veracity."

"Then I am forgiven?"

Athena had turned to gaze at the pale white moon that was rising over the poplars in the distance. "How can I blame you for something you did not intend, my lord?" The question seemed to reverberate with ambiguous echoes, and Sylvester felt as though he had heard only a fraction of what Athena had said.

"Actually it is *I* who should beg *you* to forgive me, my lord."

Sylvester leaned one hip against the stone balustrade and regarded her profile with considerable pleasure. She was a delight to look at, and if only they could get over this verbal fencing, he might find the courage to do what he should have done this morning on the lake. He would kiss her. The thought of it warmed his blood.

"I will not have you begging me for anything, my dear," he

murmured huskily. Although that was another lie, was it not? He would give half his income to hear Athena begging him to take her in his arms, to kiss her as feverishly as they had kissed in the dungeon, to lie with her and show her how much he needed her.

"Oh, but I do beg your forgiveness, my lord," she insisted.

Sylvester drew a deep breath to steady his thoughts and smiled down at her. "Whatever it is, you may be sure you are forgiven, Athena. Only tell me what you have done that is so terrible."

"I believed Miss Rathbone's letter, my lord. I actually believed you guilty of such baseness. I am ashamed to admit it," she added, turning her head away again. "But I wished you to hear me confess it before I leave."

At the mention of leaving, his heart constricted. Was she so eager and willing to be rid of him? he wondered.

Bemused at the direction the conversation was taking, Sylvester reached out to place a hand over hers on the balustrade. He felt her flinch, but she did not draw away. Deriving courage from this small victory, he raised her fingers to his lips and held them there. He felt an overwhelming desire to tell her everything he had thought, and said, and done to cause her pain since her arrival at the Castle as Perry's affianced bride. But most urgently he needed to confess that—contrary to what she imagined—he was indeed guilty of wishing to seduce her. He wanted to seduce her this very instant, here on the open terrace in the warmth of the summer darkness. He most urgently wished to crush her in his arms and feel the softness of her breasts against his chest. He felt himself harden at the thought of it.

Martin would have already done so by now, he thought, impatient with his own lack of resolve. More than likely, being the irredeemable rake he was, Martin might well have progressed beyond this point to those other delicious intimacies that Sylvester had not yet allowed himself to visualize between Athena and himself. For a brief, erotic moment, he let his fantasy dwell upon them now, and was stunned by the swell of raw desire that rippled through him.

But he was not Martin, he reminded himself firmly, quelling the wild impulses that assaulted his senses as he gazed upon Athena's soft profile in the moonlight. He had never wished to possess any of his friend's dangerous charm and disarming rakishness before. That is, before Athena had come into his life to make him feel like a gauche, inexperienced lad again. He chafed at his own inadequacies, but being who he was, Sylvester instinctively chose the safety of confession over the intangibles of seduction.

"I am not nearly as innocent as you seem to imagine, my dear girl," he said, before he lost his nerve. "Perhaps I really am every bit as guilty as Miss Rathbone painted me. Have you so soon forgotten that kiss I stole from you in the dungeon, Athena? A rather improper kiss if I recall correctly. As if any kiss between a man and his son's fiancée could be anything but improper," he added with a trace of cynicism.

Athena had turned to face him during this blunt speech, and now she gazed up at him, her eyes filled with consternation. "Oh, no, my lord," she replied hastily in a hushed voice. "That was all *my* fault. I was guilty of the utmost impropriety, I confess. The rats had driven me into such a blind panic that I became quite irrational."

He still held her fingers in his, but now she pulled loose and turned away. "I blame myself entirely for that disgraceful episode," she murmured coolly. "I am forever in your debt, my lord, for not telling Perry how I betrayed him."

Sylvester felt her slipping away from him again, retreating behind that barricade of aloofness he found so difficult to penetrate. He reacted with the fury of desperation.

"Did it never occur to you, my sweet innocent, that I betrayed Perry, too?" he demanded harshly. "At least you had your fear as an excuse. I did what I did deliberately, so the guilt is mine. Or are you going to claim that the kisses I stole during the storm were your fault, too?" He grinned wryly as she turned startled eyes towards him.

He heard her draw a deep breath. "I do not recall . . ." she began tremulously, but he cut her short.

"You do not recall us lying together in the wet grass, Athena?" he demanded, exasperated beyond endurance by his own clumsiness. "You do not recall my kisses, my touch? I checked you for broken bones, my dear. All over. Then I checked you again because I could not resist touching you. I am more guilty than you imagine, Athena. But I swear that I never meant to deceive you, sweetheart."

Sylvester saw, by the shock in her eyes that he was going about this all wrong. He groaned aloud. At the sound, Athena turned as if to flee. Instinctively, Sylvester grasped her by the shoulders and drew her roughly against him. What was it that

Martin had told him? If a woman was worth fighting for, he should do so. Fight like the devil, Martin had said, for a man might not get a second chance.

This woman in his arms was decidedly worth fighting for, Sylvester told himself through a haze of desire, as he gazed down into her startled eyes. And if he meant to win her, he had better stop dithering around and start fighting. He could not bear to consider the alternative.

Slowly and deliberately, Sylvester lowered his head. He could feel her heart fluttering wildly against his chest, but she made no move to escape. She shuddered as his lips brushed hers. They were warm and moist and infinitely inviting. Was he dreaming or had Athena tilted her face up to his?

"Athena," he whispered against her mouth. An enormous sense of joy washed over him as he pulled her closer and opened his mouth to kiss her. Finally he was bridging that gap between them.

Suddenly Athena went rigid in his arms, and Sylvester distinctly heard his son's voice calling from the terrace door. Slowing he released her and stepped back, letting out an audible sigh of frustration.

"Athena?" Peregrine called, staring out into the darkness on the terrace. "Athena, are you there?"

"Yes," Sylvester rasped, in a voice that sounded alarmingly like a snarl. "She is here, Perry. What on earth is the matter?"

Peregrine came striding along the terrace. He stopped beside Athena, who had turned to stare out into the night. He looked curiously from his father to his former betrothed, then he took Athena by the elbow.

"It is Penny, Athena," he said urgently. "Nurse came down to report that she is running a fever. Nothing serious, she says. Your aunt has gone up to her, but I thought you should know . . ." His voice trailed off uncertainly, and he glanced again at his father.

Sylvester said nothing.

Long after Athena had gone upstairs to the nursery, he stood looking out at the moonlit garden wondering if perhaps he had been born under an unlucky star.

CHAPTER SIXTEEN

Crossroads

The clock in the hall downstairs sent three sonorous chimes ringing throughout the still house.

Athena moved restlessly in her chair and opened her eyes, glancing anxiously at her daughter. Penelope seemed to be sleeping soundly, but when Athena touched her face, the child's skin was still hot and dry. She dipped the wet cloth in the lavender water by the bedside and gently wiped her daughter's heated forehead.

The doctor—summoned hastily at that late hour by the earl—had assured her that there was nothing to be alarmed about. Athena could have told him that; indeed, she had attempted to do so but was overridden by an anxious Lady Sarah, who had seconded her nephew's decision to send a carriage for the doctor. Later, she was glad she had kept her counsel and not explained that Penny often reacted to overexcitement by running a slight fever. She would not have wished to have deprived her hostess of the evident pleasure she derived from setting the whole staff on its ears to cater to the little patient up in the nursery.

Yesterday had been a day replete with excitement, Athena mused, resuming her seat and covering her knees with the rug provided by the solicitous Lady Sarah. Excitement for both mother and daughter. Not only had Sir Henry arrived to reclaim daughter and granddaughter into the family again, but Lord St. Aubyn had kissed Athena on the terrace last night. If indeed one might count that briefly tantalizing touch of his lips on hers as a kiss. Athena decided that she definitely wished to count it as a kiss. She could still feel the steady hammering of his heart against her breasts as he had held her pressed against the lean, hard length of him.

Athena closed her eyes and let her head relax into the cushions. Yes, it had very definitely been a kiss, she concluded, although as far as kisses went, that one might be termed unsatisfactory, for it had left her wildly eager for more. It had been a far cry, for example, from the kisses the earl had lavished upon her in the dungeon. Those had been kisses to make her toes curl. In fact, they curled now at the very memory. After those kisses, Athena had felt thoroughly and delightfully kissed. But last night's kiss had promised more than it delivered.

Perhaps that had not been the earl's fault, she mused, letting her mind recapture the events leading up to that kiss on the terrace. Perhaps he would have kissed her more thoroughly, *much* more thoroughly, she thought with a shiver of delight, had Perry not arrived on the scene.

But why had his lordship waited so long before he took action? she wondered. That thought had plagued Athena all the time she had been out there on the terrace with him. She had stood about expectantly for what seemed like hours, blathering on and on to cover her nervousness. And he had talked excessively as well. They had argued about guilt, she remembered vaguely. He had claimed first to be innocent of Miss Rathbone's accusations, and then, in an astonishing about-face, suggested that he was indeed guilty as charged.

Athena had been thoroughly confused.

Especially so when the earl had taken her hand and laid it against his lips. She had felt the warmth of his mouth spreading throughout her body, tingling along her nerves right down to the tips of her toes. She had been mesmerized by the glint of the moonlight on his dark hair, the rugged planes of his jaw, the unfathomable blackness of his eyes. She had reached such a pitch of excitement that she had actually prayed for rats to appear on the terrace, for lightning to split the tranquil summer sky, and failing that for an earthquake to jolt her out of her paralysis so that she might fling herself into his arms in panic.

But no such cataclysm had come to release them from the apathy that gripped them. Eventually, she had withdrawn her hand, and the earl had talked on incoherently about lying in the wet grass together, about kisses and caresses she recalled only vaguely.

And then he had pulled her into his arms, and Athena had waited, breathless with anticipation, while he had teased her with that brief touch of his lips on hers. Her heart had been ready to explode with happiness.

And then Perry's voice had shattered the moment and the bliss dissipated.

*   *   *

The dawn, creeping over the poplars in the Castle Park, found Athena rinsing out the cloth once again and bathing her daughter's forehead. The skin appeared less dry, but Penelope was still overheated and drank thirstily from the mug her mother held for her.

"May I go riding with Perry today, Mama?" she wanted to know.

Athena chuckled. "First of all, you must get better, my love," she replied, straightening the covers the restless child had dislodged. "Your pony will still be there when you are well again."

"I want Perry," the child mumbled insistently. She had called several times for the viscount, and Athena had promised to send for Perry as soon as he had breakfasted.

"Now I am going to ring for Nurse to sit with you while I change my gown, dearest," she said in a tired voice.

"I want *Perry*," her daughter repeated pettishly. "He promised to show me the new puppies today."

"What new puppies are these, dear?"

"Why, Pip and Squeak's, of course, Mama. They were supposed to have their first family last night. At least, that was what Tom said. Perry promised I might see them today."

Penny closed her eyes, seeming exhausted by this lengthy explanation. Athena brushed a wayward curl from her face and gazed lovingly at her daughter. In spite of her recent very vocal falling out with the viscount, Penny appeared to be as thick as thieves with him again. And Perry was still making his good-natured promises to the little girl. Penny would miss him when they removed to Rothingham in a few days, she mused. And the viscount was not the only Steele gentleman who would be missed.

Her ruminations were cut short by the entrance of Mrs. Easton with Penny's breakfast tray. While her aunt fussed over the child, cajoling her into taking small sips of the tisane Cook had sent up specially for her, Athena escaped to her own room to bathe and change her wrinkled gown.

When she returned nearly an hour later, the sick room appeared conspicuously crowded. Besides Aunt Mary, who was wringing out the cloth in the bowl of lavender water, Peregrine lounged at his ease beside the bed, his blue eyes sparkling with animation as he described in detail the six puppies waiting in the stable for Penny to get well.

On the other side of the bed, Lady Ridgeway sat spooning a

thin gruel into the invalid, punctuating the child's eager questions with each spoonful.

"But I *am* well, Perry," Athena heard her daughter say in a tone perilously close to a whine. "Do say you will let me see them today."

"Let us hear what your mama has to say about that," the viscount remarked with a grin as soon as he saw Athena, deftly shifting the responsibility to her shoulders.

"Oh, may I, Mama?" Penny exclaimed, turning pleading eyes to her mother. "Do say I may visit the puppies this afternoon. If I promise to eat my nuncheon without a fuss?" she added with a grin that rivaled Perry's.

"Only if your fever is gone, darling," Athena said firmly. "It is kind of you to come up so early, Jane," she added; "you cannot have breakfasted yet."

"Neither have you, I wager," the countess responded with a laugh. "Penny has been a good girl and eaten nearly all of hers, so I suggest you and I go down for ours. I swear I am starving."

Athena glanced uneasily at her friend. She had intended to avoid the breakfast room this morning, not wishing to face the earl again so soon after last night's odd encounter.

"Yes, do go down and eat something, Athena," her aunt insisted. "Perry and I will stay with Penny."

Unable to come up with a suitable excuse, Athena allowed her friend to link her arm and escort her downstairs.

To her relief, the gentlemen had already finished their repast and gone down to the stables, according to Jackson. But Athena was mistaken in thinking that Lady Ridgeway would allow her to finish her meal without recounting the events on the terrace the evening before.

"It looked so promising, my dear Athena," the countess confided as soon as the butler had served their tea and withdrawn. "Martin was so sure that St. Aubyn was ready to declare himself. How very provoking of him to waste the time conversing with you, instead of getting to the point."

"Are you telling me that your husband is forcing St. Aubyn to act against his will?" The notion was so mortifying that Athena felt quite ill. No wonder the earl had waited so long to kiss her, she thought, disgusted at herself for not realizing it sooner. Perhaps he had only done so out of pity, sensing that she expected him to. That explanation pleased her even less. But then again, she could be wrong. She wanted most desperately to be wrong.

"No, of course not, you silly goose," Lady Ridgeway exclaimed with an unladylike gurgle of laughter. "I swear you are as provoking as his lordship, my dear. Anyone with half an ounce of wit can see what ails the man."

"Well, I must be particularly feeble-minded," Athena said with some asperity, "for I confess I was at a loss to understand him last night."

"What you need is a stroll in the garden, my dear," the countess said briskly, setting down her cup and rising from the table. "You have not had enough sleep and are peevish this morning. I can tell. Come, Athena, the fresh air and exercise will do you good." She held out her hand invitingly, and reluctantly Athena rose to her feet.

"Only if you promise not to abandon me as you did last night," she murmured accusingly. "I cannot endure another hour of his lordship's odd confessions, let me tell you."

And she could not endure another half-hearted kiss either, she added to herself.

Midway through the following morning, Sylvester came to the unpleasant conclusion that Mrs. Standish was avoiding him. She had refused to meet his gaze during tea in the garden yesterday, and had escaped up to the nursery after dinner on the pretext of attending to her daughter.

This morning she was absent from the breakfast table.

Disappointed and vaguely uneasy, Sylvester spent the day escorting Sir Henry and Lord Ridgeway around the estate, stopping off at the White Stag Inn in Camelford for a hearty meal, washed down by the landlord's famous dark ale. Sir Henry was a jocular sort of man, a typical country gentleman with few pretensions to either fashion or London gossip. He was obviously delighted to be reunited with his daughter and grandchild, and repeatedly thanked his host for bringing this family reunion about.

"It was kind of you to give my granddaughter her first pony, my lord," Sir Henry remarked as the gentlemen finished up the last of Mrs. Hardy's plum tarts and called for the reckoning. "I rather envy your son the delight of setting Penelope in the saddle for the first time. If she is anything like her mother, she will make a fine little horsewoman. I remember when Athena was her age, we could not keep her away from the stables."

"That sounds just like my Jane," Lord Ridgeway drawled in his rich baritone. "I still cannot keep her away from the stables.

Her ladyship originally caught my attention when I learned she had taken out my curricle and four. I did not believe it until I saw it with my own eyes."

"Your chestnuts?" Sylvester asked in a startled voice.

Martin grinned, and Sylvester could not miss the indulgent pride in his friend's voice when he responded. "Yes, my lad, the chestnuts. And you may not believe this, but Jane drives her own curricle and owns a team of grays that I would give my eye-teeth for."

Sir Henry looked askance at Lord Ridgeway, his blue eyes bemused. "Surely you jest, my lord. And in any case, the horses now belong to you."

"You try telling that to my lady," Ridgeway said wryly, his grin growing a shade more fatuous.

"My little Athena was always a handful as a child," the baronet said with obvious affection. "And Penelope appears to take after her mother. My only regret is that I have missed so much of her life. If only I had known . . ." He hesitated briefly. "My granddaughter should have been born at Rothingham instead of in some army surgeon's tent in Spain. An army baggage train is no place for a gently bred female."

"Mrs. Standish appears to be a resourceful woman," Lord Ridgeway put in gently, and Sylvester glanced at his friend gratefully. He envied Martin his ready sympathy. As for himself, the mere thought of the hardships Athena must have lived through in Spain made his tongue freeze, leaving him speechless.

"Aye, that she is, my lord," the baronet said gruffly. "But I count myself guilty for not insisting that her father-in-law, that stiff-rumped Wentworth, be more forthcoming about his son's whereabouts when I called on him. Claimed not to know where the major had taken his new wife, and sounded as though he did not care overmuch. I should have suspected something was amiss when the eldest son came into the title and refused to receive me." He sighed gustily and rubbed a hand over his face.

"That jackanapes deserves to have his neck wrung," Ridgeway muttered viciously under his breath. "Remember him from Oxford, Sylvester?" he added. "Always a self-righteous bastard, full of his own self-consequence."

Sylvester remembered the hulking Standish heir only too well, but he was concerned now with the future not the past. Athena Standish's future. And his own, he thought morosely, which seemed to be presently at a crucial crossroads. He knew which direction his heart wanted to take, but events seemed to impel him down the opposite road, taking him farther and farther away from the woman he loved. It was a sobering thought.

"Yes, that is the impression I got when I went up to London all those years ago to see him," Sir Henry muttered, taking another deep draft of ale. "Said he had not heard from his brother in years. Now I can understand why. My girl tells me the bastard cut them off without a groat." He seemed lost in thought for several minutes, then his scowl disappeared.

"But that is all in the past now, thank the good Lord," he said to Sylvester, his good humor restored. "And I have you to thank for it, my lord. Which reminds me," he added in his hearty voice, "I hope you will forgive me if I take my two gels home tomorrow. They have been without a real home far too long, and I aim to make it up to them, believe me."

Sylvester shot a startled glance at his friend, who gave a fatalistic shrug of his broad shoulders.

He heard nothing of the baronet's conversation as they rode back to the Castle. That crucial crossroads loomed even closer than he had imagined, and Sylvester knew with appalling clarity that if he did not make the right choice, he would regret it for the rest of his life.

Suddenly he was quite sure which choice he was ready to make.

After hearing from Lady Ridgeway that the gentlemen had ridden off together and would not be back for tea that afternoon, Athena allowed Penelope to join the ladies on the lawn under the oak trees at the tea hour. As usual, Lady Sarah asked her to attend to the formalities of pouring tea, while she and Aunt Mary discussed a card party they had been invited to attend at a neighboring manor house.

The only gentleman present was Peregrine, who had entertained Penny with a boisterous game of croquet before flinging himself in a chair next to Athena. He appeared somewhat ill at ease.

"There is something of importance I wish to discuss with you after tea, Athena," he muttered under his breath as she handed him his cup. In answer to her startled glance, he added tersely, "It concerns my father."

Athena felt a tremor of apprehension at the mention of the earl. She had not set eye on him since dinner last night, but he had been constantly in her thoughts. Although she deplored her own cowardice for deliberately avoiding Lord St. Aubyn, Athena had reluctantly come to the conclusion that he had no real interest in her. At least, none that would be acceptable to her. As a result, she had thought it prudent to leave the Castle at the earliest opportunity and had so hinted to her father when he had visited his granddaughter the evening before.

Having made the difficult and painful decision to follow her common sense rather than her heart, Athena did not relish listening to Peregrine's confidences about his father. Whatever transpired between father and son was no longer her concern, she reasoned, and she would much rather not be dragged into their family conflicts.

Nevertheless, and as much as she tried to deny it, her heart yearned to hear his name spoken. A foolish piece of missishness she told herself, but once she removed to Rothingham with her father, there was little or no likelihood that she would ever encounter Lord St. Aubyn again. The idea depressed her, and she wondered if she had perhaps been premature in suggesting their early departure from the Castle to Sir Henry.

Even after the tea things had been removed by the footmen, Lady Sarah and her Aunt Mary lingered in the warmth of the summer afternoon, listening to Lady Ridgeway's spirited account of her mother-in-law's reaction to her son's unexpected nuptials to a confirmed spinster. It was Penny who eventually broke up the prolonged tea-party, demanding that Perry take her down to the stables to see the puppies, as promised.

In the dimness of one of the stalls, Penelope gave a little squeal of delight and threw herself down beside Perry's spaniel Squeak, who lay, a picture of contented motherhood, watching over six plump little bodies squirming around blindly in the warm hay.

"Oh, Perry!" she breathed, for once quite deprived of her usual chatter. "They are wonderful. What are you going to call them?"

"I was hoping that you would be able to help me find the right names for them, Penny," Perry said with a smile.

"Oh, you really mean that?" The child's voice quivered with pleasure.

"Of course, I do, you silly goose. I know you are always full of good ideas, Penny, so consider that your particular job, will you?"

While Penny was engaged in crooning to the squirming puppies, Perry drew Athena outside. "Father told me all about Miss Rathbone," he said tersely, his young face unnaturally serious.

Athena stared at him in alarm. Why had the earl considered it necessary to divulge his role in bringing Miss Rathbone to St. Aubyn Castle? she wondered. The man seemed to have a veritable compulsion to confess. Had he not unburdened himself of his less than honorable intentions towards herself two evenings ago? Confession was supposed to be good for one's conscience, but there were some secrets that might cause more harm than good if revealed unwisely. She wondered if Perry might not be cast down to learn that the Beauty had been paid to dazzle him.

"And what did his lordship tell you about that lady?" she murmured, dreading the young man's fury at his father's deception.

But Perry surprised her.

"That she was not the lady I imagined her to be." He observed her keenly, as though gauging her reaction. "Did you know that, Athena?"

Athena was tempted to deny all knowledge of the affair, but her natural honesty forbade such prevarication. "I gathered from her rather immodest behavior that Miss Rathbone was not all she pretended to be, Perry."

"Father says she is an actress!" he said with withering scorn. "An actress masquerading as a lady here at the Castle. Why did you not warn me, Athena? I made an utter cake of myself."

He suddenly sounded so much like a little boy that Athena slipped her hand into his arm and drew him away towards the enclosed herb garden She was unsure as to exactly how much the earl had confessed to his son, so she proceeded with caution.

"Actually, she was rather good at it when you consider that she was not brought up in this style," she suggested casually. "And you did not make a cake of yourself, Perry. At least no more so than a hundred other boys your age, and many much older men, too, would have done under the circumstances."

"I am not a boy," he said quietly. "And there you go again, Athena, treating me like a son instead of—"

"Because that is how I think of you, Perry," she cut in quickly, not wishing to revive their former relationship. "Your father was right, you know. You would not have been happy married to me."

"That is exactly what Father said. Dashed if I know how he could be so sure. But was there no other way of . . . ?" He hesitated. "I thought he was just being autocratic again. He often is, you know."

"I know," Athena murmured in assent, curbing the smile that pulled at her lips. "But not this time, Perry. Perhaps he was not as diplomatic as he might have been, but he is your father, and he loves you dearly. He tried to warn you, and you would not listen."

"He *forbade* me to marry you," Perry said in an aggrieved voice. "And he called you a fortune hunter, Athena. Did you know that? I could not believe it of him."

"Yes, I know that, too," she responded, wondering just how much she should tell him. "And perhaps your father was right about that, Perry. I have come to see that I did not accept your offer for the right reasons, my dear. It is a very lowering confession to have to make." She paused to pick a sprig of fragrant rosemary, crushing the dark leaves between her fingers. "Your father understood that I wanted to secure my daughter's future. He merely objected to my using you as a safe haven."

They strolled in silence for several minutes, then Peregrine stopped and gazed down at her, his blue eyes troubled.

"Father deceived us both, you know," he said with difficulty. "He deliberately set out to break up our betrothal, but he never intended to hurt you, Athena. You may be sure of that. He told me so when we spoke last night. He holds you in very high regard, believe me."

"Did he tell you so?" Her heart gave an odd little lurch.

"Of course. Father never intended to hurt either of us; you must believe that. Merely to make us see that our marriage would be a mistake. He never wished you to be exposed to . . . well," he hesitated, blushing a bright scarlet. "Father did not expect you to come upon me . . . to witness that scene in the boat house. He came after you as soon as he could, but he was too late, of course. I am so sorry, Athena—"

He looked so miserable that Athena took pity on him. "It no longer signifies, my dear," she said kindly, giving his arm a squeeze. "Put the whole unpleasant episode out of your mind. I certainly have done so."

Perry gazed down at her in undisguised admiration. "You really are a trump, Athena," he said with boyish enthusiasm. "I only wish things had been different between us, because you would make a capital wife."

"Enough of that, my lad," she said sternly. "Or do you want your father to send for Miss Rathbone again?"

Perry let out a rueful laugh at this, and Athena breathed a sigh of relief that Lord St. Aubyn had not been tempted to confess the other role he had supposedly played in the Rathbone farce. She was still at a loss to decide whether or not the earl had intended to seduce her. Not that it signified any longer, she told herself firmly. Tomorrow she would be gone, and seduction, either intended or accidental, would be a thing of the past.

They had reached the end of the brick path, bordered by thick clumps of lavender bushes, when Perry suddenly turned to her, his old mischievous grin giving him the air of a young boy again.

"Father likes you, Athena," he said, his blue eyes merry. "Likes you rather more than he wants to admit, if you want my opinion. But then you probably know that already, unless I am off the mark."

Athena came to an abrupt halt and stared at him, her breath caught in her throat. Was it possible that the earl had confessed to that kiss in the dungeon? she wondered, her heart fluttering in panic.

"Did he tell you that, too?" she murmured, trying to keep her voice steady.

"Oh, no! He would never admit to something like that. He is not one for sharing his emotions, you know. But I have seen the way he looks at you, Athena." His grin took on a teasing cast. "Rather like the way he used to look at my mother."

Athena stood as if rooted to the damp brick path, her emotions thrown into chaos.

"He kissed you that night on the terrace, did he not?" Perry asked abruptly, a naughty twinkle in his eyes.

"No . . . yes. I mean, no," Athena stammered, unsure herself as to the exact nature of that truncated embrace. "Of course, he did no such thing."

"What a slow-top," Perry said irreverently. "One would think that . . ."

But Athena never heard whatever it was one would think, because a footman had entered the herb garden and trod towards them, causing her to relinquish her hold on Perry's arm.

"Sir Henry is asking for you, madam," the footman reported stiffly. "In the library, if you please," he added before he returned to the house.

Athena glanced apprehensively at the viscount. "I wonder what can be the matter?"

Perry startled her with an impudent wink. "Whatever it is, I wish you luck, Athena," he said mysteriously, turning abruptly to amble back to the stable yard.

Athena stared after him, bemused and faintly uneasy. His remarks about his father had disconcerted her. Doubtless, Perry was mistaken, but his words continued to ring in her ears as she made her way into the house.

Rather like the way he used to look at my mother.

CHAPTER SEVENTEEN

Dream Lover

Sylvester stood behind his desk, staring absently at the long shadows cast by the declining sun on the lawn outside his window.

His mind was awash with riotous emotions, and his stomach clenched with an apprehension he had not experienced since the days before his marriage to Adrienne, when his father had attempted to dissuade him from following his heart. He had been a very young man at the time, but he had known his own heart, and the match had taken place in spite of his father's misgivings. Adrienne had brought him over fifteen years of happiness, and her unexpected death of influenza had left him emotionally frozen in its wake.

Sylvester had not thought life possible without her and had buried himself in his studies, which had been enough—or so he had imagined—to get him through the rest of his days in relative serenity if not contentment.

He had been wrong, of course. The illusion of serenity he had built up around himself had suffered a severe shock when Peregrine had brought his future bride to St. Aubyn Castle. Lady Sarah had suggested that history was repeating itself, but he had known—from the very instant he had looked into the widow's magnificent amber eyes—that his son had chosen the wrong woman.

With an audible sigh, he turned from the window, seeing again the small, defiant female who had faced him from across the huge desk during their first encounter. He had been deliberately belligerent, Sylvester remembered, and had spared her none of his simmering resentment at the unpleasant surprise Peregrine had sprung upon him by foisting an unknown widow onto the family. Perhaps that had been at the root of his dislike, he later suspected. The disconcerting discovery that his only son had made the momentous decision of choosing a wife without consulting his father had caused Sylvester to reconsider his relationship with Peregrine.

He had been shocked at the realization that, as a father, he had perhaps not done his duty by his son. Should he not have been in London with Peregrine this past Season? Should he not have taken on the responsibility of introducing the boy to London society instead of accepting Peregrine's assurance that he would be very comfortable lodging with one of his Oxford cronies?

Sylvester's blood ran cold at the thought of what other, far more damaging, indiscretions his son might have indulged in as a raw youth loose on the Town. London was teeming with brigands only too willing to lead an inexperienced youth—particularly one with rank and fortune—into all manner of unsavory situations. The choice of an unsuitable bride seemed a minor peccadillo by comparison, he had to admit, one which had been relatively easy to thwart.

The memory of just how easily he had indeed thwarted his son's mésalliance made Sylvester cringe. What had seemed like a simple and relatively harmless plan to drive a wedge between Peregrine and his betrothed had mushroomed into an ugly deception that had brought shame and unhappiness to the three of them. He himself felt doubly guilty because he had deceived both his son and Athena. Perhaps he had deceived himself as well, he mused wryly, for he had, in his arrogance, imagined he would emerge unscathed from the role he had chosen to play in the charade.

Sylvester sighed again as his thoughts returned to the previous evening. He had—or at least he believed he had—succeeded in setting things right with his son in their interview after dinner. In a show of confidence that had touched Sylvester deeply, Peregrine had refused to believe that his father had actually paid an actress to seduce him. When he realized Sylvester was not jesting, Perry had been stunned and not a little outraged at the deception, but surprisingly his first concern had been with Athena.

"You have hurt Athena far more than you know, Father," he had protested after the initial shock had worn off. "She was counting on me to give her and Penelope a secure future. I am as guilty as you for letting her down."

Sylvester felt a surge of pride at this evidence of unexpected maturity in a son he had too often dismissed as a child. There was nothing childish in Peregrine's anxiety about the welfare of a destitute widow and her daughter.

"It is fortunate indeed that she is reconciled with her father," Perry had said with a seriousness that Sylvester had never suspected he possessed. "But if she were to find herself at odds with that stepmother of hers—whom Athena once described to me as a jealous tabby—then you must promise me, Father, that you will help me settle her and Penny somewhere else. It is frightening for a gently-bred female to be alone in the world, you know," he continued, revealing a side of his nature that was new to his father. "Athena may appear to be strong, but she feared for her safety in London. I came close to fisticuffs with that scoundrel Midland at Vauxhall one evening for ogling her in that lecherous way of his."

Sylvester had heard of Gerald Ashley, of course. The Earl of Midland was notorious for his insatiable appetite for women and gambling. The thought of Athena's being subjected to that rakehell's disgusting attentions made his blood run cold.

"So I want your promise, Father, that we will offer her and Penny a home here at the Castle if she is unhappy at Rothingham," Peregrine had demanded, his tone brooking nothing less than absolute acquiescence from his father.

"After all," Peregrine had continued, obviously unaware of the effect his request had had on his father, "Aunt Sarah has convinced Mrs. Easton to take up residence here as her companion, so it would not be odd at all for Athena to stay with us, too. Would you not agree, Father?"

For a brief instant Sylvester experienced a surge of unmitigated pleasure at Perry's suggestion. He came close to confessing that he would like nothing better than to have Athena living not only under his roof but in his bed for the rest of her life. The words were already on the tip of his tongue before he repressed them. Such a confession must inevitably reveal his true feelings about Athena, and Sylvester was not quite ready to do so until he had spoken to Sir Henry. And until he had laid his heart at Athena's feet, he thought with an inward grimace of amusement at the maudlin direction of his thoughts.

So he had merely acquiesced to Perry's suggestion, surprised his son with an affectionate hug, and gone in search of Sir Henry before his courage could forsake him.

And now he waited, hands faintly damp and heart racing, for the woman who might—or might not—agree to bring joy back into his life.

*   *   *

Athena paused for a moment before she tapped on the library door. She hoped her father had not changed his mind about returning to Rothingham tomorrow. Lady Sarah and Aunt Mary had hinted again this afternoon over tea that there was really no need to go rushing off when Sir Henry had barely arrived. Lady Ridgeway had loudly and persuasively lamented her precipitate departure, remarking—with a mischievous twinkle in her expressive eyes—that had she not known better, she would imagine her friend to be running from the devil himself.

Peregrine had interrupted this piece of facetiousness with the comment that his father had confessed only this morning at breakfast that he would miss watching Penelope's progress on Buttercup, and had begun looking about for a bigger pony for her. Penny had naturally taken this opportunity to beg her mother to stay at the Castle for the rest of the summer.

When Perry had moved on—quite deliberately, Athena was convinced—to describe the exciting winter activities he had enjoyed growing up at the Castle, her daughter had confessed that she had never learned to skate and demanded that Peregrine promise to teach her. Athena was not surprised when he promptly did so.

"So you see, Mama," Penelope cried with the innocent logic of childhood, "we cannot leave before Christmas, can we?"

But leave they certainly would, Athena told herself, firmly dismissing all those wonderful reasons for staying. The reason to leave was too compelling to be ignored. She could not—would not—spend another day under the same roof with a man who gave her severe palpitations every time he looked at her.

Those blue-black eyes of his seemed to promise so much of what she needed from a man, so much of what she had enjoyed with John in what already seemed like another lifetime. Her dreams had become increasingly and disturbingly full of him. He had been no hesitant, tongue-tied lover in those dreams. Nor had he tantalized her with half-kisses, or half-spoken promises, or half-veiled glances that teased her into a frenzy of desire. Oh, no, she thought, feeling her cheeks grow warm at the memory. There had been nothing half-hearted about the man in her dreams. And if she were not to commit the ultimate indiscretion of imagining that the real man was her dream lover—a prospect that was becoming dangerously appealing—she would have to put as much distance as possible between herself and the temptation to throw discretion to the winds and reach out for what she wanted.

Pausing a moment longer to allow the color in her cheeks to subside, Athena opened the door and stepped into the library.

The room was dim with the summer dusk outside, and Athena wondered idly why her father had not rung for candles. Then it dawned on her that the man standing outlined against the window was not possessed of Sir Henry's comfortable bulk.

This gentleman was taller, leaner, and his eyes were almost black in the shadows of his face. She had no difficulty at all in recognizing him. He was the man she had, not two minutes earlier, been thinking of in highly immodest terms.

She felt the color rise again to her cheeks.

A single nervous glance around the room told her that they were alone together. Her father was not there to support her, to steady her nerves, to save her from the very impropriety she had contemplated so recently.

"I beg your pardon, my lord," she whispered in a voice that sounded like a shadow of her own. "I had thought to meet my father—"

"I know, my dear," the earl cut in. "Sir Henry has given me permission to speak with you alone, Athena."

His words washed over her incomprehensibly while Athena stared at him in dismay. Her practical self warned her to flee instantly from the man behind the desk, whose stance reminded her so vividly of their first disastrous interview during which she had likened him to a wolf. His demeanor had been distinctively predatory, she remembered. His gaze, blue-black and threatening, had raked her until she was certain there was nothing about her person he had not considered and discarded as unworthy of his son.

Now they were here alone again, but instead of fear, Athena was conscious of a heart-wrenching need for this man, who she had discovered had nothing in common with a wolf at all. He was more like a magnificent, highly-bred horse, she thought irrationally. A breathtaking animal, regal and full of restive power, but also nervous and almost skittish in his reluctance to bow his head for the bridle. Athena smiled inwardly at her fanciful notion.

This same exciting man, tantalizingly remote by day, had come to her at night in her dreams. Come to her in every sense of the word, causing her skin to tingle with delight, and her body to accept him eagerly, without the inhibitions that held her passion in check by day.

Athena closed her eyes and took a deep breath, forcing her overactive imagination to simmer down. What madness had taken over her senses? she wondered, alarmed at the vividness with which her dreams had superimposed themselves upon her present reality. What demon had possessed her to stare at a gentleman quite openly, like the veriest demimondaine, with less than pure thoughts in her mind?

She soon discovered that closing her eyes had not eliminated the danger. Images from her most erotic dreams encroached upon her consciousness more vividly in the darkness. Dizzy with the irrefutable evidence of her own desires, Athena quickly opened her eyes.

She blinked.

The earl had crossed the room silently and now stood close to her—far too close to her, she felt—his dark eyes filled with questions.

"Are you not feeling quite the thing, my dear?" he asked, his low voice setting off vibrations all along her nerves. "You are very pale." He took her hand and held it close to his waistcoat. Close to his heart.

Athena thought with nostalgia of the afternoon in the dungeon when she had swooned into his arms. She wished fervently that she could swoon at will, but she had never learned the art. And never had she felt the need for such missish subterfuge as she did at this moment.

Instead, she looked up at him boldly and regretted it instantly. The warmth of his gaze burned away any notion she had of resisting him. She had seen that same look often in her dreams, but then in her dreams she had never felt the need to practice caution. She was not dreaming now, she reminded herself sternly, and it behooved her to smother the familiar desire that was curling up inside her before she forgot where she was. And with whom. Despite the warmth in his eyes, this was not the seductive man of her dreams. This was a man who could not, or would not, kiss a willing female on a moonlit summer evening.

Deliberately, and with infinite regret, Athena broke their locked gaze and glanced furtively around her.

"I think we should ring for candles, my lord," she murmured, grasping at something solid, something ordinary and everyday in the midst of the chaos of emotions which threatened to undo her.

She heard him laugh, deep in his throat. A caressing, intoxicating laugh that reminded her again of . . . But no, she thought, quickly suppressing her imagination. This is *not* the same man. And yet the vibrations of his laugh pulsed through her fingers, still pressed against his chest, sending shivers of delight down her spine.

"If you insist my dear," he said slowly, and Athena knew he was still staring at her. "Do you, Athena?"

Was it her imagination, or had the room suddenly become dimmer and warmer? More intimate? Redolent with the smell of leather, books, Holland water. The scent of gentlemen. Or rather of one gentleman in particular. A scent that was depriving her of reason.

She drew a deep, shuddering breath and whispered, "Do I what, my lord?"

"Do you insist on ringing for the candles?"

This whole scene was so very extraordinary, she thought, so filled with tension, and promise, and the unmistakable pulsing of desire, that Athena had the greatest difficulty in separating dream from reality. This could not be reality, she reasoned, for this was the kind of scene, alive with sensuous undertones, that occurred so frequently in her dreams. It was so familiar that she knew instinctively what her next move would be. Her hand would slip, slowly, teasingly, up his waistcoat and wind itself round his neck among the thick curls that clustered there. She could almost feel the crisp texture of his hair against her bare arm.

This was not a dream, she kept telling herself, but with a shock she noticed that her free hand was already halfway up his chest, slipping through the modest folds of his cravat. She froze and would have snatched her hand away had it not felt so warm and at home where it was. Perhaps he had not noticed, she thought wildly. Perhaps she could slip it down again and things would return to normal.

"Well, my dear," he murmured softly, "*do* you?" The teasing amusement in his voice belonged to her dreams and betrayed her into responding without conscious thought.

"Anything you wish, my lord," she sighed, feeling the familiar lethargy of desire invading her limbs as she swayed against him.

His sharp intake of breath jerked her instantly back to reality, the suggestive nuance in her voice still ringing in her ears.

He must have heard it, too, for he removed her indiscreet hand from his cravat and placed a lingering kiss in her palm. The kiss lasted so long that the heat of it had reached her toes before he raised his head and looked at her, his eyes glinting with an odd intensity in the dimness.

That look belonged incontrovertibly in her dreams, and Athena trembled at the thought of what was to follow. Or what would follow, she reminded herself quickly, if she were indeed dreaming this astonishing encounter. But this was reality, was it not? The dimness that surrounded them suggested the darkness of her own room, and reinforced the illusion of the dream world she had visited so often with this man. But the heat of his kiss had felt so real against her skin. The dampness of it still lingered in her palm. And yet, that suggestive kiss and everything that it promised could only exist in her dreams. Or could it?

This delicious sensation of anticipation and the unfolding of desire happened so vividly in her dreams. Athena knew that it led to the searing kisses that melted her bones and obliterated all else from her mind except for her dream lover and what he would do to her. The pleasure they would share. Together in her dreams. But this was reality, a last remnant of sanity within her protested. The temptation to ignore the voice of reason was overwhelming, and for a brief moment, as long as eternity itself, Athena teetered on the edge, between reality and dreams.

The strain of being proper was becoming unbearable. Any moment now she would act out her dreams; she would commit—she *wanted* to commit—some irreversibly sensual act like touching that single black lock that lay curled against the pristine white of his cravat. Or laying her finger against his lips to feel the warmth of them radiating through her body.

"I once had a dream about this."

The words were out before she realized she had spoken them aloud. As they hung in the air, Athena experienced the sensation of being on the verge of reaching a crossroads, the point where dreams and reality merged.

"Only once?"

There was no mistaking the teasing amusement in his voice. Only in her wildest, most secret dreams had Athena imagined having such a conversation with a gentleman. Particularly with this gentleman, who was so close to becoming the man she had wanted him to be that she felt compelled to reveal more of the truth.

"Perhaps twice, my lord."

"Please call me Sylvester."

"Sylvester," she murmured, savoring each syllable languorously, fully aware that in pronouncing his name she was taking yet another step towards making her dreams come true.

"So have I, my sweet."

Athena could not believe what she was hearing. "You have?" she whispered, watching the whiteness of his teeth as he smiled in the dark room.

"Yes, Athena. Many times, if you must know the truth." His grin broadened, and he placed another sensuous kiss in her palm, quite as though he were deliberately set on driving her wild with desire. Was it too much to hope that he was?

She closed her eyes briefly, allowing the forbidden erotic images of him to run rampant in her mind. How much longer would she have to wait for him to kiss her? she wondered, hoping that he would do so before she became quite irrational with wanting him to. In her dreams, of course, she had often kissed him herself when the need to feel his lips against hers became impossible to resist.

She opened her eyes. At last! she thought, feeling the warm glow of anticipation extending throughout her body. He was going to kiss her. But even as she braced herself to receive that long-awaited pleasure, he continued talking.

"But in my dreams, our encounters never ended so tamely."

"I know," Athena began without thinking, provoking a crack of laughter from the earl. She was glad of the growing dimness that hid her blushes when she realized the implications of her intimate confession.

"And how is it, my dear," he remarked dryly, "that you know so much about my dreams?"

Athena closed her eyes briefly in frustration. If she did not take some drastically improper action, she thought desperately, this man would still be talking when the cocks crowed, and she would have to leave the Castle unkissed. The prospect did not bear thinking of.

"I am assuming that your dreams are not very different from mine, my lor—Sylvester," she pointed out defiantly. "And if that is so, then of course they do not end here."

The earl was quiet for a few moments. Had she shocked him

into inertia with her unladylike confession? she wondered. Then his hands moved to her shoulders, and he pulled her gently against him until Athena found herself reposing in a highly gratifying position, close enough to feel his heart beating under her cheek and his breath moving her hair.

But this was not enough for her, not nearly enough. She was anxious to move on to the next step and was wondering how to nudge this man into behaving more like her dream lover when he spoke again.

"It never occurred to me that a lady of quality might entertain such ... such ... well, such *explicit* thoughts as any gentleman."

A sound alarmingly like a giggle escaped her, partly stifled by the folds of his cravat. "Well, let me assure you that they do," she managed to say at last. "And perhaps I should remind you that I am no longer fresh out of the schoolroom."

He chuckled, and Athena wondered what outrageous remark he would make next. She snuggled her nose into his cravat and waited impatiently.

"Thank you for setting me straight on that point, my dear," he said dryly. "Then I trust—since you have admitted to the explicit nature of your dreams—that you can tell me exactly what happens next."

Athena went rigid with exasperation. She lifted her face from the pillow of his chest and stared up at him belligerently. He was doing it again, she thought with growing alarm. He was toying with her. The wily devil was going to escape giving her the kiss she had been yearning for long before setting foot inside the library. He was talking himself out of it just as he had the other evening on the terrace.

But this time she would not be fobbed off so easily, she vowed under her breath. This time the unprincipled rogue would learn that no one, not even an earl, might trifle with Athena Standish. She wanted to be kissed by the man who had invaded her dreams with a passion and enthusiasm that had whetted her appetite for the real thing. She would not be denied a second time.

Athena's anger slowly dissipated. No, she thought, she would not be outsmarted by this slippery rogue. She smiled up at him, the slow sensuous smile she had employed so often in her dreams to bring this man to heel. Her heart pounding at her own temerity, Athena took up the challenge.

"Of course, my dear Sylvester," she cooed. "Although I had not thought you in need of instruction in the art of flirtation."

"Is this a mere flirtation, then?"

"Not in my dreams it is not," Athena retorted daringly.

"Nor in mine." His voice was suddenly husky, his breathing unsteady, and his mouth so close that Athena was sorely tempted to reach up to claim it. She was so close to him that she clearly saw the corner of his lips twitch teasingly when he spoke.

"What do I do in your dream, my love?"

This was so clearly another challenge, that Athena responded without a second thought for the propriety of her action.

"You kiss me," she breathed, *you slow-top*, she added under her breath, her eyes holding his as if daring him to continue this teasing game they were playing.

Before she had time to consider how much longer she could resist without claiming the kiss she craved, Athena felt his hands on her waist and felt herself crushed intimately against a lean, hard body that fulfilled all the erotic expectations of her dreams. It also confirmed her suspicions that the clever rogue had known all along just what the next moves in this sensuous game entailed. There was little doubt that he was as ready for it as she was, and after that first little gasp of surprise, Athena pressed herself against him, more than eager to explore the feel of him.

Through a haze of desire, Athena realized that she was trembling, and that her hand had climbed his waistcoat again, and slipped round his neck in the most familiar manner imaginable. The dark curls tickling her arm were no dream this time; neither was the mouth that hovered over hers, brushing her lips so lightly that Athena moaned in anguish.

"Like this, my sweet?" he murmured against her eager lips.

"Yes, oh, yes!" Athena stood on tiptoe to reach up to him. But still he hesitated, a deep chuckle rumbling deep in his chest.

And then Athena heard a warning bell ringing frantically somewhere in the distance. She had lived through this scene before, she saw with a flash of clarity. All this had happened on the terrace, except that Perry had interrupted them and the kiss had remained unconsummated.

Not tonight, she prayed. Oh Lord, let it not happen again tonight.

Her prayer apparently fell on deaf ears for at that precise moment the door of the library burst open, and a flood of candle-light from the hall illuminated them starkly before they sprang apart.

"Father!" Perry's voice cut across the silence as he peered into the dim room. "What are you doing here in the dark?"

CHAPTER EIGHTEEN

Second Chance

"My dear Perry," a deep baritone rang out in the hall, which Athena suddenly realized was more than usually crowded, "it appears to me, old chap, as though we are all very much *de trop*. Unless, of course, your father has any news of a particular nature to impart to us."

"Lud, Martin," Lady Ridgeway exclaimed impatiently, pushing her husband aside and sweeping across the room to grasp Athena's hands, "have you no tact at all? Now tell us, my dear," she lowered her voice so that it was no longer audible above the babble from the group now spilling into the room, "has he come up to scratch?"

Feeling her breath catch in her throat, Athena stared at her in astonishment.

She was saved from having to dredge up an answer to her ladyship's leading question when Sir Henry's ample figure appeared beside Lady Ridgeway, a broad grin on his face.

"Well, my dear?" His jovial bellow rang out loudly above the voice of Lady Sarah instructing the butler to light the candles in the library. "Are we to wish you happy, my girl?"

Athena gaped at him, an uneasy sensation taking up residence in the pit of her stomach.

"Whatever are you talking about, Father?" she managed to get out through stiff lips. She dared not glance at the earl, who had stepped over to the sideboard to pour himself a glass of brandy.

"My love," Aunt Mary chided, sweeping her into a tearful embrace, "now is not the time for coyness. Has his lordship . . ." Her voice tapered off as Athena gazed at her with a frozen expression on her face. "Oh, dear," she muttered under her voice, patting her niece ineffectually on the shoulder. "Oh, dear me."

"But . . ." her father spluttered, looking blankly from his daughter to the earl. "The two of you have been shut up in here for over half an hour, Athena," he said, a distinct note of reproach in his voice. "Has not St. Aubyn told you, lass?"

"Sylvester," Lady Sarah barked imperiously, "do you mean to stand there and tell me that—"

"I have no intention of telling you anything, Aunt, standing or otherwise," the earl said tersely, gulping his brandy down as though he were in dire need of its restorative powers.

Athena thought he looked unusually put out, and she did not blame him. She was put out herself, and not a little alarmed at the implications of being discovered alone in the semidarkness of the library with a gentleman, even if that gentleman was her host.

"Father," Peregrine said, his eyes dancing with unholy amusement, "then it is true what Sir Henry has told us that you and Athena—"

"Enough!" Lord St. Aubyn exclaimed harshly. "Where are your manners, lad, that you come bursting into a room without knocking?"

"Oh, but I did knock, Father," Perry countered with what Athena could only call an impudent grin. "Knocked twice, to tell the truth, as God is my witness. But since you did not answer—"

"Did it never enter your addle-plated skull that I might not have wished to be disturbed?" the earl said icily, his face pale with annoyance. "And that will do, thank you, Jackson," he snapped at the butler, who was systematically lighting every candle he could find in the room. Athena suspected that the venerable Jackson was all agog with curiosity and wished nothing less than to be able to convey fresh gossip to the kitchens.

"I will not have you taking your bad temper out on the servants, Sylvester," Lady Sarah declared in her strident voice, breaking the heavy silence that had fallen after Jackson's unhurried departure. "Come, Mary," she added, turning towards the door. "I believe we have time to finish that chapter you were reading to me when Sir Henry made his astonishing announcement. I can see now that it was all a hum." She cast a withering glance in the baronet's direction before sweeping regally out of the room. Athena could hear her ladyship loudly holding forth on the deplorable habit of gentlemen not knowing their own minds, and their inability to act upon it even when they did, as she marched down the hall and mounted the stairs.

It seemed to Athena that they stood for an unbearable length of time listening to Lady Sarah's aggrieved voice fading slowly into the distance as she climbed the stairs to the drawing room above.

When silence had once again settled upon the tense little group in the library, Athena heard Lord Ridgeway chuckle under his breath.

"It appears that we have been somewhat premature, Sir Henry," he murmured, amusement at this glaring understatement causing his rich voice to quiver with laughter. "I suggest we withdraw to the billiard room and amuse ourselves with a game or two while St. Aubyn here gathers his wits together sufficiently to put an end to this Canterbury farce."

"But . . ." Sir Henry protested weakly, his troubled blue eyes glancing from his daughter to the earl. "No doubt this bumble-broth will sort itself out, would you not agree, Ridgeway?" He looked hopefully at Lord Ridgeway, who merely shrugged with his usual nonchalance.

"One way or another, things usually do fall into place," his lordship replied laconically, giving Athena a decidedly lewd wink before sauntering out of the room, leaving a hesitant Sir Henry gazing after him dubiously.

Athena threw her father a despairing glance as he paused in the doorway. "Please, Father," she murmured, making a pleading gesture with her hand towards her departing parent.

"You have nothing to worry about, love," Sir Henry said gruffly. "Lord St. Aubyn will do the right thing by you, I can assure you of that." This faintly threatening pronouncement was accompanied by a speaking glare at the earl, who stood rock-still, staring at his empty glass as though it held the answer to his present dilemma.

"Yes, Athena, you have *my* word on that," Perry said earnestly, striding forward to grasp both her hands in his and carry them to his lips. Suddenly, his face broke into a grin and he chuckled. "Father may be a slow-top," he murmured in a stage whisper, "but he will do the honorable thing, I swear it, my dear." His grin broadened. "I cannot tell you how happy I am that things turned out this way, Athena." Quite unexpectedly, he gave her a crushing hug that lifted her feet from the floor, then strode out of the room, whistling as though he had not a care in the world.

Peregrine's words sent a chill through Athena's small frame, and she glanced desperately at Lady Ridgeway, who had been watching the gentlemen neatly ease themselves out of the picture. Her friend returned a dazzling conspiratorial smile.

"Come along, Sir Henry," the countess said firmly, linking her arm through the hesitant baronet's and propelling him towards the door. "I think I shall join you gentlemen in the billiard room. I am accounted a pretty fair player, you know."

Realizing that the last of her supporters were about to abandon her, Athena made as if to follow. "Jane," she cried in a strangled voice, "I think I will join you if I may."

Lady Ridgeway turned a startled face, her eyes darting to Lord St. Aubyn, who was staring at Athena for the first time since they had been interrupted.

"I think you should stay here, my dear," Lady Ridgeway said gently. "Would you not agree, my lord?"

Athena heard a distinct challenge in her friend's voice, and she suddenly felt that she was being maneuvered into a situation from which there was no possible escape. It had become abundantly clear to her as she listened in horrified silence to the unfolding conversation that everyone who had witnessed her compromising presence in the library alone with the earl expected St. Aubyn to repair her reputation as only a gentleman could. To her befuddled senses it even appeared as though her father had deliberately engineered her presence here to force the earl into making her an offer. And now Lady Ridgeway was suggesting the same impossible solution to her embarrassing situation.

"I agree entirely, my lady," the earl said stiffly, with a palpable lack of enthusiasm, Athena thought miserably.

"Well, I do *not*," she sniffed defiantly, determined not to become a party to this subterfuge. "I will join my aunt in the drawing room if it is all the same with you, my lord."

She did not dare look at him, but his reaction was immediate and unmistakable. He strode over to the door and shut it forcefully in Lady Ridgeway's startled face before Athena could escape.

"You will stay here, my dear," he said conversationally, as though they were discussing the weather. "There are certain things that need to be settled between us."

He was standing with his back to the door, barring her escape, and Athena felt it would be undignified to protest a decision that had obviously been made for her. She stepped back and glanced up at him. His eyes were dark blue again in the light of the candles, and Athena turned away from him with a sigh, wondering sadly where her dream lover had gone.

"I cannot imagine what you mean, my lord," she said stiffly.

"I thought we had agreed on Sylvester, my dear."

Athena laughed shortly. "You must have been dreaming, my lord," she replied with a touch of asperity.

"You cannot know how sorry I am that you were subjected to that mortifying scene, Athena," he began. "It was not my intention to—"

"I can well believe it, my lord," Athena interrupted quickly. She could indeed believe that the sly rogue had not intended to be caught embracing her in the dark library. "But there is no need to apologize, my lord. I see that, as usual, I am as much to blame for this awkward situation as you are. I should not have dallied here alone with you. It was imprudent of me, I confess it."

Ah, she thought sadly, but what a delightful dalliance it had been while it lasted. Not that it had lasted nearly long enough to satisfy her craving for this elusive man. However much she might wish he had truly compromised her beyond any question, Athena's honesty obliged her to admit that he had done no such thing. This had not been a scene from her dreams, after all, where there had been no question that she had been thoroughly and delightfully compromised. Possessed and pleasured by the most enchanting rogue imaginable.

That dream lover had dissipated with the first glimmer of candlelight, and in his stead she was faced with a gentleman who must even now be cursing the price he had to pay for those few moments of indiscretion.

Perhaps in the eyes of the polite world they had been scandalously indiscreet. Athena could admit that it might have appeared so to those who had unexpectedly crowded into the library. But Athena was not greatly influenced by the polite world. Was not her honor unfortunately still intact? she thought. Could she in all decency force any gentleman—and in particular this one, who had imbued her dreams with passion and romance—to offer to shield her from the consequences of an act that had never occurred?

"No," she heard the earl say, cutting through her chaotic thoughts. "I should have come to the point much sooner, my dear, instead of teasing you, Athena."

"Teasing me?" Athena repeated mechanically. "You were teasing me, my lord?" She had known it all along, she reminded herself ruthlessly, and now he was confirming the true nature of his interest in her. Why then did she feel so bereft, so disillusioned? What was this dreadful pain in the middle of her chest?

"A fine kettle of fish you have got us into with your teasing, my lord," she exclaimed waspishly, determined, if nothing else, to prevent Lord St. Aubyn from ever finding out how much he had hurt her.

To her surprise, the earl seemed amused at this unladylike outburst. "We can get ourselves out of this bumblebroth—to borrow your father's words—in a jiffy, my dear, if you will only allow me to—"

"Well, you may save your breath, my lord, for I shall do no such thing," she snapped again. "And I will not have Papa badgering you into something that you cannot want, my lord. That neither of us wants, for that matter," she added with a blithe disregard for the truth. "I daresay you think you have to, but you will never persuade me that you wish for it."

"Are you saying that *you* do not wish to marry me, Athena?"

"*Marry you?*" Athena stared at him for a full minute before the significance of his words sank into her befuddled brain. When she could no longer doubt the love she saw in his eyes, she knew this was no dream.

He came to her and took both her hands in his, pressing them, as he had done before, first to his lips and then against his beating heart.

"Yes, marry me, my love."

The tenderness in his eyes disconcerted her, and she looked down at their linked hands. "Your father has given his permission, Athena," he continued softly. "And my son urged me several days ago to fix my interest with you before you got away from me."

His voice dropped into a husky whisper, so reminiscent of her dream lover that Athena's heart turned over. "I meant to speak that day at the lake, my love, but I could not find the words. Perry calls me a slow-top, and he is right. It has been so long since I have felt any desire to speak of love to a woman."

"Love?" Athena murmured, enchanted by his confession, but hesitant to believe that she was that lucky woman.

He grinned wolfishly and pulled her closer, slipping an arm around her waist. "Yes, my sweet. Love. You make me feel like a young buck again, Athena. Now, answer my question, woman," he growled, "before that son of mine interrupts us again."

But Athena was not quite ready to surrender. "How do you know it really is love?" she wondered aloud. "If I remember correctly, my lord, you thought I was a fortune hunter out to snare Perry."

She felt him chuckle deep in his chest. "Sylvester," he reminded her. "I was wrong about you, Athena. When you kissed me in the dungeons—"

"As I remember it," she interrupted quickly, sudden warmth making her cheeks tingle, "you kissed me, my—Sylvester."

He grinned and brushed her lips with his. "Let us admit that we kissed one another, my love. A thoroughly satisfying kiss, I might add. Quite unexpected, too."

"I thought you were Perry," Athena protested, delighted at his teasing.

His arms tightened around her and Athena felt her heart skip a beat. "It seems we owe Perry a good deal," the earl said. "That kiss woke me up to a number of things."

"What things?" she demanded archly, eager to hear him speak of it.

The warm light that sprang into his eyes as they raked her face made Athena blush. "I discovered that I was not immune to the charms of a beautiful woman," he whispered in a low, sensuous voice. "It proved to me that I was not yet in my dotage, and that love is as sweet at forty as it was at twenty. And I do love you, Athena," he said, his voice heavy with emotion. "Believe me, I do."

"You had a peculiar manner of showing it, sir," she could not resist pointing out, mindful of all the deceptions the man she loved had practiced upon her and Perry.

His gaze sobered instantly. "You have a good deal to forgive in that regard, my love. But once you are my countess, I will make it up to you, that I can promise."

Athena smiled a secret, satisfied smile, and lowered her lashes, letting the wonder of this man's love seep into every pore of her being.

"Well?" he urged after a brief silence, his breath warm on her cheek. "May I inform Sir Henry that he cannot take you back to Bath with him?" When she made no immediate reply, he raised her chin and gazed lovingly into her eyes. "If you are worried about Penelope, my dear, I assure you there is no need. The child is more than welcome to make her home here at the Castle." He paused, his eyes glittering with amusement. "Of course, I had to promise her a bigger horse, and sundry other things I will probably regret at a later date."

Athena's eyes flew open. "Never say you bribed my daughter, sir?" she said accusingly, although she knew her face betrayed her amusement.

One of his dark brows rose quizzically, and the warmth in his eyes brought the color to Athena's cheeks.

"I can see that I shall have to bribe you, too, Athena Standish," he murmured, lowering his head purposefully, "or I shall never get an answer to my question."

Athena sighed and tilted her face to receive his kiss. "What exactly was your question, my lord?" she murmured playfully against the warmth of his mouth. Conscious of a sudden rush of tenderness for this man whose deceptions, painful as they had been at the time, had brought her a greater happiness than she had imagined possible, Athena pressed herself more intimately into his embrace.

This time there was no hesitation about the kiss he gave her, and Athena gave herself up to it, surrendering her lips, her heart, her body, as she had only dreamed of doing with the dazzling lover of her dreams.